Seven Days At Oak Valley

By

Ruthie-Marie Beckwith

ABQ PRESS
www.abqpress.com

Copyright © 2009 Ruthie-Marie Beckwith

This is a work of fiction. Names, characters, places and incidents are either the product of the author's imagination or used fictitiously, and any resemblance to actual persons, living or dead, business establishments, events or locales is entirely coincidental.

Cover design by Michael J. Meredith

ABQ Press
Albuquerque, New Mexico

ISBN 978-0-9774161-6-5

Acknowledgements

My deepest thanks to my friends and family for their unwavering support and for believing this book could be a reality. Grateful acknowledgement is made to my initial readers, Hank Bersani, Chuck Emery, Mark Friedman, Judy Gran, Jim Lent, David Meredith, Ruby Moore, Sandy Reagle, and Steven Wiehe who read through the various drafts of this work and shared their vast wisdom regarding revisions. Many thanks are due to the 911 group at the online Writer's Village University for very specific comments at the beginning of the journey. Finally, to Judith Van Gieson and the special group of mystery writers who shared their thoughts and wise suggestions at the Taos Summer Writers Conference, this book grew up under your tutelage.

To my three sons, Matthew, Michael and Timothy,
and to my beloved husband Mark,
who walked beside me on the entire journey.

And to Bonita Scott, my sister in spirit,
whose smile lit up my world
and continues to shine in the remembrance
of all we shared together.

"Order and truth are not always compatible bedfellows.
Law is not morality.
Intelligence is not thoughtfulness.
The able do more than we know.
The evil do more than we believe.
And the good must do more than curse them."

Burton Blatt, *In Search of the Promised Land*

Oak Valley State Training School and Hospital
Laurelville, TN
(1978)

KEY

- B: Dormitory; crib cases
- K: Older Boy's Building
- D1&2: Dining Halls
- F: Older Girl's Building
- G: Children's Ward
- A: Administration
- C: Canteen
- N: Superintendent's House
- H: Infirmary & Hospital
- J: Assembly Hall
- E: Central Support Services
- M: Workshop School
- 1 — Fire Station
- 2 — Water Tower
- 3 — Steam Plant
- 4 — Security
- 5 — Garage
- 6 — Cemetery

Seven Days at Oak Valley

Chapter One

Saturday, September 29, 1978: 6:15 p.m.

Mac Jones, head of security, stood at the edge of the cemetery and watched two members of his security force and two attendants finish shoveling dirt into the grave of the latest resident to die at Oak Valley Training School and Hospital. He stroked his thinning hair as he thrust out his chest. A tense twitch in his right cheek kept time with the rippling of muscles beneath the shirt of his slightly rumpled standard issue uniform. Standing at five foot six and 165 pounds, he didn't appear necessarily big or outright menacing, but tonight, as his body continued its ominous rhythm, he noted that even his own men took care not to look him square in the eye.

    Jones had observed the arrival of Dr. John T. Cordell just moments after the makeshift pine coffin had been lowered into the ground. Cordell stood next to the grave, shuddering at the sound of each shovel of dirt thudding into the grave. His starched, white lab coat hung loosely on his six-foot frame and his hands were jammed into its pockets. His classic blond features and crisp exterior were a stark contrast to Jones' own darker, disheveled appear-

Ruthie-Marie Beckwith

ance. Jones watched one of the men scrape his shovel over the mound to smooth the top of the grave while the rest of the burial crew gathered their tools. Cordell remained at the foot of the mound, his silent presence invoking a somber mood among the otherwise boisterous men.

Jones twirled a toothpick between his teeth, scowling. He tried to gauge Cordell's reaction to the burial but the man was unreadable. The shadows of the lingering dusk masked Cordell's face as darkness began to engulf the tangle of weeds and exposed roots of the cemetery. Away from the main footpaths and roadways, this obscure corner of the grounds was the most neglected. The dead that were buried there seldom had anyone come to pay their respects.

One of the men finished the burial detail by placing a marker engraved only with the number 8627 on top of the mound. Unanchored, it would sink into the ground as the loosely piled earth settled into the grave and soon be as obscure as its predecessors.

Jones moved forward to shake his men's hands, thanking them for their effort. The men simply nodded, moving off in unison toward the dirt path that connected to Chestnut Lane, the road that led back to the parking area beside the Administration Building. Cordell waited until the men disappeared before heading for the path himself. Jones caught up with him, cutting him off before he had reached the edge of the cemetery.

"Evenin', Doc."

"Mac."

"Another one in the ground," Jones commented, pointing the toothpick at the now deserted grave.

Seven Days at Oak Valley

"Guess this makes fourteen funerals since you came on board."

Cordell glared at Jones in silence.

"Any progress in locating those missing files?" Jones continued, determined to provoke a reaction from the stoic physician. Even from five paces away, Jones could smell the strange combination of antiseptic and Cordell's cologne.

"You'll be the first to know if and when they turn up," Cordell responded. "Now, if that's the end of your interrogation for this evening, you know Dr. Jefferson's wife is holding dinner."

"You don't really like it here at Oak Valley, do you, Doc?" Jones challenged.

Cordell paused, leaving Jones with the impression that Cordell was measuring the importance of each word before replying. "I'm just doing my job as instructed, like you and everyone else. All I know is I inherited one hell of a mess."

"You never know where life's going to lead you, Dr. Cordell, particularly in a place like this." He stepped closer and leaned forward until his face was five inches from Cordell's. "For example, if Old Doc Henderson had taken better care of his colon, we wouldn't even be having this conversation now, would we?"

Cordell's eyes narrowed. Ignoring Jones' last statement, he sidestepped around him and strode toward the overgrown path.

Jones walked back and knelt down beside the grave, calling out to Cordell before he disappeared into the overhanging foliage of a red oak tree, "Hope you take better care of your colon than Doc Henderson did, Dr. Cordell."

Ruthie-Marie Beckwith

Still twirling the toothpick between his teeth, Jones knelt down and picked up a clump of dirt that had evaded the burial detail. The damp earth was pungent with the smell of years' worth of decayed leaves. He squeezed it in his palm and the loose particles fell on top of the rectangular metal grave marker that bore the number 8627. "Number eight six two seven, don't you fret none, I'm sure you'll have some company joining you here fairly soon. In fact, I'd be willing to bet on it."

Jones stood up, made one final sweep of the landscape with a turn of his head and added, "Dinner time. Hope Mrs. Jefferson has cooked up some of her famous greens." He headed down the path as the night air caught up the low echo of his laughter. The sound rumbled in the looming darkness that was soon to be challenged by the rise of the autumn moon beyond the surrounding hills.

6:30 p.m.

Tony looked over his right shoulder one last time as he swung himself off the granite ledge to grab the drainage pipe. Reaching back with his right hand, he pushed the rusty iron grate that was supposed to bar the window back in place and shimmied down the fat clay tube. He dropped to the ground with a soft thud. Pulling his long limbs beneath him, he sat with his back against the old elm that towered above the three-storied brick and granite dormitory. Looking out across the grounds, he decided to wait for the moon to rise high enough to spread its light across the deserted campus before he headed out.

Seven Days at Oak Valley

The open windows of Building K, the older boys dormitory, from which he had just emerged past curfew, made it possible to hear the shouting and crying going on inside. Shrill noises punctuated an occasional scream, sounds that were barely noticed by anyone who had lived or worked there for longer than two months. The ward staff had thrown open the windows, hoping in vain that the fresh air would carry away the worst of the odor that went with three hundred forty grown men living in four wards that had been designed to house two hundred.

The red brick building was covered with ivy, leaving the naïve observer with almost a collegial impression. White columns lifted up a revival baroque facade popular in the 1920's when the building was first constructed. At that time the groundskeepers had surrounded Building K and the other dormitories with American elms, which were later replaced with red and white oak. The elm Tony leaned against was one of the few remaining trees on the grounds that was still languishing in the final stages of Dutch elm disease.

As a sliver of moon began to rise above the water tower, Tony stood and assessed his appearance. He wondered what Debbie Allison would think of him. Black pants hung on his lanky frame, anchored around his waist with a worn brown belt. The tails of a wrinkled blue and green plaid shirt were tucked into the pants. He had been to the barber two days ago where he received the only cut the irritable little man seemed to know how to do. His dark curly hair was shaved close to his head, a deterrent to the upcoming lice season.

Ruthie-Marie Beckwith

When Tony stood at attention he reached six feet, but he typically found it more useful to hunch his shoulders in order to appear docile and anonymous. His deep indigo eyes were by far his best feature. In his younger days the Appalachian Relief Ladies, who came every Saturday to conduct games in the Assembly Hall and dispense cookies and funky tasting Kool-aid, had fussed over his long curly eyelashes and clucked their tongues at the deep dimple that formed on his right cheek whenever he smiled.

I do look kinda like Elvis, he concluded as he become older. To further cultivate this newly adopted image, he set about learning *Love Me Tender* by heart. He performed it at the top of his lungs in the dining hall, along with the required hip gyrations, whenever any of the girls walked near his table. The final touch had been the addition of a cheap, tarnished chain to wear around his neck with the top three buttons of his shirt undone.

All things considered, Tony decided that he looked pretty good. The only thing missing were shoes, but some things couldn't be helped. He set out on the lower path that ran beside Building B, where they kept the crib cases: the ones that stayed in bed all day. After it passed by Building B, the path cut sharply to the right by the dining hall and ran alongside of the garden in the back of Superintendent Jefferson's house, before rising uphill to end at Building F, the older girls' dormitory.

He figured the risk of being seen by the superintendent was pretty low since a meticulously maintained three-foot hedge surrounded the garden. He'd just have to duck down if he heard any noise.

Seven Days at Oak Valley

Besides, he was a man with a mission and his confidence was at an all time high. He looked out across the manicured lawn for anyone arriving late for second shift, hunkered down, and set out.

Dew clung to his bare feet as he loped along the path. He very much regretted the whole deal with the shoes but trading them had been a critical part of his overall plan. The Appalachian Relief Ladies, now fifteen years into their soul-redeeming mission had, with an overabundance of pride, presented him with a pair of loafers at their last volunteer gig in his building. He rewarded them in turn with his best Elvis smile and mumbled a polite thank you.

The shoes were brand new and only one size too big. Not quite his style. He'd worn them for only a day when his best friend and roommate Joey noticed how easy they were to slip on. Notorious for tripping over shoelaces, Joey's efforts at tying them rarely resulted in success. Joey offered him a trade of a whole carton of cigarettes on the spot. He'd gotten his hands on the cigarettes in a trade with the second shift custodian for the transistor radio his folks had given him on his last birthday. With Joey's cigarettes securely in hand, the whole idea of tonight's little trip had begun to take shape. Tony stuck a hand in his pocket to make sure the pack of cigarettes he had spirited out of his locker was still in place.

Tonight's plan was to give Debbie two cigarettes. If she agreed to be his girlfriend and to sneak out to meet him again this coming Tuesday, he would give her three. If there was one way to get Debbie's attention, it was through cigarettes. Every guy he knew who had managed to get under her skirt had started out by offering up a nice, quiet smoke in the

Ruthie-Marie Beckwith

bushes behind Building F. With a whole carton nestled in his locker, he figured he had it made, at least until it started to get too cold to meet outside. After that, he'd have to stand in line with the other guys to use the storage room behind the main boiler at the steam plant. Tinker, the old guy who kept the boiler going, liked to smoke, too.

Tony looked up and realized his daydreaming had brought him within a yard or two of the southeast corner of Dr. Jefferson's house. The names and tenure of former occupants of the superintendent's house quickly came to mind: Dr. Jefferson, two years; Dr. Winston, ten years; and Dr. Randall, eight years. Tony had made daily trips to the house when Dr. Winston was superintendent. He had been part of a special program that used some of the younger boys as servants.

Nowadays, he only went to the house as part of his mail route around the grounds. Every morning except for Sundays, he stood on the edge of the front stoop where he could see all of the superintendents' fancy pictures going up the wall that ran by a curvy staircase with a shiny wood railing that had a large ball on the end of the banister. Ten years ago, he'd learned how to polish that wood until he could see the reflection of his face.

A wide porch framed the entire house. A section in the back was screened in to fend off mosquitoes that routinely came swarming up from Lower Pigeon River. Ferns hung between classic columns. White wicker chairs covered with red floral cushions were grouped beneath two picture windows, intended to be a welcoming place for casual conversation.

Seven Days at Oak Valley

A large magnolia served as the centerpiece within the well-groomed shrubbery that defined the perimeter of the garden. Thorny rosebushes took up one corner and sunflowers rose above another in an effort to tempt birds into the area. Tony's favorite part of the garden was where the gardenias were planted in a circle around a concrete birdfeeder. They had smelled like Mrs. Winston's perfume. Mrs. Winston had taught him the names of all the flowers.

Tony hunkered down more and moved forward along the shrub line, ducking lower just before he would have been caught in the beam of the back porch light. On the other side of the bushes he could hear folks talking. Crouching low to the ground, he shivered. His privileges could be kissed good-by if he got caught, especially his highly prized job as mail boy. Not daring to move, he listened as the voices grew louder.

"I tell you, Winfred, if this gets out, we can expect major problems."

Did that voice belong to Mac Jones, head of security?

"I don't think we should do anything until we determine if something is missing."

That sounded a lot like Dr. Cordell. To his reckoning, only doctors who could give shots could sound like doctors.

Recognizing Dr. Jefferson's voice was never a problem. The superintendent had one of those deep booming voices that could carry clear across the grounds from Dining Hall 2 to the Fire Station.

"I just want to be crystal clear," Dr. Jefferson replied. "We don't need to do anything that will call attention to ourselves. Lord knows, the last thing we need here is a bunch of legislators breathing down our necks upsetting our residents and routine. No offense, Senator."

"None taken," replied another voice. Tony didn't recognize this voice but he figured it must be Mr. Senator, someone he'd never met before. "I know full well how tiresome my esteemed colleagues can be when they get a bug up their ass about something," Mr. Senator added.

Tony heard the men chuckle in response.

Dr. Cordell continued, "Right now, I simply want you to carry out your respective searches and report whatever you find to me first thing Monday morning. I don't want us going off on a wild goose chase, providing grist for the gossip mill. We all know how it operates at top speed around here."

Another voice cut in, "I'm just trying to point out that we might end up answering questions from some very disagreeable people for a long time."

Mac Jones? Sure sounded a lot like him.

"For heavens sake, Mac," Dr. Jefferson interrupted, "one of those little LPN's or a clerk, might just have laid them down somewhere when they were off having a smoke or something. All I want you to do is to continue looking until the damn things turn up."

Tony heard both men mumble in response followed by silence.

"Well, I trust you gentlemen will soon have this business under control."

"Certainly, Senator, just a matter of some misplaced paperwork," he heard Dr. Cordell reply.

"Yes, sir," echoed Jones.

"And Winfred," continued Mr. Senator's voice, "I do trust these files are the only ones that have been, as Dr. Cordell says, *misplaced*?"

"Yes, Roy," responded Dr. Jefferson, "all of the other records have been under my control and will remain so."

"Well, then," responded the Senator, "I'll be back up on Tuesday to check on how our other projects are progressing."

Tony decided to breathe again when he heard one set of footsteps move toward the house. Cigar smoke floated past him in the cool evening air. That would be Dr. Jefferson smoking. Anyone who'd been around Oak Valley as much as he had knew that Dr. Jefferson smoked his fancy cigars with the red and yellow band when he was upset about something. Silently cursing, he realized that waiting for Jefferson to finish his cigar could mean his date with Debbie was history.

Tony jumped at the sound of the porch door swinging open and struggled to keep from falling over into the hedge. Those hinges still need oiling, he thought.

He recognized Mrs. Jefferson's voice as she called out, "Winfred, you gentlemen had best come in now. Dinner just won't hold any longer. As it is, you'll have to tolerate a good part of it cold."

"We'll be along soon, Mrs. Jefferson," called Jones, "I'd hate to have anything you've cooked go to waste."

"We'd best move indoors," Dr. Jefferson remarked to his companions, "or she'll be fussing at me worse than any gaggle of legislators ever could."

Ruthie-Marie Beckwith

The other men chuckled again and Tony heard their steps creaking on the porch steps. The door slammed again. In one move he rose and dashed up the path to Building F, the older girls dormitory.

Seven Days at Oak Valley

Chapter Two

Sunday, September 30th: 6:10 a.m.

The cold water jarred him awake. He turned to look at the body standing beneath the showerhead next to him, instantly regretting it as suds created from the yellow soap bar trickled down his forehead and stung his eyes. The next guy in line stepped forward to take his place as he finished washing and rubbed a threadbare white towel across his face.

Recognizing Joey, one of his three roommates, he warned, "It's as cold as ever, man." Joey shivered as he took Tony's place beneath the showerhead. His blond hair was shaved in the same manner as Tony's, but that was where any physical resemblance ended. Standing five foot six, Joey's slender frame appeared smaller due to a curve in his spine and the inward angle of his knees.

"'Ways 'old," Joey complained loudly. Laughing in response, Tony dodged the worker's usual attempt to pop him with a towel and danced in the direction of the room he shared with Joey, Ben, and Sam.

Ruthie-Marie Beckwith

He and Joey were among the youngest men in the Building K, but they were among the handful that really knew their way around. Still naked, he stopped in front of the clothes room to grab something to wear and then, reconsidering, hustled back to check on Joey's progress. At the entrance to the shower room he heard the worker's laughter drown out the sound of the running water and the snap of a wet towel connecting with flesh.

"Just one more time, boy, an' then you can go," the worker was saying. "You stand there an' take it like a man, boy, and you'll be on your way."

Tony couldn't hear Joey's reply but knew better than to interfere. It would just make things worse on Joey when he wasn't around to take up for him. He stepped back around to the other side of the doorframe. He heard another snap of the towel followed by the heavy thud of a body hitting the floor. The sound of wet feet slapping furiously on the dingy yellow tiled floor gave notice that Joey was on his way.

Joey raced past him. Tony could hear the worker's cussing and hollering echo up the hall from behind.

"Damn it, you little retard, you get your skinny ass back here. I didn't say you was finished. Shit, boy, you gonna pay tomorrow! You hear me? You gonna pay!"

Tony called out to Joey, "Hey, man! Wait up!" and broke into a run behind him.

"No, 'ay!" Joey yelled back as he plunged ahead and turned the corner to the stairwell leading to their second floor room. Tony slowed, looking over his shoulder for the irate worker who failed to emerge.

Seven Days at Oak Valley

He stopped by the clothes room one more time to collect something for Joey to wear.

Joey was huddled on the floor behind his bed when he reached their room.

"Coast is clear, Joey," Tony told him, "he's not comin'. He must still be hosin' down the other guys. What d'you do to him this time?"

"'E slipt," Joey replied as he pulled on the green striped pants Tony had retrieved for him.

"Dis all?" Joey asked, looking down at the extra pant lengths that gathered around his ankles.

"Aw, quit bellyachin'. Just roll 'em up like usual. 'Sides, I was in a hurry, remember?"

Joey rolled his eyes. Tony slid his own legs into green and yellow polyester plaid and pulled them up over his butt; the pant legs ended four inches above his ankle. Joey withheld comment on the pants as Tony slipped on a worn blue t-shirt emblazoned with the picture of a chalet under which the name *Gatlinburg* was barely legible. He slid his hands over his still wet head, his fingers searching for missing curls.

Looking around the room, he acknowledged Joey's effort at pulling up their sheets, "Beds'r made."

The top sheet of each of their beds was tucked under their pillows and their folded blankets were precisely placed at the foot. Joey had learned bed making at home before his parents had sent him here and he always made both of their beds before he hit the shower. For some reason that no one had explained to Tony, bed making became a priority when Dr. Jefferson took over. Even though he knew

Ruthie-Marie Beckwith

how from his days in the special program, he always let Joey do it his own way every morning.

"Yeah," grunted Joey.

Tony stood in the open doorway facing the window. A poorly conceived renovation had used makeshift partitions that had once been white to create their room and five others just like it at the end of the hall. The outside wall wore an original coat of green paint that resembled the pea soup that had been served every Thursday afternoon for lunch for as long as he could remember.

Along the now grey partitions to the left, four beds with metal frames stood side by side. Two of the beds still sported a tangle of sheets on top of top of their plastic mattresses. One was empty and the other smelled of urine. Sam, their third roommate, was at the center of that tangle. Sam was a heavy set black man who, like Tony, was six feet tall. To others, Sam looked intimidating but was gentle as a breeze ruffling the dogwoods on a clear spring day.

The only problem with Sam was he had never stopped pissing in his bed. Tony and Joey never complained about Sam for pissing in the bed like some of the other men did to their roommates. Over the years, the workers had tried all sorts of tricks to get Sam to stop. The most recent one was making him sleep in the dirty bed. He'd get clean sheets on Wednesday, maybe.

Ben, their other roommate, was called "Downs" by most of the workers. He pretty much took care of himself, but then again, he'd never learned how to talk, so he never complained about anything or anyone. Ben's bed was empty. An early riser and famous for his huge appetite, Ben liked to be first in

Seven Days at Oak Valley

line at the dining hall for every meal. The cooks rewarded him for his loyalty with bigger portions and lots of compliments about his expanding waistline.

Tony had moved up from Building G, the children's ward, to Building K for the "older boys" four years ago on his sixteenth birthday into the room already occupied by Sam and Ben. Joey, his best friend since the affair with the Christmas ornaments, had joined him a month later.

After taking stock of his new roommates, he had made it plain that no one ratted on each other, at least no one who shared *his* room. Tony and Joey looked out for Sam and Ben because they were useless at looking out for themselves. This arrangement had its advantages for each of them and Tony's was being able to come and go when he pleased without worrying about being turned in, just as he had last night.

Paint from the pea soup colored walls was peeling around a silent radiator that stood beneath the curtainless, open windows. The iron grates, behind window screens that had long ago curled back from their edges, were red with rust. The partition walls were bare except for a picture of Joey's family nailed in place above his bed. Joey's mom and dad smiled down on their son every night.

"So, what d'you wanna' do today?" Tony asked.

Joey finished buttoning his shirt and slid his feet into the loafers. He stored the shoes in his locker along with his other collection of treasured personal possessions. Both of their lockers sat at the foot of their beds stationed like green army surplus supply guardians of their owners. Tony looked at the shoes with blatant longing but cut his eyes to the right when he realized Joey was watching him.

Joey, catching his glance, laughed and ventured, "'Apel?"

"Nah," Tony responded, knowing full well that Sunday services were mandatory for high grades, which is what they were both considered to be. The only way to get out of it was going to the infirmary instead and that was a whole lot worse than being in church.

"'Teen open," Joey commented.

"I ain't got no money and no plastic pennies, man. You know that," Tony told him, annoyed that Joey would bring up his long standing inability to buy stuff.

The mention of chapel and canteen only served to remind him that it was Visitor's Day. Sunday always meant Visitor's Day and Visitor's Day always meant moms and dads, except Tony had no mom and dad; not that he knew of, anyway. According to Miss Lambuth, Building K's social worker, he had been at Oak Valley State Training School and Hospital since he was two years old. Miss Lambuth had been the one who had finally told him that he had originally come to Oak Valley from an orphanage somewhere near Memphis. He stood quietly, his mood darkening.

"Not 'omin," Joey told him, as if reading his mind. "Mrs. G'een 'alled. Not 'omin."

Not coming, Tony knew from long experience, meant Joey had the day free. Joey's parents weren't going to make the long drive from wherever it was they lived. He knew was it was a long drive because

Seven Days at Oak Valley

that's what they told Joey each and every time when they first got out of their car on Visitor's Day.

"Martha," Tony would always hear Joey's dad say to Joey's mother, "eighty seven and a half miles. That sure is a long drive."

"Well," Joey's mother would always reply, "we had best get visiting then before we need to leave." They would then get Joey to take them on yet another tour of Oak Valley before driving him into Laurelville for a cold drink. They returned with Joey every Sunday just as the dinner siren sounded and Joey would keep to himself for the rest of the night.

Visitor's Day by and large left Tony on his own with very little to do except wander from building to building visiting old friends until he was chased away by the staff. Tony's mood lightened. Today, he and Joey would be able to spend the whole afternoon roaming the grounds together before the dinner siren went off.

"Smoke?" Tony asked Joey, sort of in consolation for his parents' absence. He lifted up a loose tile beneath the radiator to retrieve his locker key. In the winter he sometimes burned his knuckles sliding it out, but the steam plant that supplied the radiators had been shut down since early spring. He reckoned Tinker would be firing it up soon, however. The air last night had been cooler and the dew on the ground was another sign that fall had definitely arrived.

Tony unlocked his locker. The locks were new, donated this past Christmas by Wrights Hardware over in Laurelville. Tony guarded his key with great care. He didn't wear it around his neck like the other guys where anyone could just grab it and run off. Only Joey knew where he kept it hid. Joey was one of

Ruthie-Marie Beckwith

the two people he trusted in all of Oak Valley, the other being Tinker.

He reached into the locker and pulled out the same pack he'd taken with him the night before. He counted out four cigarettes, two for him and two for Joey. He slid the pack into the carton with its other Marlboro unfiltered companions. Getting a light would be a somewhat harder challenge.

"Yeah," Joey replied. He watched Tony lock his locker and return the key to its hiding place, and then added, "'Ets go."

Together they retraced their earlier steps down the dingy and poorly lit hall. Signs taped to the wall at the top of the stairs announced events that had already passed, like the Labor Day fireworks and Girls' Chorus performance. These events were always held on Visitor's Day so parents and other dignitaries could attend.

On their way back, they found Sam standing naked at the clothes room.

"Hey, Sam," said Tony.

"Where y'all goin'?" asked Sam.

"'Moke," Joey answered, gesturing with his right forefinger and thumb in front of his mouth as they passed them by. "B'fast, too," he added.

Tony took the stairs down two at a time. Joey took one step at a time, leaning on the railing as he placed each leg side by side on each stair before lowering his right foot to the next step below. Tony waited for him at the bottom of the stairs while he took his time but he could move fast when he needed to; as his dash from the shower room earlier demonstrated.

Seven Days at Oak Valley

Once outside, the two men moved behind the elm tree that had served as Tony's resting post the night before. Joey grinned at Tony, reached down and produced a minor miracle from the inside of his left shoe: a pack of matches.

"Man," Tony exclaimed, with obvious respect. "Where'd you get those?"

Like most things at Oak Valley, matches were expressly forbidden. Anyone discovered with matches could count on serious time spent in the superintendent's office followed by a lengthy stay in the tight room. Just how long of a stay couldn't be determined, because the room's dim light stayed on all the time. The only window was on the door. The smoky glass was the size of shoebox, big enough for the workers to see in, but too small to see was happening on the outside.

"Miss G'een," Joey said, wearing a sly smile. "Office 'all," he explained further, "cryin'. 'Er no see me."

A picture of Joey, leaning over Miss Lambuth's desk as she reached back to get a Kleenex for his fake tears flashed through Tony's mind. Joey, with his innocent looking face covered with tears, would never be suspected of pinching her matches. Joey, with his innocent looking face and his well-to-do parents, was never suspected of doing anything. Tony, on the other hand, worked extra hard at not getting caught.

They lit up. Tony suppressed a laugh as Joey struggled not to cough. Joey was not a big smoker. Tony inhaled and exhaled smoke rings. Smoke rings never failed to impress Joey. Tinker was the one who had taught him how, and, as a trick it was always a

Ruthie-Marie Beckwith

crowd pleaser. Too bad he hadn't had a chance to use it on Debbie the night before.

"'Ebbie?" Joey asked.

Tony took his second drag on his cigarette. "She wasn't there," he replied. Joey looked surprised. Joey had told him that Debbie was interested in him. At least, that's what Wanda Sue, one of Debbie's roommates, had confirmed. Wanda Sue told everyone everybody's business, whether they wanted to know or not.

"I was late," Tony explained. "Jefferson was in the garden with Jones. I had to wait in the bushes until they quit talkin'."

"'Aught?" Joey inquired.

"Nah," Tony replied, "I didn't get caught. But haven' t' listen to them jawin', along with smellin' Jefferson's old cigar smoke made me late to see Debbie."

Joey laughed. Everyone hated the smell of Dr. Jefferson's cigars except, of course, Dr. Jefferson himself.

"Yeah," Tony continued, "they kept talkin' and talkin'. Somethin' about somethin' missin' and it causin' a problem if some guy named Mr. Senator's buddies found out. Somethin' else about gossip and a grissly mill. Another man was there talkin' like a doctor. I figure it was Cordell. Mrs. Jefferson said she was goin' to feed 'em all a cold supper. She must've been pretty mad."

"Alk, 'alk," Joey mimicked with a deeper voice like he was Dr. Jefferson.

"Problem, problem," Tony echoed, drawing himself up to attention like he was Big Mac Jones.

Seven Days at Oak Valley

Swaggering around Joey, he pointed his index and thumb with his still lit cigarette between them at his friend. "You boys know this is a problem," he said, shaking the cigarette the way Jones did in his dinky office. "You boys know that is a problem," Tony added.

As usual, once started, Joey couldn't laughing.

"Everyone and everythin' is a problem, boys," he concluded when Joey fell to the ground laughing. Taking one final drag off his cigarette, Tony flicked it aside.

"'Befast," Joey stated in between laughs.

As if in reply, the siren sounded and he reached down to help Joey up off the grass. Joey tilted to the left and then to the right, using Tony's arm as an anchor to catch his balance.

"Got us a free day, Joey, now, that's not a problem, is it?"

"No 'ay," Joey replied. He pointed across the leaf strewn lawn in the direction of a sagging chain link fence and asked, "'Struction?"

"Perfect!" Tony agreed. "There won't be no workers around and I know just the place to sneak in. I haven't been over there since they started putting the walls up. Who knows what we'll find. We'll still have to keep an eye out for Mac or his other goons. You up to that?"

"'Ood," Joey indicated. He turned toward the dining hall.

"O.k., no exploring on an empty stomach," Tony conceded.

In tandem, they exclaimed, "Forward, march," and began walking slowly toward the squat one story dining hall in the early morning sun.

Ruthie-Marie Beckwith

7:30 a.m.

Grace watched her husband pull a pillow over his head as she fumbled for the telephone on the bedside table. Why they had installed it on her side of the bed made no sense to her. Winfred was the one who had folks calling him at all times of the day and night. On the sixth ring, she managed to pluck the receiver from its cradle and answer, "Hello?"

A minute later she shifted in the bed and rolled over to nudge him. "Winfred?"

"I'm awake," he grumbled.

"Mac's on the phone and he says it is urgent he speak with you," she informed him in a soft voice that still retained traces of her Memphis Delta upbringing.

"Hand it over," he told her while stifling a yawn.

"Mac?" he asked. He sat up and swung his feet over the side. Curious about the call, Grace stayed upright in the bed beside him, trying with varying success to overhear Mac's news.

"Winfred," she heard Mac report in his usual heavy-handed tone of voice. "I'm sorry to disturb you and the missus. You'll need to get your coat and hat, I'm afraid."

"What's going on?"

"I'm at the infirmary. You need to get down here."

"Whatever it is, Mac, can't you get someone there to deal with it? It's Sunday morning, for heaven's sake."

"I don't think anyone else'll be able to deal with this, Winfred," Mac countered.

Seven Days at Oak Valley

Jefferson switched the handset to his other ear and Grace lost track of the conversation. Disappointed, she leaned back against the ornately carved cherry headboard and waited for the call to end.

"I'll be right there," he advised Mac. He handed Grace the handset and launched himself out of bed, snatching up the pair of trousers and shirt she had laid out the night before on the antique valet stand adjacent to his closet. He flew out of the room and the next thing she heard was his voice calling to her.

She groaned and slid out of bed to go to him. The soles of her slippers swooshed against the hardwood floor of the hallway that led to the main bathroom. She rapped on the door, raising her voice in order to be heard over the sound of running water.

"Winfred?" she asked.

"I'm going out," she heard him explain through the door. "Mac's got an emergency over at the infirmary I need to see to. You go on to chapel without me. I'm afraid this may take awhile."

"But you were out so late last night!" she complained.

At that moment the door flew open. She stepped aside as he pushed by her, fully dressed with traces of shaving cream still clinging to his bushy sideburns. He covered the distance to the upstairs landing in three long steps.

"What could be so urgent on a Sunday morning?" She called out, trying to keep pace with him. She pursued him down the stairs, the ends of the sash to her robe flailing behind her.

"Winfred!" Grace cried out in exasperation. "What is goin' on?"

Jefferson continued to ignore her as he grabbed his hat and tan overcoat from the hall tree. He reached for the doorknob. Then, appearing to reconsider, he turned back to face her. Her disheveled blond hair partially concealed her hazel eyes from his penetrating gaze. His expression hardened and for a moment she thought he was going to reach out to brush it away from her face.

"Well, you'll find out soon enough," he told her. "Mac said he found Cordell dead in his office when he was making his mornin' rounds."

Grace gasped. The blood drain from her face and her whole body swayed. She flung out her arm to grab hold of the banister. She drew in a deep breath as he took another step toward her and yet another. She sensed him measuring the intensity of her response and struggled for control. Her fingers tightened their grip around the handrail, leaning on it for support.

A third deep breath supplied the strength she needed to return his probing gaze with one of her own. She brushed the hair off of her face with her free hand and raised her chin. Her stance on the first stair step made her height feel identical to his.

Grace looked him in the eye and dredged up her mother's most imperious expression from memory and claimed it as her own. Squaring her shoulders in a manner that almost dared him to do otherwise, she told him, "Then I guess you had best be goin'."

After what seemed like an eternity, he retreated and opened the door to leave. "I'll be back as soon as I'm able," Jefferson told her, closing the door behind him. She watched through the parlor window until he disappeared from sight around the corner of the

Seven Days at Oak Valley

house. Certain that she was out of his view, she sank into the one of the parlor's mismatched upholstered chairs and buried her face in her hands.

The clock on the mantel sounded the hour. The current of her discontent began to swell and she rose with it, pacing to and fro across the faded oriental carpet. John was dead. How could that be? Last night he had been here for dinner, winking and smiling at her, making her feel part of an undefined inside joke.

The other men bickered and debated over the same multitude of topics they had carried to her table for close to two years. John? John, in way she couldn't quite describe, seemed unaffected by the other men's intense obsessions. It was that particular quality that had led to their friendship, a degree of detachment from his work that she had long given up hoping to find in Winfred.

The amount of time Winfred spent running Oak Valley was directly proportional to the degree of unhappiness that had been building inside of her since they had returned to Tennessee from Oklahoma. He had promised her that this job would be different, that he would spend more time with her.

Winfred had been foolish to believe that they could leave Oklahoma behind and somehow start over with each other. Winfred, being Winfred, had only taken three weeks to get caught back up in the minutia of what it took to keep one of these places running. She, on the other hand, was still expected to serve as an ornament, regardless of how much luster had been lost when she had watched their two-month-old son's body being lowered into the grave in Enid.

Ruthie-Marie Beckwith

Now, two years later, there was yet another death. As the shock of John's death began to take hold, she experienced an overwhelming desire to flee from this horrid place. Standing in front of the beveled glass panes, Grace could see in her reflection the beginning of a fissure she had avoided her entire lifetime open up. Tears welled in her eyes and she pulled tissue after tissue from a box that made its home on the mahogany coffee table.

The weight of her grief took hold, pulling her down onto the floor and the tears she had struggled to keep from falling ran down her cheeks unimpeded. Her blue bathrobe enveloped her and within it she grew quiet. Grace pulled her knees up against to her chest and she stayed in that position long after the clock struck the hour again.

8:00 a.m.

The smell of antiseptic stung his nostrils as Jefferson swung open the glass door at the entrance to the infirmary. Outside he had passed two squad cars from the Laurel County Sheriff's department along with the beige four door Chevy Impala favored by the Oak Valley Security Force. Mac must've called them, he thought as he removed his hat and coat, and Sheriff Thomas' deputies hadn't wasted any time getting there.

He handed his hat and coat to the receptionist who stood wringing her hands behind the front desk. She was petite and in her early twenties. Her curly red hair was disheveled and her eyes were rimmed with the telltale signs of crying. He spent an awkward moment dredging up her name, Cordelia Williams, from the recesses of his memory, along with the fact that she also was going to school part-time to be a special education teacher over at Roane State.

"Good morning, Miss Williams," he said, straightening his tie as he approached her.

"It's just awful, Dr. Jefferson," she wailed as she took his things. "I mean, poor Dr. Cordell. It's so hard to believe! I got to work this mornin' at 7:00 a.m. and there was Mr. Jones, already here to let me in. Since he usually leaves me waiting at least ten minutes or so, I thought he was bein' nice because it was so chilly outside. But then he told me somethin' had happened in the buildin'. I never dreamed! The police and everything..."

Jefferson lost patience with her hysterics and interrupted. Then, to make sure he had her attention, he repeated her name somewhat severely, "Miss Williams."

Startled, she stopped talking and lost her train of thought. "Yes? I mean, yes, sir?"

"You have one of the most important jobs on this campus," he told her. "You operate the main switchboard, isn't that correct?"

Cordelia nodded.

"Then I suggest you take ten minutes, go wash your face, powder your nose and get ready to deal with an extraordinary number of calls today. And don't forget, we also have parents coming in today. It wouldn't do for them to see things all out of sorts, now would it?"

She drew herself up to her full height of five feet, two inches, and nodded, "Yes, sir. Certainly, sir. I'm sure it will be very busy today, just as you say." She reached under the counter to retrieve her pocketbook and moved out from behind the desk.

"One more thing," Jefferson told her as she headed down the hall. "Once this gets out, we may have reporters calling. You're to tell them that no one is available to respond to questions at this time. However, there will be a statement issued at 4:00 p.m. this afternoon by my office. Understood?"

The freckles on her face faded as she turned white and she froze in her tracks. "Reporters?" she repeated, flustered once again.

"Yes, ma'am. Reporters. Now, go!" he ordered. Heeding him at last, she turned quickly and hurried down the hall, her heels clicking in tandem on the ancient white linoleum block floor.

Further down the hall Mac Jones crossed paths with her as he headed to join Jefferson. Jones greeted her perfunctorily, "Miss Williams."

"Mac," Jefferson heard her reply before dashing into the safety of the ladies room.

Jefferson strode down the hall toward Jones, catching up with him in front of the elevator. "Mac, fill me in," he demanded. "What in blue blazes is going on?"

Jones pointed to the open doors of the elevator. "This way, Winfred. I'll explain as we go."

Jones pushed the down button and began briefing his boss. "They're down in the basement. He was already dead when I found him this mornin'. I was making my rounds, openin' up. His office was already unlocked, so I went in to check it out and there he was, lying face down behind one of his mountain high stacks of paperwork. Not much blood, but it sure ain't no accident."

Seven Days at Oak Valley

Jefferson stepped into the elevator with Jones, "And the sheriff's department?"

"Waitin' on you. Sheriff said the coroner's on his way. Might take a while, they had to drag him outta' bed. Seem's like he had a late night dealin' with a big ole' tractor trailer wreck down on I-40."

"So who's here?" Jefferson asked.

"There's four of 'em," Mac replied. "Sheriff Thomas, himself, and Deputies Ward, Baker, and Anderson."

"Thomas?" Jefferson repeated and smiled for the first time that morning. "That old fox?"

"Old coot, some say," Mac responded.

Jefferson's smile evaporated. Thomas was one of their biggest local supporters. For ten years running, he and his department had sponsored the annual fishing rodeo down on the Lower Pigeon River. Proceeds went to the Christmas fund.

"Please tell me there's no bad blood between you and Billy," Jefferson stated. Jones had come on board at Oak Valley shortly after failing to unseat Thomas in Laurel County's most recent hotly contested race for the Office of Sheriff.

Jones narrowed his eyes and murmured, "None that's gonna interfere with my job here, Winfred."

"This couldn't have come at a worse time," Jefferson said as the elevator door slid open. They stepped out into the hall and came face to face with Thomas and his crew.

Deputies Ward and Anderson looked ill at ease at their post by the door to Cordell's office. Thomas' face was flushed, as though he had spent the last hour running a dangerous fugitive to ground instead of pacing the basement hall. However his uniform was starched and creased and fit perfectly despite his portly stature. All manner of gadgets hung off his belt and those of his deputies. His felt hat with his silver sheriff's badge pinned to it was securely tucked under his left arm. He reached into his left pocket, pulled out a notepad and a pen, and scribbled a quick note.

"What couldn't have come at a worst time?" Thomas asked Jefferson, picking up on the two men's conversation.

Jefferson offered his hand and countered with a question of his own, "Billy, I can't say it's good to see you, not under these circumstances. How's the Missus?"

Thomas conjured up a grin and shook hands. "Just fine, Winfred. Just fine. Spendin' all my money in Knoxville, as usual. And Mrs. Jefferson?"

Jefferson smiled back. "Pestering me to retire. Wants to go to Florida and live in some kind of new fangled condominium. I told her this old hound still has some good running years left in him."

Thomas stood back, his business demeanor descending upon him like a veil. "So why is this the worst time, Dr. Jefferson?"

Jefferson drew back into his bureaucratic version of formality, replying smoothly, "Well, Sheriff Thomas, as you might recall, Sundays are visiting days here and by noon we're going to be overrun with all manner of residents' parents and families."

Thomas nodded in sympathy. "Expect any of these parents to be comin' over here?"

"No, but I'm sure once word gets out, they'll be queued up out my front door trying to find out

Seven Days at Oak Valley

what's going on. Dr. Cordell was very popular with the families."

Jefferson paused as Thomas nodded his head as though he sympathized with the challenges of facing unhappy parents.

"Furthermore, our annual accreditation survey, that is to say inspection, is less than two weeks away. That's what I meant. You know me, Sheriff, all business. Having a homicide investigation going on in the middle of that is going to make it real complicated, that's all."

Then, thinking that perhaps he had overstated his case, Jefferson backpedaled, "But Dr. Cordell's murder is certainly more important than any of my accreditation problems."

"What makes you think it's a homicide?"

"Mac here filled me in just a piece on the way over. But of course, I need to hear what you've found so far."

Thomas pointed across the hall. "Let's go into the conference room. I believe that's what it's called? Unless, of course, you want to go see the body?"

"No, Billy, if it's alright with you," Jefferson replied. "I'll take it on your word and Mac's that Dr. Cordell has joined the dearly departed."

The three men moved across the hall and sat down at a worn mahogany table surrounded by a collection of mismatched chairs in various states of repair. The white walls reflected the light from the florescent fixture above. Two dirty ashtrays sat forlornly at the far end of the table. Notices on Oak Valley official letterhead covered the bulletin board facing the door.

Ruthie-Marie Beckwith

Jefferson sat back in the chair facing Thomas and waited as Thomas flipped open his notepad.

"Well, now you understand this is all very preliminary. We've only been at it for forty-five minutes and basically we've secured the area here and rousted the coroner."

Jefferson raised an eyebrow in Jones' direction at the forty-five minutes portion of the Thomas' update. So, they'd already been at it for quite some time before he'd gotten the call, he thought. His already low opinion of Mac dropped even further. He forced his attention back to Thomas.

"I understand, Sheriff. You've just started your investigation."

"The gist of what I do know is that Dr. Cordell was found by Mac here at six forty-five a.m. face down in the office when he was opening up shop for the day. From what I can see, without the coroner havin' to point it out, he was stabbed two times. No tellin' which one did the job or if it was even the stabbin' that killed him. No weapon in sight. The door was open. Mac claims one of his men checked out the buildin' last night around ten thirty-eight p.m. and the door was locked. Coroner'll be able to shed some light on the time of death."

Jones shifted in his chair, cleared his throat and asked, "So who'll be doing the investigation, Sheriff?"

Thomas' glance at Jones made it clear that he felt Jones' was speaking out of turn. Ignoring him, he explained to Jefferson, "We're talkin' about a homicide investigation, Winfred. I'm gonna get a crew up here from Knoxville to take care of gatherin' the preliminaries, forensic evidence and such. In fact, I'm waitin' on their commander to return my call

Seven Days at Oak Valley

soon as I get back to my office. I'm gonna need y'alls full support and cooperation."

"Of, course. You've got it," Jefferson replied.

"I've got a list of names of people who work in this building that Mac here has given me. He told me that only the top floor is used on the weekend. That's where the residents who are sick are kept?"

"That's true, that is, residents who aren't sick enough to be sent to Knoxville Memorial. Our director of nursing could fill you in on who was here this weekend. Of course, Dr. Cordell made rounds each morning. He was very dedicated to his work."

"We're gonna need to know how to get in touch with his next of kin," Thomas told him.

"Dr. Cordell was single. I don't think he had anyone special. The rumor mill had him painted as somewhat of a ladies' man. His family's somewhere down in Chattanooga. I believe his mama is still living and he has two sisters. I'll have Mac carry the details over to you as soon as I can put my hands on them. Anything else I can do to help?"

Thomas paused a minute and then asked, "I know my askin' might not sit well with you, but you don't suppose there's any chance one of your residents here had anything to do with this?"

"No, Billy, I mean I don't see how. Curfew is well before ten-thirty and none of them could even get close to a knife or anything that poses any danger. No, that's clearly out of the realm of possibility."

"Well, that's all I have until the Coroner gets here. This part of the building will be off limits for a while, I'm afraid," Thomas concluded.

"That won't be a problem," Jefferson said. "You'll keep me posted, Billy?"

Ruthie-Marie Beckwith

Thomas nodded. Jefferson stood up. Jones rose and left the room as Thomas and Jefferson shook hands once again.

"Terrible business," Jefferson added.

"I suppose you'll have all those Nashville officials breathin' down your neck over this one, Winfred." The men walked together to the elevator. It opened as they approached and Jefferson stepped inside. He nodded in agreement at Billy as the elevator door. Alone in the elevator, he pressed the button for the main floor and reflected. "I suppose I will. I suppose I will."

1:00 p.m.

Shortly after noon, a small trickle of cars entered the main gate. The guard station was unmanned, a Sunday courtesy for families who, tired after long drives, need not be delayed any further from visiting their loved ones. The drivers passed by the rustic brown and yellow Oak Valley State Training School and Hospital sign replete with the Tennessee State Seal beneath which read, "An Accredited Facility". The vehicles kept to their right as they followed the Dogwood Loop to Assembly Hall, the central check in point for Visitor's Day.

Tony and Joey watched from the vantage point of a lofty perch on the water tower. They had decided to postpone their trek to the construction zone until after the weekly parade concluded. Tony kept count as one by one the vehicles parked in orderly fashion and their occupants emerged.

Seven Days at Oak Valley

"Well, Joey, that's it," he reported. "Forty-two. The Coles just pulled in and you know they're always the last to get here and the first to leave."

Hearing no response, he turned and faced his roommate. "You already knew they weren't comin', Joey," he stated when he saw how Joey's watery eyes were staring at the narrow road.

"Aw, come, on," he told Joey as he began climbing down from their perch.

Joey followed, still watching the road.

"We gotta' get going, Joey," Tony told him when they were both on the ground. "We're wasting time and besides, you know they'll be here next week. You know they've never missed two weeks in a row. I swear they'll be here next week. Now, come on, let's get goin'."

He grabbed Joey by the arm and started dragging him in the direction of the athletic fields. Joey began to move on his own steam and Tony let go. They followed the Dogwood Loop until they hit the Lost Creek turn off. Tony barely slowed as they crossed the road but Joey came to a full stop and began to search his pockets. Sensing that Joey was no longer following, Tony stopped and turned.

"'Teen," Joey said and pointed north to the dining hall across the lower path where the Canteen was also housed.

"I told you, Joey," Tony said, struggling to keep his temper in check. "I ain't got no money or plastic pennies. You do what you wanna' do. I'm going to check out those new buildings."

Tony waited to see if Joey was going to follow, but Joey stood his ground, grinning. He slyly pulled his right hand out of his pocket holding a dollar bill.

Ruthie-Marie Beckwith

Then he pulled his hand out of his left pocket, revealing another dollar bill.

"'Eat,' Joey told him.

Joey was full of surprises today, Tony thought as he took in Joey's offer to treat him. He held off long enough to give Joey's offer the consideration it deserved and then announced his decision.

"On the way back. The siren'll ring like always before they close. We'll have time to go check it out then."

Joey looked crestfallen but he followed him across the street. "'Kay," he said.

Tony came to an abrupt stop as he and Joey came around a bend in the road. His eyes got wide as he took in the squad cars from the sheriff's department parked beside a hearse in front of the infirmary. Cop cars were never a good sign, except when it was time for the annual rodeo, which he knew had long since passed. Whatever the problem was, it had nothing to do with him. He whistled low as Joey collided into him from behind.

"Joey!" Tony hissed as he recovered his balance and grabbed Joey in the process. Joey righted himself and faced Tony with a puzzled expression.

"Man," Tony admonished as he pointed toward the squad cars, "you don't pay attention to nothin'!"

Joey turned to look. Two uniformed men emerged from the front door of the infirmary along with another man dressed in a dark rumpled suit.

"'Uts goin' on?" Joey whispered.

"Nothin' good," Tony told him. "Not when cop cars are here. We're gonna have to go around."

Seven Days at Oak Valley

Joey shook his head in agreement and turned back. Tony remained still a moment longer, taking in the scene and then fell in step with his roommate.

"We'll have to see what we can find out later," Tony told him.

"Yeah, 'ater," Joey agreed.

Tony slowed his pace to Joey's more laborious gait. Beside him, Joey moved one foot in front of the other, struggling as his uncooperative muscles catapulted him side to side like a top ready to give in to the forces of gravity. They covered the remaining distance to the construction site in twenty minutes.

Tony headed for the spot where the chain link fence wasn't anchored to the ground, an oversight on the part of the construction foreman. He inserted his fingers into the metal mesh at the bottom of the fence and pulled. Joey dropped to the ground and shimmied through the gap.

Once on the other side, Joey repeated Tony's action of pulling on the fence as Tony slid forward to join him. They both stood up and made a half-hearted attempt at brushing the dirt off their clothes. Pleased with his own display of prowess, Tony decided to let Joey take command of their exploration as a reward for getting the matches.

"So, where to?" he asked.

Predictably, Joey pointed to the building where the construction effort had progressed the furthest. Outside walls were in place along with doorways. Glass cubes had already been stacked and mortared together to form a row of three four-feet-square windows beneath what would be a one-story eave.

"Good choice," he affirmed and headed off in that direction.

Ruthie-Marie Beckwith

The construction crew had shown up early last spring. Tony and Joey were able to track their progress by simply watching out their dorm room window since Building K had the best view of the construction site as well as the cemetery. The heavy equipment had been brought in by way of a new road built expressly for that purpose, Redbud Lane, which ended at Lost Creek Road. To the north, the site was accessible by way of Chestnut Lane, a rarely used gravel road that had until now served only as access to the cemetery.

Construction had begun in earnest following a ribbon cutting ceremony attended by the Governor, several legislators, all the school's employees, a handpicked group of residents that included Joey, and their families. Following the ceremony, Joey had carried the news about the purpose of the construction back to Building K. Ten new cottages, the word had been, along with another dining hall for the complex. Tony had been the one to get the scoop on who would be moving to the cottages once they were completed.

"Wheelchairs," he announced to his roommates at the dining hall the day after the ribbon cutting ceremony. "The wheelchairs and babies are the ones that get to move. Looks like we're still stuck in old Building K."

After the purpose of the construction had been laid bare, Tony made it an integral part of his daily mail route, even though there would be no official mail to deliver there for some time to come. He kept the rest of his roommates up to date on the construction crew's progress, filling them in on what the crew members' names were, the steps involved in

Seven Days at Oak Valley

pouring a foundation, and other information gleaned by standing at the fence for long periods of time and watching.

On weekends he'd slip into the abandoned site and scour the ground for discarded hardware. Occasionally he found a tool set down and left behind by a careless construction worker. All the treasures he found were stored away in his locker.

Today Tony was letting Joey take the lead. Joey had sneaked into the site with Tony only once before and that had been early on. This was his first trip back since the plumbing fixtures had been set and cinder block walls had begun to take shape. Tony scoured the ground looking for treasures to add to the collection in his trunk. He followed Joey as they went from foundation to foundation.

Two hours later, at the last foundation that had been framed, but was yet to be poured, Joey shouted and reached down into a mire of mud and rubbish directly in front of him. Tony moved to his side and whistled low as Joey extended both hands and tugged at the tied knot of a black garbage bag.

"You lucky dog," Tony exclaimed. He glanced around and gestured for them to move behind one of the new walls being raised in the center of the complex. "Don't want anyone to see you looking at your buried treasure," he explained, making no effort to disguise his envy of Joey's discovery. "Let me see!"

Joey hesitated, struggling with the knot. Recognizing his frustration, Tony took hold of the bag, tore a hole in the side, and handed it back to Joey. Joey put his hand into the hole and pulled out a white shirt wadded into a ball. Puzzled, he handed the shirt to Tony and reached in again, pulling out a brown men's loafer that was quickly joined by another. Tony eyed the shoes with unveiled longing as he shook out the shirt.

"Really stained," Tony observed. He held it up for Joey to see. In the light, the brown stain took on a reddish hue. Two one-inch cuts near the left pocket triggered a thought that Joey observed aloud.

"'Ood."

Hoping to conceal a growing concern over their find, Tony shook his head. "Nah. That's not blood. It's just your 'magination getting control of you, Joey. That's probably spaghetti sauce from last Wednesday's dining hall special." He wadded up the shirt and handed it back to Joey. "Put it back in the bag," he instructed. "Won't do no good to put that into the laundry bin. Besides, probably never see it again, anyways. The shoes, now, they could be cleaned up."

"Yeah," Joey agreed. He held the muddy shoes out to Tony. "'Ry 'em."

Tony slipped one foot and then another into the shoes. He couldn't believe how well they fit, only once before had he had a pair of shoes that fit that good. As he slipped his feet out of the shoes he noticed that his right heel was covered with the reddish color of clay mixed with mud. "Nice," he commented as he held them out to Joey.

"You 'eep," Joey told him.

"Really?" Tony asked, stunned by his good fortune. "You are the best roommate a guy could *ever* have! Wish I'd had these babies last night!"

Tony slipped the shoes back on while Joey stuffed the shirt back into the black bag and closed it with another knot.

Seven Days at Oak Valley

"Can't believe someone threw these away!" Tony said as he helped Joey push the bag into a crevice in the incomplete masonry of the wall. Shielding his eyes from the sun, he looked back across the grounds. "Looks like it's getting late. You go on to the Canteen without me. I'm gonna head over to the steam plant and see if Tinker is back."

Even though he knew Tinker had left early the day before and wasn't due to return until tomorrow, he was always happy to have an excuse to visit the steam plant. He and Tinker had been tight since the first day Tony arrived at Oak Valley, at least to hear Tony's side of the story.

Joey waited as Tony held up the weak spot in the chain link fence and slipped through ahead of him.

"'Ater, 'gator," Joey told Tony as he followed behind him.

"Don't spend all your money in one place," Tony advised him. They headed west along the lower path and then turned off in different directions.

2:00 p.m.

Jefferson glanced up at Grace as she placed a glass of iced tea on the table next to his chair. He'd been on the phone for an hour after he'd gotten back from his regular Sunday lunch with the president of Oak Valley's Parent Guardian Association. His eyes were drawn to her lithe figure as she gracefully leaned up against the archway to listen to his side of the conversation he was having with Dr. Andrew White, the assistant commissioner of the Tennessee Department of Mental Health and Mental Deficiency. A coughing sound coming from the black receiver

Ruthie-Marie Beckwith

pressed to his ear drew him back to the matter at hand.

"Yes, sir," he responded into the mouthpiece. "Dr. White," Jefferson asserted, "I am familiar with departmental procedure."

He suppressed a yawn as his boss continued to dictate instructions regarding the matter of Cordell's death.

"No, Sheriff Thomas didn't say whether he was going to bring the TBI into it."

"Yes, I know this is state property and all and it really is the TBI's jurisdiction. But you know as well as I do that county sheriffs have their own opinions about what does and what doesn't fall within their purview."

Hearing no response to that observation, Jefferson took advantage of the lull in conversation to shift White's attention to another problem that Cordell's death had created. "Now that Cordell's dead, I'm going to need a back up Medical Director until personnel can get someone over here for us."

"Yes, sir, I'll do that," Jefferson continued, jotting a note on the legal pad perched on the armrest of his chair. "I'm sure Mike over at Pleasant View or Janice at Rolling Hills would be happy to share the services of their Medical Director during the interim. I need to call them anyways about putting off our monthly superintendents' meeting. I'll give them a ring as soon as we finish up."

"One more thing I'm sure you'll want to know," Jefferson continued. "Senator Russell was here yesterday, snooping around."

"Yes, I know it was Saturday," Jefferson replied with a little more force than he intended. He knew full well that legislators usually confined their business hours to Monday through Friday. "That's why I'm bringing it up. He said he was on his way back from Bristol and just thought he'd stop by."

"No, he left last night around nine-thirty. Said he still had a long drive ahead of him. Had to get back to Nashville. Said he'd be back on Tuesday to get brought up to speed on the construction."

"Yeah, I know his committee is raising cane about the delays," Jefferson remarked, becoming more defensive with each minute the conversation continued. "Apparently his esteemed committee members think I'm somehow responsible for all the rain we had last spring."

"No, sir, I'll tow the company line," he responded. "My report will only have the facts and figures they've requested."

"Yes, I'll send it to you as soon as it's finished tomorrow."

Jefferson hung up the phone and reached into his left pocket to retrieve his handkerchief. He mopped his brow with his left hand as he reached into his briefcase to remove a single piece of paper. His wife's handwriting filled a page of her custom ordered stationary. Dated three days ago, it was addressed cordially to Dr. John T. Cordell. The contents of the note however, appeared to him to be far more than cordial.

Jefferson looked up at Grace as she stared at the paper.

"Grace," he told her, "we need to talk."

Ruthie-Marie Beckwith

3:45 p.m.

Thomas hung his hat on the antlers of a buck mounted on the wall of his office and sat at his desk. Deputy Ward stood in the doorway waiting for instructions. Thomas looked up to tell him that he could go on home for the day when the phone rang. Waving Ward off, he picked up the receiver while simultaneously hearing Julie, his administrative assistant call out, "TBI on Line 1."

"Thomas," he answered while leaning over his desk to pick up a stack of pink "While You Were Out" message slips.

"Sheriff Thomas," he responded, emphasizing each syllable as he flipped through the pile, noting that half of them were illegible and the other half lacked information about the caller. He grimaced at one where Julie had written, "Some guy called". The final three had been taken by Deputy Ward and were marked URGENT, each one a call from Andy Knowles over at the Laurelville Daily Register.

He groaned and turned his attention back to the telephone, interrupting the caller in midstream. Holding up his fist, he ticked off the primary points he always made whenever confronted with representatives from the TBI, raising a finger as he stated each.

"I am aware that this is a case of a suspicious death on the grounds of state facility. And, yes, I am aware that the esteemed Tennessee Bureau of Investigation is always willing and able to assist with any investigations relative to situations such as this on state property. I am also aware that this state facility is located within the boundaries of Laurel

Seven Days at Oak Valley

County, the jurisdiction of which falls within the purview of the Laurel County Sheriff's Department. We have the situation well in hand and will notify you when we have something to report."

Without giving the caller a chance to respond, Thomas slammed down the phone, muttering, "Hell and damnation. Took them long enough to figure out one of the state's employees isn't going to report to work on Monday."

He pulled a yellow pad out from the center draw of his desk and began making his first set of case notes. His deputies would be processing the official documentation, but he always liked to capture his own thoughts and observations. First impressions always ended up having some real bearing on a case.

Thomas wrote out the location of the crime and the name of the deceased. Under <u>Crime Scene</u> he noted, "struggle evident, forensics pending". Under <u>Motive</u>, he put a series of question marks, no telling what was going to crawl out from under the rocks at Oak Valley when he started turning them over. Finally, he added <u>Suspects</u> to the list under which he wrote, "too damn many". As the largest of the state's centers for the retarded, there was no end to the number of employees, or residents (regardless of what Jefferson had to say about it) who may have had some knowledge of what had happened to Cordell. He'd most likely find himself hip deep in a political cesspool before the facts of this case were uncovered. He sure hoped his waders were big enough to keep any of it from sticking to him.

Ruthie-Marie Beckwith

5:00 p.m.

Tony kept his eyes on his tray while Wanda Sue sat next to Joey chattering on about the events of the day that he and Joey had missed while off exploring the construction site. Why Joey had chosen to sit by her, he couldn't fathom. He looked at her eye to eye, and he didn't particularly like what he saw. Her mousy brown hair was cut bluntly into the shape of a bowl, the only other style the Oak Valley barber might someday master, and her face was covered with acne that still erupted despite her being in her early thirties. Today she was dressed in a brown plaid skirt that fell in a crooked hemline above chubby knees and a dull cream blouse with the telltale splotches of spaghetti sauce down the front.

She gave Tony a cursory glance and said loud enough for everyone within earshot to hear, "Debbie was real disappointed, last night, Joey. Debbie thought your friend was gonna come visiting." Tony cussed under his breath and continued to spoon the rest of his peas into his mouth.

Wanda Sue giggled at Tony's discomfort and asked, "So what did you and Tony do today, Joey?" pronouncing Tony's name "Tah-o-ony" as if it had three or four syllables instead of two. I didn't see your folks' car over in the parkin' lot when I said good-by to my mom and dad."

Joey's mood shifted from enjoying the teasing his friend was getting to irritation at being reminded that his folks hadn't made the long drive for Visitor's Day. He glared at her and bragged in response, "'Struction."

Seven Days at Oak Valley

Tony grunted a warning at Joey, but Joey, having been provoked continued, "'Splore".

Wanda Sue leaned forward, now showing greater interest than normal in what Joey typically had to say, "Exploring?"

"Joey," Tony said, growling another warning.

Joey continued ignoring his roommate and gesturing to his own shirt, he added, "'Oody."

Wanda Sue's eyes grew large. She shifted her gaze to Tony who stood up abruptly, cutting off the conversation.

Facing Wanda Sue, he gritted his teeth and squeezed out, "We didn't find no bloody shirt, Miss Wanda Sue Blabbermouth. Just some bag of trash that had dirty old rags in it." Then turning to Joey, he ordered, "We're leaving, Joey, now!"

Wanda Sue backed away as Tony pushed his past her to Joey's side. She turned and walked over to the table across the room where Debbie sat watching the whole exchange.

Tony resisted the temptation to look across the room in the women's direction and picked up his tray. Joey stood and lifted his own from the table as well. The green compartments on Tony's tray revealed traces of tomato sauce, the only evidence of their meal of spaghetti, peas, a slice of white bread, and a store bought cookie. Joey's tray was similarly empty with the exception of the cookie that Tony eyed with considerable interest.

"Aren't you gonna eat your cookie?" he asked, deliberately changing the subject.

"No," Joey replied.

"Well, then," Tony responded and reached out with one hand to snatch it off the tray. Joey dodged

Ruthie-Marie Beckwith

Tony's effort by attempting to turn sideways and lost his balance in the process. His tray grazed the head of the resident seated directly behind him at the adjacent table who yelled out in anger more than pain. All heads in the dining room went up to locate the source of the commotion. Tony did his best to appear nonchalant as Joey pocketed the cookie and moved on. The worker stationed near the overloaded conveyor belt that bore trays back to the dish room moved toward them.

"Now look what you've done!" Tony exclaimed in annoyance.

"'You 'id," Joey retorted, continuing toward the conveyor belt with his head down. As he reached the end of the aisle, the worker moved to block his path.

"Gonna write you up for that, saw the whole thing. You hittin' him in the head with your tray," the worker began as he pointed at Joey.

"'Ipped," Joey replied in his own defense.

"Startin' a fight, I say. That's what's goin' in my report and that's what the supervisor is goin' to read first thing in the mornin'," the worker smirked. "You goin' t'be on report, boy. Now I'm just wonderin' what yo' momma and daddy are gonna say about that."

Joey winced at the word "fight" and repeated his defense, "'ipped."

"C'mon, man, he told you he tripped," Tony cut in.

"You probably the one what put him up to it, Mr. Sassy Ass," the worker responded. "Guess you both gonna have to be in my report."

Tony's bravado faltered and he looked around the dining hall for the reactions of the other

Seven Days at Oak Valley

residents. Two hundred and fifty heads went down like a slow moving ocean wave as his glance swept the room. His eyes landed on the other worker stationed just inside the door. The white-jacketed figure left his post and moved toward them. Joey shifted his weight from one leg to the other as Tony moved closer to his side. The second worker stopped three tables away from the three men.

"I say he tripped," the second worker spoke out. "From where I was standin', he tripped." The clatter of forks against compartmentalized trays ceased. The first worker stepped aside as Joey made his way around him.

The worker hissed, "Later, boy. No report means you pay anyways. Me'n my friends, we know just the thing to do with retards who like to start fights. We'll be making our rounds one night this week. Better be on the look out and you better have somethin' good to give us."

Joey watched wide-eyed as the worker formed a fist with his right hand and punched it into his open left hand. "Puny as you are," the worker continued, "it won't take long for us to collect. Money or goods, don't make no difference to us. Don't forget."

Tony inserted himself between the worker and Joey. Joey stepped back and turned toward the dish room. Heads around the dining hall turned to stare at him, a tacit commentary on the tension he'd created in the hall. At the dish room, Tony moved deftly around Joey, shoved his tray into an empty crevice, and strutted out of the building. Joey waited for another crevice to appear, slid his tray into it, and made his way to the door.

Ruthie-Marie Beckwith

Once outside, Tony turned to face his roommate. His face was red with frustration.

"Why do you want to go and cause somethin' like that over a damn cookie?" he demanded.

Shifting his weight from one foot to the other, Joey muttered, "'portant."

Tony's anxiousness from the dining hall coalesced into real anger. "Look, Joey, and you listen up!" he shouted. "You told that fat blabbermouth Wanda Sue about us being at the construction site and even worse about finding that shirt. You just nearly got us busted over a damn cookie. I want to know what's so 'portant about a damn store bought cookie that almost cost me my privileges for a week."

Pointing toward Building B, Joey repeated, "'Portant."

Tony exhaled in total frustration. "Important enough to get you onto the list of guys they come after? Oh, just get outta' my sight before I hurt my best friend."

"'K," Joey grunted in response as he swung around and moved down the sidewalk. Tony made a point of stomping off, making as much of a ruckus as he could across the lawn toward the middle of the Green. He sat down on the grass with an air of defiance and watched Joey disappear through the front door of Building B.

5:45 p.m.

The late afternoon sun was sliced into dusty ribbons as it passed through the wooden Venetian blinds in the office of the superintendent. Jefferson sat behind a massive oak desk that faced a bank of curtainless windows. The windows provided a view of the expanse of grass that made up the Green and its surrounding environs. The desk had been part of the office since opening day and remained in its original location. Like Jefferson, each of his predecessors had appreciated the vantage point it provided for observing the vast majority of the institution and its occupants.

Ten minutes later Jones' short but stolid frame passed by the window. Jefferson heard the sleigh bells that his secretary had tied to the doorknob jingle as front door opened and closed.

"In here, Mac," Jefferson called out.

"I'll be there in a minute, Winfred," Jones called back. "I need to use the can."

Jefferson waited, drumming his well-manicured fingers on the edge of the blotter. Mac appeared in the doorway and removed his hat.

"Long day," Jefferson commented as Jones took his seat in the dark leather chair in front of his desk.

"Too long," Jones agreed.

"Mine apparently started forty-five minutes later than Sheriff Thomas' crew," Jefferson snapped. "Any particular reason it took so long for you to call?"

Jones fidgeted with his hat and stared at a spot on the wall just past Jefferson's right shoulder. He began, "The policy is . . ."

"Don't give me that, Mac," Jefferson interrupted. "I wrote the damn policy and it doesn't say anything about waiting forty-five minutes before contacting the Administrator-on-duty, which happens to be me." He stood up, placed his hands on the desk, and leaned forward. He thrust his neck out an additional three inches, putting his face within inches of Jones who had shoved his back as far as it would go into the leather upholstery. Jefferson lowered his voice and returned to his seat.

"I don't like being sand bagged, Mac. I don't like it and I won't have it. I'm sure personnel could offer up any number of security employees to take your place. Do I make myself clear?"

"Perfectly," Jones answered, followed with, "sir," almost under his breath. He started to rise out the chair, but Jefferson motioned for him to remain seated.

"So, how goes the investigation?"

"Which investigation do you want to start with?"

"Let's start with the late Dr. Cordell," Jefferson told him. "I'm sure that took up the majority of your time today, keeping Thomas' deputies entertained."

Jones retrieved his notepad from his left shirt pocket, flipped through the first two pages and began, "Well, the coroner finally showed up around ten-thirty. Based on his initial examination, he figured Cordell was dead between eight to ten hours before I found him."

Jones stopped giving his report long enough to wonder aloud, "What could Cordell have been doing in his office at that time of night on a Saturday evening?"

"Beats me," Jefferson replied, "Maybe he was still looking for those files he misplaced. Go on."

"So, Sheriff Thomas asked him about the cause of death. The coroner said he'd have to wait until the autopsy to be sure, but likely as not, it was one of those stab wounds I told you about."

"Anything else?"

Seven Days at Oak Valley

"Oh yeah, seems we might have found the murder weapon."

"How so?"

"Well, after the Coroner shoved off and they'd finished interviewing everyone on the day shift at the infirmary, I started taking Deputy Anderson on a tour of Oak Valley. Thomas and the other two stayed behind to finish searching the building."

"They find anything?"

"Anderson and I'd gone through three buildings and had just hit the Canteen when I had a call from one of my men about a problem at the steam plant, possible break in. You know how some of the boys like to hang around that place."

Jones digressed, "I've told you before that we need to do something about keepin' them away from there. One of these days one of 'ems gonna get hurt."

"So, what else?" Jefferson prompted to get him back on track.

"Well, that was just about an hour ago. So the deputy decides he'd just follow me over since I was headed that way. We got there and sure enough, the door was wide open but the lock wasn't torn up. Tinker must not have locked up proper when he left out on Friday. Anyways, Anderson decides he wants to do an official search bein' as how he's already there and all. So, he goes on in ahead of us. We followed 'im in and stood around talkin' and watchin' while he poked around for a while and then suddenly he pulled out a hanky and reached behind boiler number two."

"And . . ." Jefferson jumped in, trying to get Jones to come to the point.

Ruthie-Marie Beckwith

"And, low and behold he pulls out a letter opener, one of those fancy silver kind like folks get as an award. Anderson held it out to me. *NAMD Fellow* was on engraved on one side of the blade and nineteen seventy-six was engraved on the other. We both looked it over and I swore that it looked like there was dried blood left in the engraving. So Anderson got on his radio and called over to Thomas. Thomas came drivin' up in his car leavin' a trail of dust clear back to Dogwood Circle. They bagged the thing and said they were going to have it tested to see if it could be the murder weapon."

"So there you have it," Jones concluded.

"Are they going to question Tinker? He's been here so long I think he came with the place."

"I believe they plan on it but it seems like Tinker called in today. Sheriff Thomas called over to his house and his nephew answered the phone and said something about Tinker and his missus' having to drive over to Cleveland to go to some funeral. Looks like he'll have another one to go to when he gets back."

Jefferson ignored Jones' allusion to Cordell's funeral, "So they're finished with their search?"

"The deputies think they are," Jones replied. "Me, I don't know for sure. Thomas said he had a bunch of people he wanted to interview and that he wanted to get with you first thing in the morning. He said to tell you he wants to avoid disrupting folks' routines as much as possible."

Jefferson sat back in his chair. "That's Thomas, all right. You can always count on him being as neighborly as possible. But he's as sly as they come. Keep your eye on him and keep me updated."

"You can count on it."

"They didn't turn up those missing files when they searched the infirmary, did they?"

"Nope, no files."

"Well, they're bound to turn up somewhere. You've checked with the supervisor over at Building B?"

"Twice," Jones replied, "and both times, no files. Who knows, maybe they're sitting on Senator Russell's desk for all we know. He's always been real interested in your and Old Doc Henderson's little experiments."

Jefferson cut him off. "You know if Russell had the files, he would have told us as much last night. No, Cordell must have put them somewhere. He was as absentminded as they come sometimes."

"Well, things sure ran a whole lot smoother when Doc Henderson was in charge, I'll grant you that," Jones agreed. "But then again, if you and old Henderson hadn't always been so gung ho about getting your names written up in some medical journal, we wouldn't have this problem, now would we?

"I've told you before, Mac, it's important research," Jefferson retorted. "If Doc Henderson had paid attention to the new research protocol Health, Education, and Welfare sent down from Washington, we wouldn't have a problem now," he complained.

"I just don't see why y'all got your backs up so much over a bunch of shots and watered down Kool-aid."

"That's neither here nor there," Jefferson countered. "The important thing is to find those records and turn them over to the Alternative Power

Board in Piney Bluff like we're supposed to. And," he added, "before Cordell's replacement and the accreditation team shows up."

"I'll stay on it, Winfred," Jones said defensively, "but you need to figure out what you are going to do if they don't turn up."

"All I can say is a few subjects less in this project won't hurt the results any."

"That's all up to you Ph.D. and M.D. types. Us security types just wish you'd pay better attention to keepin' things locked up around here."

Jones began to rise to his feet but Jefferson motioned again for him to keep his seat. "One other thing I need to add to your plate."

"Like I don't have enough already?"

"I've been doing a review of the procurement records for this year. I'm getting a report ready to give to Senator Russell who has that god awful oversight committee breathing down his neck," Jefferson said, studying Jones' face.

Jones looked him coolly in the eye and said, "And?"

"It seems like we've been going through a somewhat higher than normal rate of dietary and housekeeping supplies. I don't know but I may need you to do some checking for me. I'd hate to think we have a theft problem."

Jones held his gaze as he replied, "Just let me know where and when you want me to start. So is that all?"

Jefferson nodded as he stood up behind his desk. "That's more than enough."

"Well, I'm off to grab some grub. I'll keep you posted. Don't forget to lock up, Winfred," Jones

Seven Days at Oak Valley

admonished. He adjusted his hat and offered up his hand.

Jefferson shook it, saying, "Never have and never will."

Jefferson stood by the window and peeled the wrapper off a cigar as he watched Jones cover the short distance between the Superintendent's Office and the Security Office. He retrieved his cigar cutter from his top desk drawer and used it to neatly slice off the tip of one his special order Partagas cigars.

Bringing the cigar to his lips, he held a worn Zippo lighter to the other end, warming it slightly before letting it touch the flame. Drawing smoke into his mouth and savoring the taste, he made a mental note to place another order soon. Since the embargo, it had been harder than hell to get a decent cigar, but maybe these Nicaraguan Habanas would suffice as a temporary substitute.

He watched the Green as shadows gathered, marking the end of a long and dismal day. Clouds of smoke accumulated around him as he fished in his pocket for his keys. Movement on the edge of the Green caught his eye and he made note of Tinker moving along the perimeter, most likely on his way to the steam plant. Must've gotten back earlier from the funeral than he'd planned, he thought, as he turned out the lights and locked the door behind him.

6:00 p.m.

Joey made his way up the main hallway of the building where the crib cases were housed. Every

Ruthie-Marie Beckwith

Sunday this was part of his ritual way of dealing with his parents' departure after Visiting Day.

The building was usually quiet and understaffed. He had been visiting Building B every Sunday for as long has he could remember. The first job he'd had after his parents left him at Oak Valley was scrubbing the cribs in Building B. All of them. The supervisor who'd assigned him that job had said something about breaking his spirit. He didn't know anything about that but, while he scrubbed cribs, he'd gotten to know the building inside and out and made friends with a couple of the boys who lived there. The job had lasted six months before the supervisor decided he was ready to go over to the workshop and do contracted piece work for plastic pennies.

As Joey passed by the nurses' station, he shot one of his winning smiles at the sole person behind the desk who failed to even glance up from the soap opera digest that held her attention. He made his way to the elevator, pushed the button and entered through the parted doors.

Stepping out of the elevator on the second floor, he glanced back and forth down the hall. Directly ahead of him the hall led to the solarium, a curved, screened in space that had been intended to afford the residents in this building with fresh air. Instead, it now served as storage for a tall heap of broken wheelchairs, portable toilets, bedpans, and other things Joey couldn't begin to name. Beneath the solarium on the first floor was a porch the same shape as the solarium that also housed a similar collection of discarded supplies and equipment.

To his right the hall led to the women's ward, part of Building B that was clearly off limits to him.

Seven Days at Oak Valley

Joey turned left and moved down the hall to a set of swinging doors. At this point he realized he needed to use the bathroom. He took two more steps and pushed open a door with both his right hip and arm.

The bathroom hadn't changed. From the entrance he could see all the way across the bathroom and through another open doorway into the men's ward itself. Along one wall was a row of six unused and unenclosed commodes.

In the center of the room were two concrete slabs resting on bases that had been donated to Oak Valley by Mr. Samuel Pullman. On the bathroom wall was an old black and white picture of him standing next to two big square blocks of marble as they were being loaded onto a flatbed truck with the name Pullman Quarry painted on the side of it. Each of the concrete slabs had a four-inch tall rounded edge with a drain at one end. The name, *Southern Embalmers Supply Company*, was engraved on a brass plate attached to the side of each slab. Hooks suspended from the ceiling above each slab held hoses with a sprayer attached at the end just like those Joey had seen in the dish room of Dining Hall 1.

A naked man, whose pasty white legs were spilling out over the edges, occupied the slab closest to the door. His arms were flailing around his head in a futile effort to keep the cold water from the hose away from his face. His head flung back and his whole body arched as the water sprayed over his torso and rushed toward the drain at the far end of the slab.

"Just a few more minutes, George, and your bath will be over," the worker said to the man as he began a long garbled string of "arghhs," and "ughhhs". The worker noticed Joey out of the corner of her eye just as he finished urinating in the commode farthest from the door.

"Hey, you, hand me one of them towels," the worker ordered. Joey grabbed a threadbare towel from the stack on a metal table and handed it her. She grunted in recognition as Joey attempted a greeting and pointed toward the open door to the ward.

"Oh, it's you, Joey. Yeah, go ahead. I gotta' finish George, here," she told him as she began toweling off George's shivering body. Joey nodded and moved through the doorway.

He looked around the room at the rows of metal-framed cribs lined up five wide and ten deep. Fifty men shared this space when they weren't being bathed, wheeled over to the infirmary, or laid out on a gym mat while the workers changed their linen. The smell of urine mixed with sweat assaulted his nostrils sharper than Sam's yellowed sheets ever had. His gaze took in a pile of dirty linen in the middle of the second aisle and another at the end of the fourth. He looked around for another worker and seeing none, proceeded down the first row.

Faces with vacant eyes from within the mental cribs stared past him. Joey stopped at each crib and called the occupant's name. At the sound of his voice, one or two of the occupants in each row would try to turn their heads in his direction or respond with a smile. The workers had grown accustomed to his regular Sunday visits and were amused by his mimicking of their caretaking. As such, he knew the names of all residents assigned to Building B. He also knew, from being asked to point out individual

Seven Days at Oak Valley

residents, that some of the newer workers were still struggling to match his achievement.

Turning right at the third row, he cut between cribs, and stood next to the crib nearest the pile of dirty linen. He reached into his pocket to retrieve the cookie before looking over the railing.

"'Aniel," he said as he held the cookie out over the rail. ""Ook, p'esent."

He stopped talking as he looked down and realized the crib was empty with only a plastic mattress left to greet him. Puzzled, he slid the cookie back into his pocket and looked around the room, noting that the gym mat in the far corner was unoccupied. He had just finished retracing his steps through the rows to the doors when they swung open, startling both him and the worker who was rushing through them.

He looked down at his shoes and waited until the second worker had caught her breath before he looked up with a puzzled face and asked, "'Aniel?"

The worker looked at him with a puzzled expression of her own and repeated his question in an effort to understand, "'Aniel? What you talkin' about, boy? 'Aniel?"

Pointing toward the pile of dirty laundry, he repeated, 'Aniel."

Understanding crossed the worker's face along with a mixture of apprehension and consternation. She held back even as he continued to point and repeat, "'Aniel?" and then even more emphatically, "'Aniel!"

The worker interrupted him, "Daniel, yes, I know, Daniel. That one, Daniel, well, well, he passed on yesterday mornin', right after breakfast."

Ruthie-Marie Beckwith

Not waiting for Joey's reaction, she rushed on, "Joey, you been around long 'nuf to know how things are in this here buildin'. Easy come and easy go. That's the way it's always been and that's the way it's always gonna be. Now then, you done visitin' everybody for today?"

Joey waved his arms and shook his head in confusion.

Ignoring his distress she said, "Well, then, I guess you best be gone."

He began moving toward the door, shuffling his feet across the gray linoleum.

"Go on with you now, Joey!" she scolded. "Curfew time's almost here and I don't want to be the one responsible if the supervisor finds you here in my buildin' after that siren goes off, ya' here?"

Joey mumbled an acknowledgement and pushed himself through the door. Retracing his steps, he went back to the elevator and waited again for the doors to open and swallow him up. Making his way out of the building, he dug his hands deep into his pockets, hung his blond head down, and hunched his back as grief laid its heavy burden upon him. Near the end of the sidewalk he pulled a handful of crumbs out of his pocket and scattered them across the neatly edged lawn.

6:30 p.m.

Tinker paused on the threshold of his dominion. Things seemed out of place since he had left on Friday. The door to the boiler room stood ajar. The discarded oak chair he'd patched up was leaning up against the wall instead of its normal location next to

Seven Days at Oak Valley

boiler number one. His tools were scattered from one end of his workbench to the other.

They'd gotten back early, mainly because his wife didn't get on too well with his folks. Rather than get into all of their past differences, he'd gotten his coat and loaded himself and her into the car, mumbling his final respects as they drove off. His wife had wanted him to stay home tonight, maybe even go to church with her, but he'd heard enough preachin' at the funeral to last him at least a day or so.

So, he'd told her, with the cold front coming in and as damp as it was getting at night, he thought he'd better get over to the plant and try to get the main boilers up and running, at least the one whose pipes ran to the infirmary and children's wards. Old as that particular boiler was, he'd told her, he might be there all night getting it to cooperate.

Right before he'd left for Cleveland, he'd gone over to the infirmary basement to check on the pipe valves and make sure they were ready for another run. Dr. John had been there in his office, hard at work, too. Guess that was the lot in life doctors had to be prepared for, patients needing things at all hours of the day or night.

Tinker leaned against the workbench and surveyed the damage. When he got hold of the youngin' who'd stirred up this mess, he'd be wishin' he'd been messin' with the inside of Dr. Jefferson's office instead of Tinker's steam plant. One by one, he began picking up his tools and returning them to their designated locations on the pegboard above the bench.

Noting the ashtray at the far end with its contents of fine white ash, he sniffed the air and reconsidered.

Ruthie-Marie Beckwith

The lingering smell of cigars seemed stronger, now, somehow. Maybe Jones had been here smoking a cigar he'd lifted from Dr. Jefferson's office on one of his so called "security checks". That could explain the mess. He and Jones had never seen eye to eye on how to treat the folks here, particularly Tony. Although this was way past the pranks Jones had pulled on him in the past.

He was reaching to put his saw up on the topmost peg when the lights went out. "Jones, is that you?" he hollered out but was met with only the hiss of the sputtering, recalcitrant hot water boiler. "Jones," he repeated as crossed the room and moved through the door to the entrance, "you've already made a mess of my shop! Enough is enough. . ."

Just as he passed through the doorway he felt a blow glance off the back of his skull. His hand shot up to where he'd been struck and he pulled it away, wet with his blood. "What the. . .?" he shouted as a second blow rained down.

Barely, just barely, as he drifted into darkness, he heard a familiar voice fading into the distance.

"Shouldn't have been out wandering around in the middle of the night where you don't belong, Tinker, seeing things you ought not to have seen. Now we're all gonna be cold for a little bit longer."

9:45 p.m.

Grace called out to Jefferson as he stood in the garden, smoking his last cigar of the day. "Winfred," she beckoned, "Mac's on the phone. Says it's urgent. Again."

Seven Days at Oak Valley

Jefferson flicked the cigar across the garden and watched as it landed in the rose bushes. "Damn," he said aloud to himself and then shouted out to Grace, "tell him I'll be right there."

Grace held the door open as he climbed up the steps to the porch. Slipping past her, he felt her shudder as his shoulder grazed hers. He sneered at her reaction, "You're going to have to get used to me being this close again, Grace." He took a strand of her hair, rubbed it between his fingers and murmured, "Maybe even closer."

"Mac's on the phone waiting," Grace reminded him in a voice that was almost a plea.

Jefferson flashed her a mocking grin. "Later, then," he responded. He strode into the house and picked up the gold toned wall phone they had recently had installed in the kitchen. Its long cord reached into the parlor and onto the back porch. He stood at the door watching Grace as he mulled over her reaction.

"Winfred?"

Mac's voice coming through the receiver drew him out of his contemplation.

"Yes," he answered. He listened in silence and then responded, "I'm on my way." Hanging up the phone, he headed toward the hall tree. Grace followed him to the front hallway and stood beside the stairway banister.

Jefferson filled her in on Mac's call as he slid on his hat and coat. "Seems one of Thomas' deputies stopped back by the steam plant looking for Tinker. Found him hanging from one of the rafters. This is going to take a while." He stepped toward her,

Ruthie-Marie Beckwith

attempting to place a kiss on her forehead. As she drew back, he said, "Don't worry about waiting up."

Seven Days at Oak Valley

Chapter Three

Monday, October 1st: 7:30 a.m.

Jefferson had been hard at work for over an hour despite the late hour he'd returned home the evening before. He was analyzing the most recent procurement reports when he heard the bells on the front door jingle. The click of his secretary's pumps on the hardwood floor echoed upward to the twelve-foot ceilings. He waited to give her time to put up her things before pushing the button on the intercom.
"Mrs. Fisk?"
"Yes, Dr. Jefferson?" came a crisp reply over the intercom.
"I need the procurement files from dietary, housekeeping, and medical supplies for fiscal years 1977 and 1978."
"Yes, sir," Mrs. Fisk answered, "but I believe they're all in storage. It could take a couple days to locate them."
"That won't do. I need them by lunchtime."
"Yes, sir," Fisk echoed. "Lunchtime. I'll see to it."
Jefferson sat back in his chair and looked out the window. Signs of fall were more present every day as the leaves of the oaks and dwindling elms outside the Canteen displayed a canopy of gold and red amidst

the green. His peripheral vision caught the solitary figure of Tony Ervin working his way down the lower path toward the mailroom. He could also see the stream of therapists and aides reporting in for the day shift in the Children's Ward. After the construction was completed and the children were relocated to the cottages, he would no longer be able to tell who was straggling in past the eight o'clock duty time.

Thinking about the construction reminded him of his second task of the morning; reviewing the construction foreman's change requests and weekly report. The abundance of rain last spring had wreaked havoc with the overall project's timeline, which now lagged three months behind. Intermittent rain over the past two weeks had hurt the schedule even more. He was counting on fair weather this week to make it possible to get back on track, which would go far to solving at least one of his myriad problems. Cost overruns associated with the delay were one of the items he was due to explain during his Tuesday meeting with Russell.

Jefferson gathered up the procurement reports and tucked them back into their manila folder and returned them to the green hanging file as the intercom buzzed again.

"Yes, Mrs. Fisk?"

"Sir, Dr. Ford from Rolling Hills is on the phone for you."

"Put him through."

Stroking the key to the file drawer in his hand, he said, "Dr. Ford, it's good to hear from you. We're in a bit of a fix and were hoping that maybe you could help us out."

Seven Days at Oak Valley

7:45 a.m.

Tony leaned against the counter listening to the chief mail clerk chatter into the phone about her weekend. She went on and on about her grandchildren and daughter. The assistant mail clerk handed the bundles of mail to Tony over the counter while his boss launched into yet another anecdote about her son. Tony clutched the bundles of official looking letters and magazines and carried them to where his mail sack hung on a hook near the door. He slid the mail into the sack and returned to the counter, anticipating another load.

The assistant gave him a puzzled look and told him, "There ain't no more mail, Tony, so just get along now."

Tony hunched his shoulders down and pointed to the shelves behind the counter where three boxes languished unceremoniously in a disarray of brown paper and twine, one of which had Joey's name on it.

"This one looks like it be for your roommate, Tony," the assistant had pointed out the Friday before. "But you can't take it today. It ain't been inspected yet. You can carry it on over to your building on Monday."

So, today being Monday, Tony asked, "Packages need deliverin'?"

The assistant turned to face the shelves, gave the packages a cursory glance, and turned back to Tony. "Nope, nothing today. Now you just get along. Folks'll be waitin' for their mail."

Disappointed, he turned and slung the strap of the mail sack over his head.

Ruthie-Marie Beckwith

"See ya' later, alligator," he called as he went out. Letting the door slam behind him, he paused to eavesdrop on the mail clerks. Stepping off the sidewalk, he edged his way to below the open window, close enough to hear the assistant clerk exclaim, "That boy is somethin' else." The clerk then called out to his boss, who was still on the phone, still talking about her family. "When we gonna ship this package over to Tony's roommate in Building K?"

"I haven't gotten to it, yet," the chief mail clerk responded. "There are some jeans in there that look like they'd fit my youngest grandson, if you know what I mean. I'll get the package fixed back up this afternoon and Tony can carry it over to Building K tomorrow."

His suspicions proving true, Tony ducked down and sprinted away from the window, his anger driving him forward up the hill and away from his designated route. He ran as far as the parking lot behind the administration building before he realized he could run right into Dr. Jefferson. Drawing three deep breaths, he counted to ten like Tinker had told him to do whenever he was close to losing his cool.

He wished he could go right to Tinker with this problem, but Tinker had left town to go to his nephew's funeral over in Cleveland. He would just have to wait, even if it meant Joey wouldn't be getting his jeans, at least, not this time.

Seven Days at Oak Valley

8:00 a.m.

Jefferson sipped at the cup of tea, now lukewarm, that Fisk left on his desk earlier. He had spoken with the assistant commissioner and filled him in on the night's events. He'd left off telling him that he intended to track down Sheriff Thomas himself to see if there was anything Central Office could do to assist.

He dictated six memos, including one announcing the arrangements for Cordell's memorial service, indicating that similar arrangements would be made for Tinker as soon as details from his family were forthcoming. With that unpleasant task completed, he buzzed Mrs. Fisk. "See if you can get through to Senator Russell's office for me."

"It's only 7:00 a.m. in Nashville, Dr. Jefferson."

"Senator Russell is an early bird like myself," Jefferson responded. "He usually tries to get in early to get the jump on colleagues."

"Yes, sir. I'll get right on it."

Moments later, the intercom buzzed again. Jefferson pushed the button and Fisk reported, "Senator Russell is on the line for you, Dr. Jefferson."

Jefferson picked up the handset and put it up to his ear. Then, reconsidering, he held it out six inches from his head. Russell had a solid reputation of talking so loudly into the phone that having a speaker phone like the ones reputedly in use over at Piney Bluff would be unnecessary.

"Good morning, Senator Russell," he said into the phone. "How's the state legislature this fine October morning?" As anticipated, Russell's reply came through loud enough for Mrs. Fisk to hear in the next room. He came around the desk and attempted to close the door, but the cord wouldn't reach and he came close to knocking over the Tennessee state flag that Mrs. Fisk insisted on being on display.

"You know good and well that fine esteemed body is in recess, Jefferson. But I'll tell you one thing, these damned committee meetings are making me old before my time."

"Well, Senator, there are some that say you were old long before you were elected to the senate," Jefferson told him, abandoning his effort to close his office door. He'd just have to keep one ear open for the sleigh bells.

"Now see, here, Winfred," Russell retorted, "if that's the case, then you are well past the deadline for moving to Florida that Mrs. Jefferson set for you not less than five years ago."

"You got me there, Senator, so why don't we just keep our ages to ourselves and get right to the business of the day?"

"What's on your mind?" Russell asked, but before Jefferson could respond, he added, "Terrible news about Cordell, and that colored boy, too. I supposed that's why you're calling."

"Yes, that would be the case, Senator. Dr. Cordell's untimely demise has added somewhat to my load."

He sat back in his chair wondering how Russell might have gotten the news of Cordell's death so quickly, let alone Tinker's. Mac Jones sprang instantly to mind. He swallowed his growing anger to focus on Russell's increased meddling.

Seven Days at Oak Valley

"I suppose you want to postpone our meeting tomorrow afternoon?" Russell asked.

"Well, as a matter of fact, that would be a very kind gesture on your part. Would you have time in your busy schedule for, say, Wednesday morning instead? Of course, you could always plan on coming to dinner afterwards. You know my wife is very fond of your company."

"Your wife is the best cook east of the Cumberland Plateau," Russell commented, "so that's a mighty tempting offer, but no, I'll need to get back. You know well and good I've got the New Construction Oversight Committee breathing down my neck. I don't need to remind you how much I need those figures, Winfred."

Jefferson leaned forward, placing his left elbow on his desk. "Hopefully, we'll be able to get that all cleared up once we have our meeting and go over the numbers. You'll have my report ready for you to carry back with you when you leave."

"You've got a lot on your hands, Winfred," Russell conceded. "Keep me posted about the investigation. Do you think Thomas will get to the bottom of this quickly? You don't think he'll get any harebrained ideas about bringing in the TBI, do you?"

"The TBI won't be around if Thomas has anything to say about it. Right now the sheriff continues to believe we're squarely in his jurisdiction," Jefferson replied. "I, for one, am not going to argue with him on that."

"Good luck to you," Russell told him. "See you Wednesday at 9 a.m. sharp."

Ruthie-Marie Beckwith

Jefferson sat back in his chair again forming a pyramid with his fingers. Through the blinds he could see Thomas coming up the path toward his office. He glanced at his watch, noting the time. Eight fifteen. Right on schedule.

8:30 a.m.

Tony kicked at the leaf strewn dirt path that he used as a short cut between Building N, the workshop and Building M, Central Support. Stopping at the workshop always slowed him down and not because they had a great deal of mail. No, every morning, Monday through Friday, he showed up at the workshop and had to stand and listen to Mrs. Dawson, the workshop supervisor, go on about proper work habits and how he could easily end up back at the workshop if he messed up even once.

Today had been no different, except she had taken one look at his bare feet and launched into a second lecture about his appearance. She had gone on and on about looking his best, like anyone who had to get clothes out of a cardboard box the size of a television could do any better. But, no, she never took that into consideration.

"Anthony Bedford Ervin," Dawson admonished through clenched teeth as Tony winced at the sound of his full name, "and just where are those new shoes I know the Appalachian Relief Society presented you with just last week?"

Tony suppressed a smart remark as he stood staring at his bare feet. Still savoring the enormity of Joey's find, he'd left the shoes they'd found in his

Seven Days at Oak Valley

locker and opted to go barefoot one more day. "Dunno," he replied instead.

"You don't know," Dawson responded with exasperation, "A brand new pair of shoes and you don't know! Well, I wonder how, if you can't keep up with a new pair of shoes, you can be responsible enough to deliver the mail all over Oak Valley."

Tony held his tongue, trying his best to appear remorseful. He took a chance and batted his eyes at her the way he had seen Elvis do it to the girls in one of his old movies. Then, in a deep voice that he hoped sounded a lot like Elvis, he said, "Mrs. Dawson, I promise I'll look for 'em just as soon as I finish my route today."

Mrs. Dawson was unmoved by Tony's Elvis impersonation. "Well, Anthony, you had best see that you do." Then, finally running out of steam, she added, "Now get on with you, you have a schedule to keep, you know. And don't dawdle at the superintendent's house either. Mrs. Jefferson has enough to do without being troubled by the likes of you."

Tony nodded, trying not to show his relief at his impending release from her lecture.

"And one more thing," Dawson said, "stay away from the steam plant as well. I know how you like to go up there and pester that poor old man. Well," she continued, "there won't be any pesterin' today or any other day from now on. Sheriff Thomas' deputies are up there right now tryin' to figure out why it is your old friend Tinker strung himself up."

With that final devastating blow, Dawson spun around, the door closing before Tony could muster any type of reaction. After exiting the building, he walked the short distance to the infirmary and forced himself to enter, hoping that someone inside would be able to tell him more about Tinker. He stopped at the empty receptionist's desk, reached into his mail sack, fished out the bundle labeled infirmary and placed in the tray labeled IN. His hand automatically moved to the tray labeled OUT but, surprisingly, it was empty. Not wanting to leave without any information about Tinker, he decided to wait until Miss Williams returned.

He leaned up against the wall next to a dusty fire extinguisher. A cheap frame on the wall next to the extinguisher held a map of the building with arrows marked in red pointing to all of the exits.

Tony started as the director of nursing and a uniformed man emerged from her office, their conversation spilling over into the hallway.

"That's all I know, Sheriff Thomas. The weekend was routine. We only had three residents in the infirmary. Two had symptoms of a stomach virus and one had a severe seizure. Bringing him here was just a precaution, you see." Her voice dropped to a conspiratorial whisper and she added, "His father is on the Board of Trustees."

"I see," Thomas commented. "So no disturbances? Dr. Cordell seemed his usual self?"

"Well," she hedged when she noticed Tony staring at her. Tony looked away. "He did come in on Saturday morning. He had us all going through the records room looking for some files that he said the accreditation survey team would need for their upcoming review. We were at it for more than three hours before he let us stop. He told us they must

Seven Days at Oak Valley

have already been sent over to the administrative building."

"And that's it?" Thomas asked.

"Yes, other than that it was a routine weekend," she concluded.

The door to the ladies' room swung open and Cordelia emerged, clutching a wad of tissue in her hand. Her eyes were still red and she dabbed at her nose as she returned to her seat behind the receptionist's desk. She was just replacing her headset when a phone line buzzed and she swiveled in her chair to take the call.

"Oak Valley State Training School and Hospital," she stated in crisp, professional syllables. "How may I direct your call?"

She cocked her head to listen to the caller stated a request, then answered, "No, ma'am, Dr. Jefferson is not taking any calls from reporters at this time. He will be issuing another statement about. . ." Cordelia took a deep breath and then continued, "about Dr. Cordell's death at ten o'clock tomorrow morning."

Cordelia cocked her head again and Tony crept toward her desk, listening to her businesslike responses. Cordelia spoke into the phone again, "No, I don't know where the statement will be made, you might want to check at the Guard booth as you enter the grounds. I'm sure they'll be able to direct you to the right location. Thank you for calling."

Cordelia turned back in her seat, noticing him for the first time. Tony felt numb and more confused than he had been in a long time.

"Dr. Cordell's dead, too?" he asked.

Cordelia stood up from her seat and glanced at the mailboxes. She picked up the incoming mail and pulled the rubber bands off the bundle.

"Yes, Tony," she replied in little more than a whisper. "Dr. Cordell died sometime Saturday night. I'd have thought you'd know more than the police by now, what with how you scamper all over this place at all times of the day and night."

"What about Tinker?" Tony added, forcing the words out past a lump the size of a brick that had lodged in his throat. Cordelia stopped sorting the mail and looked up at his devastated expression.

"One of the sheriff's deputies found him last night, Tony," she told him gently. "The deputy went up to check on the steam plant 'cause earlier they'd found a letter opener hidden there and the sheriff thinks this is very important. He was looking for Tinker to tell him about it."

Tony inhaled sharply.

"Anyways," Cordelia continued, "that's where they found him. I'm sorry, Tony, I know he was your friend."

Tony swallowed hard and exhaled. His head had started pounding and his heart felt like it was going to bust out of his chest. He pointed to the box labeled "OUT".

"Any mail to go out?" he asked.

Cordelia sighed, "It doesn't look like it today, Tony." The phone rang again. "You best be about your business," she told him, her green eyes full of compassion as she swiveled back in her chair. "We both have work to do. Work'll help take your mind off of things," she added. "Trust me, I know 'cause

Seven Days at Oak Valley

that's what I've been trying to do for the past twenty-four hours."

Tony took a final look down the hallway where Sheriff Thomas stood waiting for the elevator. Thomas stared blankly in his direction, a look that most people had around Oak Valley residents, a look that always made him feel invisible. So, ghostlike, he drifted to the main door and let himself back outside into the morning sun.

11:00 a.m.

After leaving Oak Valley, Thomas decided to head over to Lyla Jean's City Café for lunch. Situated on Main Street just before it ended at the historic courthouse, Laurelville's most prominent meat'n'three not only served up the best yeast rolls in East Tennessee, anyone involved in the legal doings of Laurel County could most likely be found at this time of day sitting at the community table. As he had hoped, Bob Forrester, Laurel County's former coroner and newly appointed medical examiner, had squeezed himself on the far side of the table between Judge Robinson (who only ate lunch with the fellahs during election time) and one of the county's two public defenders.

Thomas watched from the door as the stout, balding man shoved the last spoonful of his homemade banana pudding into his mouth and then he called out a general greeting to all. "Afternoon, gentlemen."

"Sheriff," the men responded, almost in unison.

Thomas caught Forrester's eye and signaled for him to follow as he made his way to a vacant booth

Ruthie-Marie Beckwith

adjacent to the restrooms. Lyla Jean materialized in an instant with a glass of ice and a pitcher of sweet tea. Taking out her pad, she chatted with the one of the county's more reputable bondsmen while Thomas studied first the menu and then squinted at the blackboard where the day's specials were written out.

Thomas handed Lyla Jean the menu and dictated his order, "I'll have the vegetable plate with fried okra, green beans, creamed corn and tomatoes along with a basket of those yeast rolls of yours." Lyla Jean trotted off to the kitchen and Thomas took a huge swallow of his tea. Like any other self-respecting southern man, sweet tea and yeast rolls were two of his biggest weaknesses.

Forrester caught up with him after stopping to chat with one of the county commissioners two booths away.

"Busy week," Forrester commented.

"Too busy," Thomas agreed as Lyla Jean appeared with a second glass of tea that Forrester accepted with a nod.

"I suppose you must have chased me to ground to get an update," Forrester observed. "On Monday you're usually over at the state park's buffet."

"I figured that since the legislature saw fit last spring to have the county commissions appoint their own medical examiners instead of being elected coroner by the citizenry, that this where you'd moved your office," Thomas observed.

Forrester shot Thomas a sardonic grin. "Well, Billy, the good news is I don't to have to campaign year round." Forrester patted his stomach, "The bad news is I'm gonna put on quite a few extra pounds if

Seven Days at Oak Valley

I keep having to track down those gentleman to this establishment."

"If you're as pressed for time as I am, you know that sometimes there are sacrifices to be made," Thomas commiserated. "You know, Bob, its gonna take a while for folks to get used to the change," Thomas advised him. "Trying to get my own men to make the change feels like a losing battle."

Out of the corner of his eye, he saw one of Forrester's new bosses tip his hat in their direction as he stood up from the community table. Thomas shot him a short salute.

Forrester took a swig of tea. "It'll happen, it's just gonna take time, that's all. I guess you want me to cut to the chase, Billy. I can give you the short version on Tinker and none of the tests are back yet, you understand..."

Thomas scanned the room as Forrester pulled a spiral bound notebook out of the breast pocket of his coat and flipped it open. Noting no obvious eavesdroppers, he motioned for Forrester to continue as he slathered a huge dollop of butter onto a piping hot roll.

"...that much being said, I can tell you the man didn't die from being hung," Forrester finished.

Thomas raised an eyebrow and took a swig of tea, "Now that's very interesting..."

Forrester continued, "I found blunt force trauma to the back of the head. Three blows, with either the second or third most likely the cause of death. His widow is already fussing at me to let loose of the body."

"Tinker was a fixture. He must have been there almost since the place first opened. Who could have possibly had it in for him so bad?" Thomas reflected. "Then, to try to cover it up as a suicide? Or even to look like a lynching?"

Forrester blanched at the word "lynching", returned his pad to his pocket and fell silent. Thomas, noticing the newly minted medical examiner's expression as he began clicking his pen, retracted part of his musings. "Don't worry, Forrester, no indication so far that there was any racial motivation. Tinker was pretty well regarded in these parts. That's what makes this so damn puzzling."

Thomas noticed a couple with a baby moving into the booth adjacent to his and placed a ten-dollar bill on the table. Recognizing that the interview was over, Forrester stood, shook his hand, and made his way back to say his good-bys to the community table. Thomas sat back, pondering this new puzzle, as the best and the brightest of Laurel County's legal establishment began speculating on who would win the Governor's mansion in November.

11:15 a.m.

Jefferson looked up from his desk and saw Tony coming up the path toward his office. He glanced at his watch, noting the time. Right on time. Tony hadn't drifted off course today. That made it two days in row. At least something at this institution was going right.

He reached into his pocket and fished out the key to the file drawer. Through the door he could hear Mrs. Fisk typing away. Her new IBM Selectric typewriter was quieter than her old manual and it

Seven Days at Oak Valley

had definitely increased both her speed and accuracy. Unlocking the file drawer, he retrieved the folders he had secured there earlier that morning and placed them on top of his desk.

He flipped through the pages until he found the document he was looking for — the final memorandum he had received last Thursday from the now deceased Dr. Cordell. Typed neatly on official letterhead, Dr. Cordell expressed regret at having to inform the superintendent of what appeared to be a pattern of missing medical supplies. Ever the efficient Dr. Cordell, Jefferson thought to himself as he read further. Except, perhaps, for inadvertently sending it along with a carbon copy of a letter addressed to the assistant secretary of the United States Department of Health, Education, and Welfare.

Jefferson set the carbon copy aside and continued reading Cordell's monthly pharmacy inventory. It appeared that upon completion of the monthly pharmacy inventory, a significant amount of drugs, primarily Valium and amphetamines were missing. Cordell respectfully requested an official investigation into the missing items.

Setting the report aside, Jefferson examined the carbon copy. It appeared to be only a draft. He could only pray Cordell hadn't had the chance to mail it and that it wasn't in the three boxes of paper Thomas's deputies had hauled off, all the while assuring the director of nursing that they'd respect the confidentiality of any information about the residents that might turn up. Most likely it was with the missing files, he thought, hoping that they would stay missing until Thomas was finished sniffing around.

Through the door, Jefferson heard Mrs. Fisk make a muffled comment about Tony's shoes.

Mrs. Fisk opened the door a crack and whispered, "I just thought you might want to know, sir. Tony's here with the mail."

"I'll be out in just a minute," he told her. He returned the documents once again to the file drawer, re-locked it, and pocketed the key. He stepped out of the office and Fisk stood up, pointing to a tower of files, two feet tall, on the corner of her desk.

"I have those records you requested this morning, Dr. Jefferson."

Jefferson stifled a groan, forced a smile, and said, "Good work. You can just leave them on my desk. I'll look at them when I get back from lunch."

Jefferson turned to Tony, "Ready for lunch?"

"Yes, sir," Tony responded.

They walked together toward Dining Hall 2. Jefferson enjoyed walking the circle at lunchtime. A long time habit that he had cultivated, he considered the walk to be part of his unofficial "rounds".

"I suppose you know by now that Dr. Cordell is dead," Jefferson stated plainly.

"Yes, sir, Miss Williams told me that this morning when I brung her the mail."

"Tinker, too."

"Yes, sir," Tony murmured.

"Sheriff Thomas is here looking into things," Jefferson told him. "I don't want you residents to worry. You let your friends know that, now."

Seven Days at Oak Valley

"Yes, sir. No one's talkin' about it right now. Everything's been real quiet in all the buildings."

"Well, that's as it should be, isn't it?" Jefferson responded.

Tony turned up the walk that led to the dining hall. Jefferson walked on deep in thought, toward the cutoff leading to the lower path.

11:45 a.m.

Joey had already been through the line and was halfway through his meal when Tony joined him. Tony placed his plastic tray on the table and swung his legs over the bench that was connected to the table. Dining Hall 2 didn't use chairs like Dining Hall 1. Scanning the room, he located Ben sitting off by himself. He kept looking but didn't locate Sam.

"Where's Sam?" he asked Joey in an accusing tone of voice, implying that Joey had been negligent at looking out for him.

Joey reared back, looked him in the eye and said, "'Ight 'oom."

Tony moaned in response.

"'Eed in bed," Joey explained.

Tony pieced together the story over the course of lunch. Sam had wet the bed again. The weekday shift had arrived and two of the workers had decided to rub the soiled sheets in Sam's face. In response, Sam had taken several swings at one of them. Maybe with any luck, Tony thought to himself, Sam had managed to bust one or two of them in the nose. As it was, it had taken three more staff to drag him into the "tight" room.

"'Ay 'as 'eal' 'ad." Joey commented. "'Acket."

—87—

"They must have been really mad," Tony observed, "if they put the straight jacket on him." Then he asked, "How long?"

"I 'ouldn't find out," Joey answered.

"Well," Tony replied as he picked up his fork, "there's nothin' we can do about it right now."

Half-way through his green beans, Tony reported, "Cordell's dead."

"'Ready know," Joey replied.

"Tinker, too," Tony told him.

"'Ready know," Joey said, adding, "Sorry. 'Eally sorry."

Tony shrugged his shoulders and scraped his spoon along his tray. News sure did go around fast, Tony thought, but then, the infirmary was right next to the workshop building.

Trying to impress Joey with one last additional piece of news, he related, "New grave marker at the cemetery, Number 8627."

Joey put his head in his hands and didn't respond.

Tony looked at him, trying to figure out what was wrong. Joey usually looked forward to the news he gathered as he went around the campus.

"Joey," Tony finally asked. "What's got into you?"

Turning to face him, Joey heaved his shoulders and started crying.

"Come on, man, what's goin' on?"

Joey took a deep breath and cried, "'Aniel."

"Daniel who?"

"B," was all Joey could say and then he repeated, "'Aniel."

"One of the ones in with the crib cases?" Tony asked, finally putting it all together.

Seven Days at Oak Valley

Joey simply nodded.

Tony picked up his spoon, considering this news. Lifting a watery, pale spoonful of orange Jell-o to his mouth, he thought about Building B. That's where Joey had gone off to yesterday. That explained another new grave at the cemetery.

"Joey," Tony said to get his attention, "many other crib cases been dyin'?"

Joey stopped crying and looked deep in thought. "'Ots," he answered. "All 'ick. 'Ots 'ick."

This news didn't make much sense. Sick cases went to the infirmary. But, he never saw crib cases in the infirmary anymore.

"Did they send him to Knoxville?" Tony asked him.

Joey shook his head, "'Ont know."

Weird, Tony thought as he polished off his apple.

"I gotta' get back to work." Tony said. Then, lowering his voice he added, "Sorry about Daniel." He stood up and picked up his tray.

"Sorry, 'bout O' 'Inker," Joey replied.

"See ya' later, alligator," Tony told him without his usual enthusiasm. He moved toward the conveyor belt to deposit his tray.

Joey made a dispirited effort at smiling. "'Ile, c'ile," he called after him.

1:15 p.m.

After lunch, Tony stuck to his route, moving faster than normal in and out of the remaining buildings, wanting to make enough time for a possible delay at the Superintendent's house. Dawson's admonishment from the morning drifted

Ruthie-Marie Beckwith

back into his mind, but he pushed it aside. Mrs. Jefferson had a cookie or some sort of treat for him everyday since he had taken over the route from Charlie Edmondson. Charlie had been shipped back to the workshop after he'd been caught taking change out of Mrs. Fisk's pocketbook. What a low grade, Tony thought.

When he reached Building K, he placed the mail on the supervisor's desk and then decided to risk being late at Mrs. Jefferson's house in order to check on Sam. He slipped by the day room where guys who couldn't work at the workshop spent their days rocking, staring at their fingers, or sleeping on plastic furniture. On his way to the second floor, he stayed on the lookout for housekeeping staff that barely kept the floors and commodes clean.

The tight room was at the end of the hall. Tony stood on his toes and looked through the wire-reinforced glass. The walls were the same pea green color as his room but the window was closed and boarded up. By angling his neck to his left, he was able to see Sam's naked body. The workers must've gotten the jacket off him when they got him in the room, he reasoned. However, as he looked more closely, he could see the shackles around Sam's ankles and wrists that bound his large pudgy body to a metal frame under a thin plastic mattress.

A small trail of drool had made a path from one corner of Sam's mouth and pooled on the mattress beneath him. Sam's eyes were closed and Tony waited until he saw Sam's chest rise and fall slowly. Relieved, he thought, he's just asleep. He turned and scampered down the stairs and was out of the building before anyone knew he'd been there.

Seven Days at Oak Valley

He rounded the path behind by the garden and peered over the hedges where he had hidden Friday evening. All of his frustration came flooding back to him, but he pushed it aside, just like he had pushed aside the news of Tinker's death. He had plans to catch up with Debbie tonight at the Monday night movie in Assembly Hall. He made his way to the sidewalk and climbed the porch steps. Catching his reflection in the window of the door, he ran his hands over his head. He still resented his miserable haircut.

Mrs. Jefferson opened the door before he'd had a chance to push the bell.

"Afternoon, ma'am," he said politely. "Mail?"

A puzzled look crossed his face when he saw the red rims around her eyes. Concerned, he asked, "You okay, Mrs. Jefferson?"

"I'm fine, Tony," Mrs. Jefferson told him. "Just hay fever, I suppose. I don't think I'll ever get used to this East Tennessee air."

As she turned aside to retrieve two envelopes from a small table in the foyer, Tony craned his neck to catch a glimpse of the portraits lining the wall along the stairs. She handed the mail to Tony as he reached down in his sack. Finding only one letter, he looked into its opening to check for more, but saw only brown folders that weren't in any kind of envelope. Puzzled, he placed the mail Mrs. Jefferson had given him in the outgoing compartment. He handed her the envelope and told her, "Only one letter for you, today, Mrs. Jefferson."

"Well, that's fine," she told him. "I don't have any fresh cookies today, Tony." She went on to explain, "What with all that's been goin' on, I just didn't have a chance to tend to my bakin'. Another time, okay?"

Ruthie-Marie Beckwith

"'Nother time be just fine, Mrs. Jefferson," Tony said, somewhat distracted by the letter she still held in her manicured hand. After almost a year of carrying the mail, he would have recognized Dr. Cordell's handwriting anywhere.

"Thank you, anyways," Tony told her politely.

"Better get along, Tony," she told him as she closed the door. "You don't want to be late turning in your sack."

Tony waved to her as she looked at him through the window. Then he retraced the steps he had taken along the lower path on Saturday night. However, before he crossed over Dogwood Loop to reach the Central Support Building that housed the mailroom, he sat down under an oak tree with his back to the road. Reaching into his sack, he pulled out the brown folders.

He ciphered out the names and markings on the folders, exactly how Tinker had taught him. There were four in all and each one held at least an inch worth of papers. The name on the first file didn't mean anything to him. He jumped slightly when he looked at the number on the second one, 8627. On the corner of the folder he read the name, Daniel A. Stroupe. Daniel was the name of Joey's friend who was dead.

The number on the third file was familiar, too. He'd just seen it at the cemetery on the marker next to number 8627. The name on the fourth file, he instantly recognized--Joseph Patrick Marcum. Why was there a file with Joey's name on it with this bunch, he wondered. Looking around to make sure no one was approaching, he turned each folder over. On the backside, the words, Piney Bluff Alt-er-na-

Seven Days at Oak Valley

tive Power Board, were stamped in black next to a small sticker in the shape of a triangle. At the bottom of the triangle he sounded out the word, "ra-di-o-act-ive" and below that the word "sub-ject" followed by another number.

More dead people, he thought to himself. Lots of dead people turning up at Oak Valley it seemed. But why was there a file in there with Joey's name on it if he wasn't dead? He sat for a few more minutes in the shade wondering how the folders had ended up in his sack and what to do with them now that he had them. He decided that they must have been left in the outgoing mail tray at the infirmary by mistake on Friday and he had picked them up when he picked up the mail. Even though it wasn't totally his mistake, he'd get the blame for it anyways.

The conversation from earlier that day when the director of nursing was telling Sheriff Thomas about the files came back to him. Dr. Jefferson had been looking for files, too. These had to be the ones. Now he was really in trouble. He shoved the folders back into the sack and leaned against on the tree, deep in thought.

The folders were sittin' in his sack since Friday and nobody'd noticed. So, he'd just carry them back there tomorrow on his route and slip them onto Miss Williams's desk when she wasn't looking. Let her get the blame, he concluded, it was probably her fault anyways. With that decided, he stood up, looked around to make sure he hadn't been noticed, and made his way back to the mailroom.

After hanging his mail sack in its designated location, Tony promised himself that after dinner the first thing he'd do would be to get with Joey and Ben

Ruthie-Marie Beckwith

and see if they could come up with a way to keep Sam out of trouble. In the meantime, he figured he'd hang out around Central Support and see if he could find out anything else about Tinker.

2:30 p.m.

    Jones knew without looking at his watch that it was time for his afternoon break at the Canteen. He looked up at the sky as the sun moved behind a darkening cloud. To the west, he saw more dark clouds moving in. Not wanting to be late, he picked up his pace on the lower path. He arrived at the Canteen just in time to catch the door for one of the teachers from up at the school. She exited with her arms full of paper plates, napkins, and forks.
    "Thank you, Mr. Jones," she acknowledged as he tipped his hat to her. She was a pretty little thing with dark wavy hair and a small waist.
    "Where might you be going with all those supplies?" Jones asked. "You aren't robbing the place are you? I'd hate to have to put you under arrest..."
    "No, Mr. Jones, I filled out all of the proper forms to get these priceless paper goods," she retorted, then explained. "We going to start working on table manners tomorrow with the lower grades."
    "Won't that be a waste of time?" he commented. "I've never seen none of 'em eat like anything better than an animal..."
    "Well," she interrupted, her voice acquiring a sharper edge to it. "That's probably because they've never had any proper instruction, now isn't it?"

Seven Days at Oak Valley

Sensing that he'd somehow blundered, Jones tried for safer waters. "Would you like a hand getting that up to the school building?"

"No, thank you," she responded as she turned and stepped off the small porch. "I think I have things well in hand."

Jones watched her juggle her supplies as she climbed up the hill. She disappeared behind the hedges and he entered the Canteen. Seeing no other women present, he hollered to the male clerk sitting behind the cash register, "Independent women are the worst."

"Got that right," the clerk responded. The door to the small kitchen swung open and one of the residents who was clearly from Building K entered, carrying a plastic dish tray full of clean glasses. "Just set it over there," he instructed.

"Got ya' a new helper?" Jones asked.

"Yeah," the clerk responded. "Another one of Jefferson's new fangled ideas. Seems to think some of these folks can actually hold down a real job. So, I get to be the one to have to waste my time trying to prove him wrong."

Jones nodded. "Lots of new 'jobs' appearing around here since Jefferson took charge. Don't worry, things'll get back to normal as soon as they come up with a new replacement. They always do."

"Got that right," the clerk agreed. "Ready for tonight's run?"

Jones cut his eyes to the resident who moved around the room, wiping off tables. Intent on carrying out his responsibilities, he appeared to be ignoring them.

Ruthie-Marie Beckwith

"Same time, same place," Jones instructed, keeping it brief just to be on the safe side. He looked at his watch and announced, "Gotta' go." Three long strides took him to the exit and he chuckled when the door slammed behind him.

5:00 p.m.

Mrs. Fisk was gathering up her pocketbook and scarf along with her hat and coat when Sheriff Thomas stepped through the front door. "I believe he's waiting for you," she observed. She stuck her head into Jefferson's office. "I'll be leaving now, Dr. Jefferson. Sheriff Thomas has just arrived."

Thomas opened the door for Mrs. Fisk and then stepped into Jefferson's office.

"Afternoon, Billy," Jefferson said, gesturing to one of chairs in front of his desk.

"Winfred," he replied as he sat down. He looked casually around the room, taking in the worn carpet and book-lined shelves. On the credenza behind Jefferson he noted the framed picture of his wife. The wall above the credenza displayed Jefferson's framed diploma from Memphis State.

On the wall next to the diploma hung three framed certificates. Thomas noted that one named Assistant Superintendent Jefferson as the 1974 employee of the year at the Golden Fields Training School and Hospital, another institution outside Memphis. A certificate from the National Association on Mental Deficiency conferred fellowship status on Dr. Winfred Jefferson in 1976. Another plaque was from the Parent and Guardian Association for distinguished service while he was in assistant

Seven Days at Oak Valley

superintendent at the Enid State Developmental Center in Oklahoma. Thomas wondered how Jefferson's wife had fared so far away from her Memphis Delta roots.

With a quick glance he took in the empty top of Jefferson's desk. He hadn't seen the top of the desk back at his own office for years.

"Been busy?" Thomas asked.

Jefferson sat back in his chair. "Just finished up going through two whole years' worth of paperwork, Billy. Nothing more relaxing than reading purchase orders and inventory reports."

Thomas reflected on the amount of food and other supplies an operation the size of Oak Valley must go through in a year, let alone two. "I don't imagine I have quite the same amount of those kind of records to go over as you do, Winfred. Mostly I just have to worry about keepin' a good supply of coffee and toilet paper on hand."

Jefferson chuckled. "Well, we do go through our share of both of those. Toilet paper has to be rationed out here. If we don't, the residents would probably keep the commodes stopped up from now until the Second Coming."

"Yeah, I got the same problem with my inmates."

"Inmates," Jefferson repeated. "Well, Billy, that there's a problem that I don't have. The department keeps the dangerous ones over in Nashville at Central State. Totally locked up with no chance of a trial or parole. Neither of us have to mess with them anymore."

Leaning back in his chair, Thomas observed wryly, "Well, you've got some kind of dangerous one runnin' 'round here last couple days."

Ruthie-Marie Beckwith

Raising his left eyebrow, Jefferson asked. "What kind of progress are you making?"

"I can't give you all the details, yet, anyways. We've been here for two days and you've had two deaths. First, as we pretty much knew, Dr. Cordell was clearly murdered, sometime late Saturday, early Sunday mornin'."

"And?"

"My boys and I finished talkin' to everyone over at the infirmary to get the gist of what Cordell had been doin' Friday night. Everyone seems to think things were goin' along pretty much normal like. Nothin' out of the ordinary. He came and checked on those patients over there for the flu and told your head nurse he'd be back first thing Saturday mornin'. Forrester put the time of death somewhere between 11:00 o'clock p.m. and 1 o'clock a.m. He identified two stab wounds, one nicked an artery near the heart and the other went dead center, up under the ribs, and through the heart."

Jefferson grimaced and asked, "Death was instant then?"

"Yeah, didn't take too long. Didn't allow any time to call out, anyways. So, most the people that work over there at the infirmary say Cordell was your typical doctor, except a couple of employees intimated that he was some kind of ladies' man, but discreet. Least ways, they never saw him with anyone. Might just be rumor or envy on their part. Though, some might say he was a good lookin' man. Bein' single and a doctor and all, could get some ladies' blood pressure goin'.

No one said a thing about there bein' hard feelings' between him or anyone. His mama and

Seven Days at Oak Valley

sisters down in East Ridge didn't know of anyone who bore him any ill feelings. Basically, I'd say we got no leads along with the complication of my boys finding your steam plant operator less than 24 hours later."

"You think Tinker's death has something to do with Cordell?" Jefferson asked.

Thomas paused while considering how much information to share. "Maybe, then again, maybe not. Deputy Ward's been followin' up on Tinker's death. He seems to think it might be a suicide."

"Suicide?" Jefferson echoed. "Tinker?"

With his gut telling him for some reason to lean on the suicide angle, Thomas continued. "Well, Ward talked to Tinker's widow this mornin'. Seems like he was pretty torn up 'bout the funeral they'd gone to down in Cleveland; somethin' 'bout his sister's son runnin' off the road over on Highway 127 near Signal Mountain. Pretty much split the car in half when it got stopped by a hickory tree. 'Nothin much left of the boy." Thomas paused, appearing to visualize the crash in his mind.

"Anyways, soon as Tinker got back Sunday afternoon, she said he insisted on comin' over and workin' to get the boilers fired back up. Said he was worried 'bout the cold front comin' through and wanted to get ready for it. She said he told her not to hold supper for him and left around five thirty."

"I'll need to get my secretary to send her a note," Jefferson mused.

"Ward said she was really torn up," he agreed. "Ward figures Tinker got over here, found that letter opener missin' and what with bein' so torn up about his nephew, he decided to just hang himself instead

Ruthie-Marie Beckwith

of dealin' with turnin' himself in for stabbin' Cordell."

"So, the letter opener Ward found was the murder weapon?"

"Don't know, yet. Takes a while to do all those fancy tests we do nowadays. I should be gettin' somethin' back 'bout that tomorrow afternoon."

"Exactly how did he do it?" Jefferson asked.

"Seems he used some yellow nylon rope. You know, the kind used to tie a boat up to the dock. Could've been left over from last year's rodeo. He stood on what was left of an oak chair, the kind you see in libraries. It was lyin' on its side like he kicked it over. He could've kicked it some afterwards. That nylon rope's got quite a bit of give to it. His feet nearly touched the ground as it was."

"Did he leave any kind of note?"

"No, no note."

"Old colored man like Tinker? Probably couldn't read nor write anyways," Jefferson observed. "Well, looks like you and your men might have this whole thing wrapped up pretty quickly, Billy." He reached behind him to the credenza and withdrew two Partagas from an antique humidor.

"Cigar?" Jefferson asked.

"No, thanks," Thomas replied. "My wife'll fuss at me big time if I come home smellin' like cigar smoke. She'd probably try to pour tomato juice all over me like she does when the dogs have been out chasin' skunks."

Jefferson laughed and returned one cigar to its companions. "Another time, then," he said.

"Certainly. I'll definitely be lookin' for one come time for the Fishing Rodeo."

Seven Days at Oak Valley

"Well I hope you won't have to wait that long."

Thomas tilted his head in the direction of the humidor. "Nice piece."

"My wife presented that to me on our first anniversary," Jefferson explained. "She said it was given to her family by Batista himself. Her family was in tobacco and it seems Batista had taken a special interest in one of the strains her granddaddy had cultivated. She said her granddaddy personally shook Batista's hand."

Thomas let Jefferson's revelation about his wife's background filter through the long list of questions about Jefferson's past that was forming in his subconscious. The past two years time he'd spent sponsoring those fishing rodeos hadn't netted him as much information about Jefferson as he'd gained in the last twenty minutes.

Sensing the tail end of another thread Thomas decided to give it a tug, "So besides helping to keep all those Appalachian Relief ladies on track with their volunteer work, what else does Mrs. Jefferson do to pass the time? We don't see her very often over in Laurelville."

Jefferson stiffened in his chair. "What my wife does or doesn't do with her time certainly can't be the focus of your investigation."

Thomas forced a smile and held his arm up with his palm open, "Now, hold on there, Winfred. I didn't mean to imply anything of the sort. It's just that my wife often wishes that Mrs. Jefferson had seen fit to take up her predecessor's seat their weekly bridge games."

Thomas watched Jefferson shift back into congenial mode. "Well, then, Sheriff. I'm sorry you're going to be the one to report back that somewhere along the way Mrs. Jefferson developed a distinct dislike for the game of bridge."

"An unfortunate condition. That being the case, I'm sure my wife will continue to make do with the parson's wife. At least until the parson finds out! He doesn't care for card playing or dancing for that matter," Thomas concluded. He glanced out the window and saw that the sun had sunk to a point where it appeared to touch the top of the mountain ridge.

Thomas rose and slipped on his hat. "I didn't realize it was getting so late, Winfred. I need to be gettin' home for my dinner. I imagine you need to be doin' the same."

"Thanks for keeping me posted," Jefferson replied. He stood and moved around the desk. "I'll walk out with you, Billy. Let me just get my coat and hat and lock up here."

"No problem. I'll just step outside while you take care of what needs to be done."

Thomas opened the door and stepped across the threshold onto the narrow concrete porch of the administration building. At the tip of his nostrils he could still smell the rich aroma of Jefferson's cigar. It wasn't too unlike the cigar odor that had lingered in the closed, damp space of the steam plant. He took a deep breath of the crisp fall autumn air to clear his head. Now that Tinker was out of the picture he wondered who was going to crank up those boilers.

Seven Days at Oak Valley

6:30 p.m.

Grace laid her fork and knife across her plate and rose to begin clearing off the table. Jefferson slid his plate toward her and she picked it up in one graceful movement and headed toward the kitchen. Jefferson followed behind, carrying a blue flowered serving bowl and platter.

"Will you be going out again, tonight?" she asked him in a tone that implied that she hoped the answer would be yes.

"No," Jefferson told her, "two late nights in a row are enough for me. I'm just going to read the paper and maybe watch the game." He placed the dishes on the counter beside the sink that Grace was filling with hot soapy water. "The pot roast was good," he added as an afterthought.

She nodded at the compliment. Jefferson reached over to brush aside a strand of blond hair that had come loose from the simple chignon she always wore. At his touch, she turned her head aside, submerged her hands into the water and began moving a yellow sponge across the plates. Holding them under the faucet, she rinsed each plate and set it in the dish drainer that stayed on the counter next to the sink. Jefferson moved up behind her and brushed his lips across the nape of her neck.

Crying out, she brought her left hand up out of the water. A rivulet of red ran down from the inside of her thumb and dripped back into the water. She jerked a striped towel off the rack and wrapped it around her hand.

"The glass just broke in my hand," she exclaimed.

Ruthie-Marie Beckwith

"Here," Jefferson reached out for her hand. "Let me take a look."

She jerked her arm back. "I can see to it. I'm sure it just needs a bandage." Moving around him, she hurried up the carpet-lined stairway, with the ghosts of her husband's predecessors staring down at her. "I'll be back down in a few minutes."

Sliding the brass bolt to the bathroom door in place, she opened the medicine cabinet and fumbled for the gauze and tape. She unwrapped her hand and used one of the sterile gauze pads to apply pressure to the wound. Good sense told her that the inch-long cut really warranted a few stitches. However, she was in no mood for the drive into Laurelville to seek out a strange physician. John would have had her patched up in no time, she told herself.

Removing the gauze, she ignored the blood collecting in the cut. Using her medicine shears, she deftly formed a makeshift butterfly out of the sterile tape. Gritting her teeth, she pulled the edges of the cut together and neatly placed the butterfly. That should do, she thought. If not, she'd have one of the nurses look at it in the morning.

With one hand she splashed water on her face and used a facecloth to dry it off. Her reflection in the medicine cabinet mirror revealed a make-up free complexion that only recently had begun to collect small wrinkles around the corner of her eyes. In the last two days, she felt as though she had added another twenty years to the twenty-nine that she had lived until the moment the telephone had rung.

"Damn it, Grace," Jefferson voice drifted up to her. "Are you all right? What's taking you so long? Just let me take a look at it!"

Seven Days at Oak Valley

"I'm fine," she answered as she opened the door. She walked into view and forced a smile.

Looking down at him, she repeated her reply without believing she would ever be so again. "I'll be all right," she stated flatly, holding her hand out for him to see as she descended the stairs. "See, I'll be just fine."

7:00 p.m.

The lights in Assembly Hall flickered but did nothing to impact the noise level. Wooden chairs scraped against the floor as three hundred of Oak Valley's 1,186 residents grew restless. A frustrated recreational therapist struggled with threading a 16mm film through a projector that was aimed at a white sheet strung across the stage in the front of the room. The night's feature, Snow White, lurched noisily onto the makeshift screen as the film caught in its grooves. The hall filled with applause and the noise level dropped as the lights were brought down.

Tony sat in the seat directly behind Debbie, who was sitting next to Wanda Sue. He leaned forward and whispered, "Hey, Wanda Sue, trade with me."

Wanda Sue giggled and rolled her eyes. She nudged Debbie who didn't appear to object. He squeezed through the chairs and sat down to the right of Debbie as Wanda Sue rose and found a seat further down the row. Running his hands over his head, he shifted his chair closer to Debbie, who kept her eyes focused on the movie flickering ahead. As the melody of Whistle While You Work filled the hall, he moved his arm around her shoulders, resting it on

Ruthie-Marie Beckwith

the back of the chair. Debbie leaned back slightly against his arm.

"I'm sorry I didn't make it, Friday, Debbie, I really am," he told her in his most contrite tone of voice.

"I waited a long time," Debbie responded, leaning forward in her chair again. "Almost got caught, too," she pouted.

"I'm sorry, I said." He moved his arm to rest on her shoulders. "Tomorrow night? I promise I'll make it up to you."

"Maybe," she answered. "Maybe not."

He rubbed her shoulder with his hand, leaned over, and decided to try one of his best Elvis lines. "You know," he said in a deeper voice, "you have the prettiest eyes."

Debbie leaned into his body, letting him run his fingers through her hair and coyly told him, "Somehow, I don't think it's my eyes you are so interested in, Tony Ervin."

She raised her face and his lips grazed hers as he slipped his hand under her top, cupped her breast, and gave it a gentle squeeze. Debbie's hand up was halfway up his thigh when Wanda Sue tapped her on the shoulder. Startled, Debbie drew back.

"Staff," Wanda Sue whispered, pointing to the worker making her way toward them.

Tony and Debbie leaned apart as the worker shook her finger in their direction. They kept their eyes glued on the screen. The film flickered and came to an abrupt stop.

The lights went up and the recreational therapist shouted, "A short break now while I change this reel. Ten minutes." She then threw herself into the

Seven Days at Oak Valley

process of rewinding the first reel so she could thread the second.

The other residents around the hall stood and stretched. Those who used wheelchairs wheeled around, jockeying for a better position during the second half of the show.

Tony scowled as he saw Charlie making his way toward him. He stuck his hands in his pockets and turned to Debbie, "Tomorrow?"

Charlie came to a halt by Debbie's side as she replied, "I said, maybe."

Debbie smiled as Charlie put his arm around her and asked, "How's my girlfriend?"

"You're late."

"Sorry," he responded. "I couldn't find you in the dark."

"Tony did," she replied.

Charlie glared at him. "Well, I'm here now. I'll take over from here, Tony Ervin."

"Walk me home after the show?" Debbie asked putting her arm around Charlie's waist.

Wanda Sue's giggle from behind made Tony clench his teeth. He looked at Charlie and then in an effort to recover his pride, told Debbie in his deepest, huskiest voice, "Later, darlin'." The lights began to dim once again. Not interested in the movie, and really not interested in watching Debbie with Charlie, he turned and stalked out of the hall.

Outside, the night was almost as bright as inside the hall. The moon was rising above the trees and stars were slowly emerging across the cloudless sky. Shadows of the trees surrounding the hall crisscrossed the leaf-strewn paths and sidewalks.

Ruthie-Marie Beckwith

He patted his shirt pocket checking for the two cigarettes he had ceremoniously placed there along with Joey's purloined matches. He decided to hike over to the athletic fields to smoke both cigarettes all by himself.

His thoughts turned to last year's Special Olympics as he made his way through the trees and crossed over Dogwood Loop. The path to the Athletic Fields was used primarily in the spring when the workers from Special Olympics showed up to help stage the annual track and field games. Tony had a collection of blue and red ribbons secured in his trunk along with a medal he had won when he was sixteen for the hundred-yard dash. Now that he was the mail boy, he didn't have time to go to the spring training sessions. That was o.k. He valued the liberty his job gave him, even if it didn't pay anything.

Tony smoked the two cigarettes slowly and practiced making smoke rings that drifted off into the evening air. After this evening it looked like he was going to have the whole carton of cigarettes to himself. Wanda Sue and Debbie could just go stuff themselves. There were other girls in Building F who would appreciate a real man when they saw one. Charlie Edmondson, he almost choked as he stood up and thought, what a loser!

The movie had to be ending soon. He needed to be getting back to his building before he was missed. The sound of a truck engine running caught his attention as he crossed over Pine and was skirting around the northwest corner of Central Support. He halted and stepped into the shadows. He retraced his steps, deciding to take a different route. Realizing

Seven Days at Oak Valley

his mistake as soon as he saw the headlights of the truck, he jumped back and ducked down.

9:00 p.m.

The sheets rustled against the plastic mattress cover as Joey shifted position in bed. Ben's snores had started up moments after the night nurse had given him his pills and he wasn't going to wake up for nothing. The workers still hadn't brought Sam back. No telling when they'd let him out of the tight room after he had taken a swing at them. Rumor had it that Sam had actually given one of them a bloody nose. He shivered and pulled the sheet closer to him.

Tony hadn't closed the windows yet so the air was chilly and the sounds of the night outside crept into the room. A faint chirp of crickets and the rumbling motor of trucks drifted down the hill. Joey wished he could go to sleep, but it seemed like every little sound made his heart start pounding. He rolled over, faced the door and watched the light flicker beneath the doorway. Familiar footsteps up and down the hallway reassured him that the night staff was making their first of two bed checks.

Things had gotten complicated since he and Tony had moved up to Building K. Life seemed harder. Even though they visited almost every Sunday, his folks seemed further and further away. Sometimes he didn't feel like he was part of their family at all anymore. Tony seemed more like family, and, as a best friend, he couldn't do any better.

The sharp scrape of a chair along the hallway penetrated the quiet of their room. Joey froze. "'Ello," he called out, "'Ello?" The sound faded and

Ruthie-Marie Beckwith

was followed by soft thuds as though someone was dragging a body down the stairs. Body? Why had he thought of something like that? Maybe because that was how they usually brought Sam back. Plus, he was scared, more scared than he would ever admit to Tony.

Joey knew Tony did his best to watch out for him, but Tony couldn't keep it up around the clock, and those bullying workers knew it. They'd been after him for the past two months, ever since they found out his folks sent him stuff every month. He never did understand how they knew whenever he was about to get something.

Joey tried to think of things he could do to get try to get them to stop. Nothing that wouldn't make matters worse came to mind. Telling on them would just make them mad and who knew what they'd do to get back at him. He wasn't sure his folks would believe him, anyhow. They thought Oak Valley was the best place in the world for him. They really did. He tried to tell them he wasn't learning anything here, but they didn't seem to think that mattered much.

The sound of books dropping in the hallway made him jump and he almost fell out of bed. Someone must have dropped some of those big notebooks the staff wrote things down in, he reasoned. He wished Tony would get back soon. He wished he'd gotten that package his folks had promised him. He wished he could talk better and walk better and do just about everything better. But mostly, he wished Tony would come back soon.

Seven Days at Oak Valley

9:45 p.m.

"Just two more boxes to load," Tony heard a voice shout.

He wondered what anyone could be loading at night. Regular deliveries came during the day, first thing in the morning when everyone was busy getting dressed and heading for breakfast.

"Hurry it up," he heard another voice order, realizing with a start that the voice belonged to Mac Jones.

Jones continued, "This is probably your last run for a couple of weeks. Too much goin' on here right now."

The other voice responded, "Yeah, what with Cordell dead like a stuck pig and Tinker hung up like an old piece of laundry, Sheriff Thomas must be sniffing all over the place. Too bad, though, holdin' off will really cut into our profits."

"Well, with any luck, Thomas will get his man and things'll get back to normal," Jones replied.

"You wouldn't happen' to be the man he's huntin' for, would you Mac?" the other voice said jokingly.

Tony held his breath waiting for Jones' reply.

"Now, you know me better than that, Pete. I'm a whole lot smarter than whoever it was that left a body where everybody and their mama would be sure to find it."

The other voice laughed, "You gotta' point there, Mac."

Tony heard the tailgate slam and a truck door close. "I'm outta' here," the voice named Pete hollered.

"I'll be in touch," Jones replied.

He looked for the truck's license plate as it moved up the drive, JBL 486. As it turned left on Lost Creek Road, he noticed that the truck didn't have one of those gold round stickers on the side. All of the state trucks have those stickers, he told himself, wonder why this one doesn't?

The sound of the truck disappeared into the night as he walked around the back of the building, trying hard not to make a sound. At the northeast corner he had no choice but to step out into the open. As he did so, he bumped right into Mac Jones who must have come around the building from the opposite side.

Tony caught himself and stared at his feet.

"Evenin', Tony," Jones said.

Tony remained quiet.

"Cat got your tongue, boy?"

"No, sir."

"What you doin' out?"

Tony hedged, "Movie night."

"Movie night," Jones repeated. "Isn't that up at the hall?"

"Yes, sir."

"So what you doin' down here? Smokin' again?"

"No, sir," Tony responded. He shivered slightly, glad that he had already smoked his cigarettes. Forcing himself not to touch the pants pocket he had stuffed the matches in, he shifted his weight from one foot to the other and looked up. Behind Jones' back, he saw Miss Williams emerge from the shadow of the infirmary building and walk hurriedly toward the parking lot. He watched as she ducked down between her car and another parked alongside it.

Tony yanked his gaze back to Jones and tried to hide the curiosity that he was sure was pasted all

Seven Days at Oak Valley

over his face. "I was walkin' Debbie Allison back, after," he tried as an explanation.

"I see," Jones responded, a knowing smirk crossing his face. "So Debbie's back at her building now?"

He worked at not scowling at Jones' smirk. "Yes, sir, safe and sound."

"So you just takin' the long way back? Out for a nice evenin' stroll?"

"Nice and quiet out here. It's always real loud inside 'til everyone settles down."

"Real quiet, huh?" Jones raised an eyebrow.

"No noise, no fightin', no cars, no nothin'," he replied. Then added, "Sir."

"Just you and me out here beneath the stars, 'eh, Ervin?"

"That's it, Mr. Jones, just you and me and the man in the moon."

"Well, you best get back, boy. I guess I'd better walk on up with you, make sure you don't get lost again. Terrible thing to get lost in the dark."

"Yes, sir, be right terrible, I guess."

"Come on, boy, I ain't got all night."

Tony willed his legs to move and he fell in behind Jones. He put his hands in his pockets, fingered the matches, and whispered a prayer of thanks as they covered the short distance to Building K.

At the front door, Jones stopped him. "I'll be seein' you around, Ervin. Guess I better keep a closer eye on you."

Cursing himself for having done something to attract Jones' attention, he answered, "'Aw, Mr. Jones. You don' have to do that. I'll be good, I promise."

Ruthie-Marie Beckwith

"You best see that you are. Now get on inside. It's late."

Tony pulled the door open as Jones headed toward the parking lot where his security car was parked. Screams and crying echoed through the corridor as he moved past the vacant desk at the front. At least one thing was going in his favor, he thought, the night worker who manned the front desk hadn't come in yet. With that thought he moved down the hall and took the steps to the second floor two at a time.

10:00 p.m.

Jefferson rolled over in bed and turned on the reading lamp he kept on his bedside table. Next to him Grace's naked body shifted and the covers slipped down from her shoulders to just above her breasts. Her hair fanned out on her pillow around her head like the corona of the sun on a bright summer's day. He resisted touching her, choosing instead to watch her chest rise and fall peacefully in sleep.

Swinging his feet out over the side of the bed, he stood and crossed the room to collect his robe from where it lay across a yellow chintz upholstered chair. His bare feet were cold but a quick look around the room did not reveal the location of his slippers. He pulled on his tasseled burgundy loafers instead and slipped quietly from the room.

Once downstairs, he paced back and forth across the living room floor, dwelling on their floundering relationship. After the baby's death, it had begun sliding down hill like a vein of coal that was being

Seven Days at Oak Valley

washed off the side of a mountain by a pressure hose. Now, he only felt the pressure and the decline. She'd promised him when he'd agreed to come back to Tennessee that things would be different. It seemed like she was never going to get over the loss of their child. Then today, it had all come rushing back. Thomas' probing question about Grace had opened the door he had slammed shut back in Enid.

He'd been cautioned early on by no less than a few of his colleagues that a younger woman wouldn't necessarily rise to the occasion of being a the wife of a superintendent but she'd proved them wrong when she turned out to be the perfect hostess. No doubt the result of her upper crust, Memphis upbringing. She had provided the veneer he lacked when it came to social gatherings, lovely and accommodating at every turn. Despite his higher education, he had no grand illusions about the lack of social graces that went with his backwoods background. Indeed, learning to play golf was his one concession to the increased stature that came with his current position.

The only other criteria he had needed for admission to the old boy network thus far had been his knowledge and long experience with hunting and fishing. Grace, of course, had no interest in those manly activities, so he'd been free to enjoy them to the fullest with the local bureaucrats and occasional state government official. Even so, he'd thought he'd made it clear to Grace that it would only be a matter of a few years before he'd be free to retire and then they'd be able to travel to the extent that she'd always wanted.

Travel, he thought. Maybe that was what the current state of affairs called for; a nice little trip over to Gatlinburg to take in the fall foliage. They could stay in one of the hotels that came with a hot tub and she could relax and let him pamper her to her heart's content. Who knows, maybe she'd even get interested in pampering him in return. It was getting to be the perfect time to take in the leaves, he could tell from the changes on the grounds that fall seemed to be racing in like a pack of greyhounds ever since Labor Day.

Just one or two small details to take care of before they'd be able to slip off, he thought as the idea began to take shape in his mind. He'd have to run the accreditation team through their paces and get to the bottom of his procurement problems. Then he and Grace could take a few days just to themselves, even before he'd finished the chore of replacing Cordell.

With the thought of Cordell, the contents of the note he'd confronted her with come crashing back into his consciousness. She'd denied everything, of course. He was treating her for depression, she'd explained. Depression.

Dear John,

I can't begin to tell you how much your kind attention and support has meant to me since you came to Oak Valley. Without you, I'm not sure what I would have done. I've felt so alone here and having someone who cares about the same things I do has made all the difference. Our talks together have made me think that perhaps I can make a change in my life after all.

Grace

Seven Days at Oak Valley

The note was just an expression of her appreciation, she'd said. Did she take him for that big of a fool!

He stopped pacing and reached into the humidor on the sidebar in the living room for one of the cigars she kept on hand to share with guests. He picked up the cutter by its side. He sliced the tip with a quick downward thrust. Sniffing it once, he pulled out his lighter. Reconsidering, he stopped in midair and decided that he'd step outside for a smoke before going back to bed. He walked into the hallway and slid his coat over his robe. A slow, peaceful smoke in the fresh air always served to clear his mind.

10:30 p.m.

Tony lay in his bed listening to Sam snore. Two workers had carried him in just after Tony finished crawling into bed. Sam was out of it and Tony decided they must have given him a shot or something. Four male workers had dumped Sam unceremoniously on his bed, eyed Joey who was pretending to be asleep, and left the room.

Tony looked over at Sam who lay naked on top of his blanket. He crawled out of bed and struggled to get the covers up over him. He checked Ben and Joey's beds out of habit. Ben lay on his side with his covers over his head. Joey hadn't moved a muscle since Tony had opened the door and slipped inside.

He climbed back in his own bed, but couldn't settle down. "Joey, are you still awake?" he whispered.

"Yeah," Joey whispered back.

"What do you think about Dr. Cordell dyin' all sudden like?"

"No 'ore 'ots," Joey replied.

"No more shots? Is that all you care about, Joey? A whole lot of people 'round here seem pretty torn up about it. Even Mrs. Jefferson. I could tell she'd been cryin' when I dropped off her mail."

"'Ay 'issin."

"What kissin'? Who was kissin'?"

"'Ordell an' 'iz 'effson," Joey confided.

"When d'you see Cordell and Mrs. Jefferson kissin'," Tony asked, his tone one of extreme doubt.

"'Ast 'eek, 'uesday," Joey said, adding, "'Inker, 'oo."

Tony rolled over and considered Joey's story. Dr. Jefferson had gone to Greeneville last Tuesday, the same day the Appalachian Relief Ladies had given him the shoes. If Tinker saw Dr. Cordell and Mrs. Jefferson kissing, he wondered what else Tinker might have seen.

"Reckon Dr. Jefferson found out about it?"

"Inker 'aid not my 'izness." He yawned. "Go 'eep now."

Knowing Joey, he'd be lucky to get even a part of the whole story out of Joey. Deciding to let the matter drop for the time being, Tony laid awake on his back, full of questions

"I'm sorry about Daniel," he offered.

Joey rolled over in his bed to look at him. Moonlight streamed through the uncovered open window, casting a web-like shadow of the grate onto the wall behind them.

Joey took a deep breath and then laboriously told him, "I sorry 'bout 'Inker, oo."

Seven Days at Oak Valley

Tony pulled his blanket tighter around him against the evening chill and the sheet beneath him slid across the plastic mattress all the way up to his butt. Wiggling uncomfortably, he reflected aloud, "Lots of people dyin' at Oak Valley, Joey. Can't help wonderin' what's goin' on."

Thoughts about the missing files and scene with Mac Jones at Central Support crossed his mind. He considered telling Joey about them and decided against it.

"'Eep," Joey replied.

"You go on and sleep if you want to, Joey, I've got some ponderin' to do."

"'Areful," Joey cautioned.

"I know how to look after myself, Joey. Don't you worry."

"'Eep," Joey said again. He rolled back over, turning his back to the window.

Tony laid on his back and stared at the hole-pocked tiles in the ceiling. Sam continued to snore while Ben lay as still as a rock on the bed next to him.

Tony thought back to his confrontation with Charlie at the hall earlier. That had been nothin' compared to runnin' into Mac Jones. He thought about Tinker. He thought back to the first birthday present he had ever gotten. He'd been ten years old when Tinker had handed him a box with the Sunday comics wrapped around it. Inside he'd found a real Timex watch. It was busted now, but Tony still had it, stowed away in his trunk. No way Tinker would suicide himself, he thought resolutely. No way Tinker would've hung himself. Somethin' was goin' on and he owed it to Tinker to figure it out.

Ruthie-Marie Beckwith

"Yeah, Joey, I'll be careful," he whispered as sleep overcame him.

Seven Days at Oak Valley

Chapter Four

Tuesday, October 2nd, 6:30 a.m.

Tony shivered as he walked back down the hall, dripping water as he went. The windows had been left open all night and the moist chill air brought goose bumps to his flesh as his bare feet slapped against the linoleum. He clutched his clothes for the day in his right hand, a pair of plain brown pants and a lime green t-shirt. He put the ones he'd picked out for Joey on his bed and began to dress.

He slid the pants up his long legs and for once, they ended neatly at his ankles. He made note of the color and style knowing it was unlikely he would ever find the same pair in the clothes room again. Concluding that it had gotten too damp to be running around barefoot, he slipped on the loafers he'd pulled out of his trunk before he'd headed to the shower. Tomorrow, he'd see if he could lay his hands on some socks, too.

As he pulled the t-shirt over his head, he moved to the window to take his first look at the day. Fog had rolled up from the river during the night, filling the valley as though it was a crack in a sidewalk. The grounds were concealed. The mist refused to yield to the scant streaks of sunlight emerging behind the mountains. On fall days, fog in the mountains could last almost until lunchtime. He eyed the gray clouds hugging the top of those mountains and began grumbling about the possibility of rain.

Tony's grumbling drew a harsh yell from Sam, who lay tangled up in amazingly dry sheets.

"Sam," he said, "you need to be gettin' up. You'll miss breakfast if you don't get movin'. You know they won't save nothin' for you. Matter of fact I might just eat your share if you don't show up before I need to head out for work."

He started laughing at his own joke but stopped as Sam turned to glare at him. One of Sam's eyes hit home with a full malevolent stare, but the other was swollen shut and crusted with blood.

"Damn," he exclaimed as he moved to the side of Sam's bed. "Sam, your eye looks awful."

Sam's hand flew up to his eye and he winced as he gently touched it, "Owwww!"

"It looks pretty bad," Tony observed, leaning over Sam's face to get a closer look. The sheet fell away when Sam tried to sit up. Tony looked down and whistled low at the mottled array of dark purple splotches that stood out against Sam's dark skin. A trail of bruises began just below Sam's neck and traveled down his chest and stomach with no end in sight. Sam groaned. Tony stepped back and stretched out his arm to offer a hand.

Sam took Tony's arm and used it to pull himself up. He swung his legs over the side of the bed and groaned again as he tried to stand. Tony moved to his side as he slipped against the sheet and the plastic mattress.

"Man," he exclaimed. "They really worked you over hard this time, Sam!"

"I don't feel so good, Tony."

"You don't look so good."

"My stomach feels bad, real bad."

"No shower for you today. You can hardly stand up!" After making sure Sam had stopped swaying, he turned to leave the room.

"I'm gonna go get one of the new workers to help you," he explained.

Sam shook his head. "No way! You gotta' do it, Tony. 'Else they be all over me again."

The fear behind Sam's refusal was familiar. His own experience with asking for help and getting hurt in response had taught him that you couldn't count on the workers to be sympathetic, especially if they were trying to cover for one of their own.

Tony turned back to face Sam. "All right. Well, I'm just gonna go get you somethin' to wear, all right?"

Sam nodded.

"I'll bring them back and help you get dressed," he told him as he formulated a plan to avoid the morning shift. "Then, I'll walk over to the dinin' hall with you. I have to get to work after that but maybe one of the other guys'll can make sure you make it to the workshop."

Sam nodded in agreement and then clutched his stomach and started to shake. Tony picked up the sheet that had fallen to the floor and wrapped it gently around Sam's shoulders.

"I'll be back in a flash," he said as he left the room and headed back down the hall to the clothes room.

Two naked bodies approached at a fairly quick pace; Joey and Ben. He handed out a pair of pants and a shirt to Ben and told him, "No more underwear left, Ben."

Ben made a face and hung his head. "Got yours back in the room," he told Joey, "along with Sam." He gave Ben a look that clearly told him to move along. Ben took the hint and began shuffling slowly toward their room.

"Sam's not doin' so good," he explained to Joey. "I'm gonna help him get over to eat. You need to see he makes it to the workshop."

"'K," Joey replied.

Looking up and down the hall for signs of the morning staff, he whispered, "We better get a move on, then, or I'll get in hot water for bein' late."

8:00 a.m.

Andrew Ford, MD, had made himself at home in one of the three mismatched chairs positioned across from Mrs. Fisk's desk. His right leg, crossed at an angle over his left, served as a makeshift desk on which he was scribbling notes across a yellow legal pad. The door swung open and Mrs. Fisk's sleigh bells announced Jefferson's arrival.

Ford rose, clutching the legal pad in his left hand as he extended his right. Jefferson shook his hand, noting the firm grasp of what seemed to be impossibly long fingers. He pointed Ford toward the direction of his office as he handed Mrs. Fisk his coat and hat.

Seven Days at Oak Valley

"Split pea soup out there," he commented. Frowning, he added, "Don't reckon' we'll be seeing any construction work going on today."

"No, sir," Fisk replied. "I hope it doesn't make you fret too much, Dr. Jefferson. WKRP said it's supposed to all blow over today. Maybe they'll be able to get back to it tomorrow, first thing."

"Nonetheless," Jefferson told her, "I'd give a lot to see those concrete trucks over at the site pouring concrete. It would serve to get a lot of people off my back." Jefferson led Ford into his office and sat at his desk.

"Please, sit down, Dr. Ford," he said. "We appreciate you helping us out here on such short notice. Dr. Cordell's death sure has put us in a bind. Besides the tragedy of the thing, the accreditation team is due here next week."

"We all try to be team players," Ford responded. "It's a shame about Dr. Cordell, though, he was a fine physician."

Jefferson sat back in his chair to take his measure of the man before him. Ford had to be approaching fifty. He was tall, athletically built and sported a respectable tan. Before his death, Doc Henderson had expressed high regard for him, as a physician as well as a golfer. He'd served as the medical director at Rolling Hills State Training School over in Nashville for the past five years and was known across the country for his treatment of residents with severe behavioral disorders.

"Most of the medical services department is in pretty good shape," Jefferson went on. "I hope you won't find too much to be done other than routine patient care. Dr. Cordell had finished correcting most of the problems pointed out by last year's peer review team."

"I do believe that's the case," Ford responded. "I spoke with him just two weeks ago. He told me they were wrapping things up and the only thing outstanding was a problem with a few misplaced files."

Jefferson stiffened at Ford's mention of misplaced files. He wondered to what extent Ford was aware of their contents. "From what Dr. Cordell reported to me, I don't believe anything in those files was relevant to what the accreditation team will be reviewing. His team was still trying to track them down, but if they don't turn up, it shouldn't be a problem."

"I don't disagree with that," Ford said. "John told me they were just back up records to routine blood work and vitals, part of a new quality control system Dr. Henderson had started implementing before he died."

"So," Jefferson put in, anxious to move on. "I hope from being on the peer review team you'll feel pretty comfortable being at the helm until we can get a new doc on board?"

"Other than the double duty, I think I'll be just fine," Ford said. "You have a fine director of nursing and the folks from Knoxville Memorial who run the clinics do a good job. The staff should give me an overview today and then I should be able to give you a firm take on my schedule."

"That'll work," Jefferson said. He stood up, "I guess you'll be a busy man for a while. Hope it doesn't hurt your golf game any."

Seven Days at Oak Valley

Ford stood up, taking the hint that the interview was over. Indecision clouded his expression before he asked, "Any word on what happened to Dr. Cordell?"

"None that I can share at this point," Jefferson replied. "The Sheriff is still investigating. With any luck, he'll be able to wrap this whole thing up pretty soon."

Ford turned and left the office. Jefferson moved to the window and watched Ford stride across the Green in the direction of the infirmary. Through the fog he could barely make out the patrol car parked out front of the building. He burst out of his office, grabbed his hat and coat, sparing only a moment to inform Fisk, "I'll be over at security."

8:15 a.m.

Tony approached the infirmary, fretting about the delay Mrs. Dawson had caused in his schedule. He'd tried to avoid her by sneaking in through the classroom wing. Just his luck she'd be covering for one of the teachers who hadn't come to work. Mrs. Dawson had caught him unaware as he stood watching the kids in the trainable room struggling to put together the same puzzles they did every morning.

Tony couldn't figure out why the kids were called trainable. Already pieces were strewn from one end of the room to the other as puzzle time disintegrated into a chaos fueled by boredom and confusion. It didn't seem to him that they were being trained at all.

He stood in the hallway, chafing at his daily dressing down, the only redeeming part of which

Ruthie-Marie Beckwith

seemed to be the fact that he was wearing shoes. As soon as Mrs. Dawson had closed the classroom door, he pulled himself erect and strutted past the workshop. He paused to sneer at Charlie Edmondson and wink at Debbie. She was bound to come around eventually. Charlie was sure to mess up somehow and then he'd be able to just slide right into Charlie's place.

Tony saw a patrol car parked in front of the infirmary entrance and stopped. Deciding to take the long way around, he entered through the basement door. Yellow streamers hanging askew in the hallway by Dr. Cordell's office caught his eye. He walked past the elevator and whistled low when he realized the door to the office was ajar. After looking up and down the hall to make sure no one else was coming down the hall, he let his curiosity get the best of him. He'd never been in a room where a dead person was found. So, he slipped into the office and stood in the center of the room.

The smell of the same nasty cleaning detergent housekeeping used in his building assaulted him. It was much stronger and he reasoned that they had worked hard to clean up whatever blood must spill when someone gets stabbed. His eyes searched the linoleum tiles for traces of blood but saw only the remains of a puddle of mop water that had drained downward to beneath the bookcases.

The floor not being level probably left a lot of things to roll down hill. He moved over to the bookcases, knelt down and ran his hand under the bottom shelf, hoping to find a coin or two but expecting only dead bugs and paper clips. Footsteps in the hall caught his attention just as his fingers closed around a small metal object. He froze, hoping that he was far enough away from the door to avoid being seen. The footsteps grew louder, faded and then stopped. He heard the bell of the elevator and the elevator doors open and close.

Tony let out the breath he'd been holding for what seemed like hours and opened his hand to reveal a cufflink with a blue stone in it. What a great find! Examining it closer, it looked like part of the stone must've gotten messed up with some of Dr. Cordell's blood. He shivered and thrust it into his pocket. Best to get out of there before he got caught.

Avoiding the elevator, Tony circled back around to the front of the building and entered just in time to see Miss Williams arriving. He hunched over his shoulders and leaned on the counter. Cordelia looked up as he reached for the outgoing mail.

"Good mornin', Tony," Cordelia greeted him.

"Mornin'," Tony replied. He placed the mail in his sack, pulled out the bundle labeled infirmary, and handed it across the desk. Deciding to take a gamble, he added, "You were workin' late last night."

Cordelia stopped sorting through the mail and looked up. "How would you know that?"

"Saw you," Tony responded, "standin' over by the trees and then hidin' by your car." Then, spotting an opening for possible collaboration, he asked, "D'you see what I saw?"

Cordelia hesitated. "And what might you have seen, Tony?" she asked at last. "I remember seein' you talkin' with Mr. Jones."

Tony wavered, but he felt sure she'd seen more than that, so he ventured, "Saw somethin' wrong, I think. 'Less I'm wrong and them trucks were s'posed to be cartin' stuff off in the middle of the night."

"I hardly think that's the case," Cordelia admitted. "Anyone else see me, you reckon?"

"Naw, no way. Big Mac, he was only concerned with gettin' those trucks outta' here and chewin' on me," Tony reassured her. "You did a real good job of hidin'."

Cordelia stepped closer, leaned over the counter and whispered, "Bet you see a whole lot of things other people don't notice 'round here, Tony Ervin."

"Nothin' that most folks 'round here'd care about," he answered cagily.

"And what might be so uninteresting?" Cordelia asked.

"Oh," Tony tried to suppress a self-satisfied smile. "Somethin' like a license plate number to one of them trucks you saw last night."

"Really?" Cordelia asked, raising an eyebrow that sent half of her freckles skittering across her face.

"JBL 486," Tony boasted. "Have to be good with numbers to do the job I do."

Cordelia scribbled the number down on a pink pad and looked back up. She told him, "Sounds to me like that is something you're pretty good at, Mr. Ervin."

Tony puffed out his chest as though it was expanding with the very air of her approval. Batting his eyelashes at her, he boldly replied, "Nice to be noticed by someone as pretty as you, Miss Williams."

Cordelia let him down gently. "Well, don't let it go to your head, too much. Other people besides Mr. Jones might take notice and I'm not sure that's somethin' you necessarily want, is it?"

Seven Days at Oak Valley

"No," he agreed. "'Tention always brings trouble."

"Anything else I can do for you today?" Cordelia asked.

"Well," Tony considered. "There is one more thing that someone might need to know."

"And what might that be?" she asked.

He plunged ahead. "My roommate, Sam, over there in Buildin' K, he ain't feelin' so good. I'm just a little bit worried, understand, 'cause he was holdin' his stomach this mornin' and his eye was all swollen and kinda bloody. Sam, he wouldn't ask nobody for help, so I was kinda hopin' that maybe somebody over here might take a look at him. Just to make sure he's okay."

"I'll mention it to one of the nurses," Cordelia told him.

"Thanks," Tony said. "Well, I better get goin'. The mail must go through!"

Cordelia smiled and shooed him out the door.

8:30 a.m.

Jefferson was standing by the window looking out over the back parking lot when Jones entered the Campus Security Office. Jones removed his coat, slung it over the back of his chair and sat down behind his desk. He waited for Jefferson to speak and when a minute had gone by he concluded that maybe he should initiate the conversation.

"So, how's the new Doc?" Jones asked.

"Not much of a view," Jefferson commented as he continued to look out across the back parking lot.

"I see enough of what goes on here," Jones retorted.

"Not enough to keep our Medical Director and steam plant operator from getting killed," Jefferson countered. He swung around and sat down in the only chair available.

"Seem's like you're pretty tightly wound 'bout somethin' this mornin', superintendent," Jones observed. Anxious to shift Jefferson's attention away from him and onto something else, he asked, "How's the new Doc?"

"Ford'll be fine," Jefferson told him. "He's been down the road and back again. He's not one to ask a whole lot of questions or give a whole lot of answers, for that matter."

"I hope you're right about that," Jones said. "Too much goin' on right now for a body to get all curious about and such."

"Ford will be fine, I said," Jefferson snapped, becoming more erect in his seat.

Jones hoped Jefferson didn't move around too much in that chair during his impromptu visit. The upholstery was worn and the pants of his boss's tailored suit were greatly at risk of snagging on a wayward spring. Jefferson seemed to be in a foul enough mood as it was.

"Any word from Thomas?" Jefferson asked.

"Not today. He's still over at the infirmary, rummaging around. Other than that, business is slow in the murder solving department."

"How are things going in the file finding department?"

"Slow there, too," Jones reported. "Those files don't seem to want to be found. But, I've still got

Seven Days at Oak Valley

feelers out, so maybe they'll turn up here pretty soon."

Jefferson eyed Jones suspiciously. "You wouldn't be holding back any significant leads, now would you, Mac?" he ventured.

Jones glared at Jefferson. "Hell, Winfred," he answered, "for all I know, they're stashed away somewhere in the bowels of your own office. God Himself probably couldn't say how much paper you've managed to bury there over the past two years."

"Well, we can only hope that's the case, because they're very unlikely to resurface under Mrs. Fisk's less than efficient jurisdiction," Jefferson hedged.

"So, what's really on your mind this mornin', Winfred?"

"Too much, as usual. I managed to put off my meeting with Senator Russell. At least until tomorrow afternoon."

Jones withheld comment. He'd been wondering how Jefferson was going to handle the Senator's latest foray into Oak Valley's operations. Russell had told Jones that morning to lay low and let him deal with the Superintendent. Jones, by nature, wasn't one to let any of his hens wander off unattended, never could tell when one would come home to roost.

"Have you had a chance to check into those missing supplies?" Jefferson asked. "Sure would make my report look a whole lot better if I could say where the problem might lay."

"No, Winfred," Jones began as he shifted in his chair. He collected his thoughts and decided a little deflection might be in order. "I did, however, come across Tony Ervin wandering around in the dark last night—"

"Surely you don't think Tony has anything to do with any missing supplies, Mac?" Jefferson inserted.

"I don't know about that," Jones responded. "But he does seem to think he has the full run of the place. Maybe that mail job you gave him has given him delusions of grandeur. Was pretty uppity with me."

Jefferson put his hands together, formed a steeple with his fingers and brought the point to rest beneath his chin. "Well, seems like I might need to have a little talk with our mail boy," Jefferson conceded. "He has been reliable but he certainly could use a lesson in showing some respect for the rules. Can't have the residents thinking they can run around any time of the day or night as they please, now can we?"

"I'm not sayin' he's a thief," Jones added, knowing full well that Tony had always been one of Jefferson's pet projects, but knowing better than to outright say as much. "But it wouldn't hurt for you to knock him down a peg or two every once in a while," Jones cautioned.

"I'll handle it, Mac," Jefferson assured him. He stood up and slipped on his coat. "Mrs. Fisk will be organizing a search party for me if I don't report back to headquarters. Check in with me later."

"Will do, Winfred," Mac told Jefferson as he followed him out the door. "As a matter of fact, I think I'll just wander over to the infirmary and see if the sheriff has any kind of update for us this morning. I'll get back with you."

Jefferson veered off to his right toward the administration building. Jones headed in the

Seven Days at Oak Valley

direction of the infirmary and met up with Tony as he was turning to enter Building K.

"Forget somethin' Tony?" Jones asked, gesturing toward Tony's dormitory.

Tony stopped and answered, "No, Mr. Jones, just deliverin' the mail like I'm s'posed to."

"Well, see to it you don't get sidetracked," Jones warned. "Too nasty a day to have to go organizin' a search party for some boy who don't know how to stay put."

Tony nodded and responded in a low voice, "Yes, sir."

Jones gestured for Tony to move on and watched him until he disappeared through the front door of Building K.

9:45 a.m.

Cordelia waited for Sheriff Thomas to emerge from the basement. She was hoping he'd appear when she was normally scheduled for a break but thought she could improvise if that wasn't the case. She sat down at typewriter, typed out a quick note to Thomas and slipped it into an envelope along with the copy of Dr. Cordell's memo about the missing supplies.

Dr. Ford summoned her to meet with him at nine and she carefully took notes as he dictated the names and positions of possible callers. She tried not to stare at his fancy suit. She decided he might have worn it just for his first official day.

"The lab coats are in the linen closet," she told him, trying to be helpful. She thought it would be a shame for something to happen to his Sunday best.

Ruthie-Marie Beckwith

"I'd be happy to show you where they are," she offered.

"That would be nice," Ford responded. "Just as soon as we're finished."

Cordelia took notes for another fifteen minutes. Ford stopped and looked at her.

"Do you have any questions, Miss Williams?"

"No, sir," she answered. "I believe I've got it all down. I'll type it up and post it by the switchboard."

Ford opened the door and ushered Cordelia through.

"So," he began, "point me in the direction of those lab coats."

Cordelia smiled. *He sure is friendly for a doctor*, she thought to herself. She reached up to fluff the back of her hair and explained.

"Take the elevator down to the next floor and then turn right. At the end of the hall, take another right and you'll see a door on your left marked "clean linen".

Cordelia walked with him toward the elevator and was startled as the door opened and Sheriff Thomas emerged along with one of his deputies. Sheriff Thomas was quite memorable, but she still hadn't been able to keep his deputies sorted out. She waited until the elevator doors closed behind Ford before she called out to Thomas. He stopped and waited for her while signaling for his deputy to go on without him.

"Yes, Miss Williams?" he asked.

"Um. . .," Cordelia began as she glanced around to confirm the absence of any other staff. "I, um, have that information you requested," she murmured

Seven Days at Oak Valley

as she handed him the envelope she had prepared earlier.

Thomas looked puzzled, but accepted the envelope and slipped it into his shirt pocket behind his note pad.

"I'm sure you'll find it all in order," Cordelia told him. "If you have any questions," she improvised, "please come find me. Poor Mr. Jones is just run ragged. I'll be happy to help you any way I can."

"Really, now," Thomas began, his tone indicating that he might have the wrong impression about why she wanted to help.

Cordelia jumped in, not wanting Thomas to draw the wrong conclusions, "Dr. Cordell was a gentleman. Surely you've figured that out by now from talking to everyone here."

"I'll take a look at this," he told her, appearing to at least be trying to catch her meaning.

"I appreciate it, Sheriff," she responded.

Thomas turned away from the desk, fingering the envelope in his pocket as he flagged down his deputy. Cordelia moved out from behind her desk and watched the two men head up the hill. She hoped Thomas wasn't headed over to the Security Office to ask Jones about the contents of the envelope.

10:15 a.m.

The door to Miss Lambuth's office was closed which meant she was either gone, talking on the phone, or smoking a cigarette. Tony knocked and heard the faint sound of a chair scraping against the linoleum tile. The door swung open and a small gray cloud emerged, followed by Miss Lambuth.

Ruthie-Marie Beckwith

Tony stepped back and offered a cheerful greeting. "Mornin' Miss Lambuth."

"Good morning, Tony," Lambuth replied. "Any mail for me?"

"I put all the mail up on the box like I'm supposed to," Tony told her. "But I think I saw one or two letters with your name on 'em."

"So what else do you need?" Miss Lambuth asked.

"I was wonderin'," Tony looked down at his feet, struggling with the nature of his request. "I was wonderin', I was really hopin' I could go to the service, you know, the service for Tinker."

Lambuth didn't appear receptive and Tony prepared himself for the sure to be instant answer of "No".

"I'll see what I can do, Tony," Lambuth told him instead. He shook his head, not sure he had heard right.

"Really?" Tony asked.

"Yes, really," Lambuth told him. "Come back after you're done today and I'll let you know. Don't get your hopes up, though. You know how hard it is to schedule a community outing without any notice. But I'll see."

Tony flashed her one of his best Elvis smiles. "Uh, thanks, Miss Lambuth. I'll just go get those letters for you."

He rushed back to pulling out the two letters with Miss Lambuth's name on them, he hurried back up the hall. "Here you go," he told her as he thrust the letters into her hand.

"Thank you, Tony," Lambuth told him. "You'd better be getting on, now."

Seven Days at Oak Valley

"I will," Tony replied. "I just need to check my room for my poncho. I think I left it up there."

"Well, go ahead and take care of that," Lambuth told him.

Taking the steps two at time, he wondered if Sam had made it over to the dining hall. He hoped so because the day shift didn't like it when an extra person was left behind on the ward. Besides, he didn't want anyone to see what he was gonna do. He turned into his room and was relieved to find it empty.

He walked to the radiator and knelt down, moving the tile that concealed the hiding spot for his key. As he opened his trunk, sprinkles of rain begun hitting the open windows. Hesitating only a minute, he reached into his mail sack and removed the missing files. Since she'd been so nice to him this morning, he'd given up the idea of getting Miss Williams in trouble for losing the files everyone was so upset about. And, she was pretty when she smiled, even if her red hair was kinda frizzy.

He removed a bundle of plastic and shifted things around in the trunk so that the files were completely covered. Outside the rain was picking up. He felt droplets of water that were carried inside by the wind when he returned his trunk key to its place beneath the radiator. He stood up and moved to the windows. Ignoring the footsteps he heard coming down the hall, he reached out to pull the first window in to close it. The footsteps stopped and he looked over his shoulder to see the day shift supervisor standing in the doorway.

Ruthie-Marie Beckwith

"And what might you be doin' here, Tony," the supervisor asked as she moved to the other window and reached to pull it closed.

"I, um, I," Tony started.

"Yes?" she asked.

"I came to get my poncho," he answered, grateful now for the rain he had been dreading all morning.

"Okay, so you've got it," the supervisor observed.

"Yes, m'am, I do," Tony told her as he reached for the bundle. He unfolded it and slipped the plastic over his head. The gray plastic was torn in several spots, but it would have to do.

"Well," Tony began as he picked up his mail sack, "I need to be getting on back to work."

"See that that's all that you get to doin'."

Tony took the stairs down two at a time and all but ran down the main hall to the front entryway. He pulled the plastic hood over his head and plunged out into the rain.

11:15 a.m.

One more stop to make before it was time to meet up with Dr. Jefferson, Tony thought as he made his way up the path that led to Chestnut Lane. The leaves on the bushes lining the path were bright red, and Tony hoped they were bright and bushy enough to hide him from view. When he reached Chestnut, he walked along the side of the road. Just a quick detour, he told himself, as he turned left onto the path that led to the cemetery.

Tony's shoes squished in the mud as he moved along the cemetery edge, scanning the nameless grave markers, some of which had their numbers obscured by weeds. He noticed the red dirt still piled in clots on top of a fresh grave. Moving closer, Tony noted the number on the grave marker, 8627, chiseled into a six inch square piece of granite. Yep, that was the number on Daniel's folder that he'd left laying in his trunk. Tony wondered if anyone would be able to find his grave after he died, with only a number to go by.

He stepped back and his left foot landed in a hole that hadn't been quite filled in by the burial detail. His shoe instantly filled with muddy water. "Damn," he muttered out loud. Standing on his right foot, he pulled the shoe off, tipped it over to empty it, and put it back on. That accomplished, he circled around the cemetery. Altogether, he counted fifteen mounds of dirt that didn't have much grass or weeds growing over them. Those would be the ones who died this year, he reasoned.

Looking at the numbers, he recognized another, 8432, that had been on one of the folders. Two of the people who had their names on those folders were dead for sure, he thought to himself. He shuddered and moved back to the cemetery path. He didn't want to be late for lunch, now that he had something important to tell Joey. He just wasn't sure exactly what it was or how he was gonna explain it.

11:45 a.m.

Jefferson looked at his watch when he finally saw Tony pass by his window. He moved into the vestibule and grabbed his coat and hat.

"I'm off to lunch," he told Fisk. He opened the door to let Tony pass by, tilting his head down to keep the rain off his face.

"You're late," Fisk called out.

"I know," Tony replied as he closed the door behind them. He handed Fisk the mail and rushed out to join Jefferson.

"You're late," Jefferson observed as Tony fell in step with him on the upper path.

"Sorry," Tony told him.

"Been wandering around in the rain?"

"No, sir."

"I don't like to be kept waiting," Jefferson reminded him. "So where were you?"

"I stopped to get my poncho," Tony explained.

"You should have taken it with you when you left this morning," Jefferson admonished. His eyes swept the tall figure beside him. The poncho was torn in several places and couldn't be a very good defense against the miserable weather they'd been having. His gaze trailed down Tony's torso to note that Tony's pants ended at his ankles for once, and, remarkably, he had shoes on. Looking closer, however, he realized that these were not the shoes that he knew Tony had received from the Appalachian Relief Ladies.

He narrowed his eyes. "You haven't been over at the construction zone recently have you?"

Tony failed to answer. Jefferson paused mid-step to look Tony square in the face. "Mac Jones tells me he found you wandering around last night after curfew."

"It wasn't past curfew," Tony countered. Jefferson shot him a look of complete disbelief.

Seven Days at Oak Valley

"Well, it might have been just about curfew," he conceded.

"I've got enough on my mind right now without having Mac Jones come see me to tell me that I've got a resident wandering around in the dark after hours," Jefferson told him.

Tony was silent, his expression hidden by the hood of his poncho.

"Well, see to it that you get in before curfew," Jefferson said, emphasizing the *before* to make his directive crystal clear. "You know, Tony, they've built a new prison in Nashville that's meant for boys like you who don't know how to stay put and follow the rules. I'd hate to be the one who had to fill out all of the paperwork to send you over there."

Jefferson stopped, trying to determine his lecture had been sufficient. Hearing no reply from Tony, he decided he'd gotten his message across.

"Well, get on to lunch now." Jefferson ordered when they reached the turn off to the lower path. As Tony picked up his pace in the direction of the dining hall, he called out one more admonishment, "And be on time from now on!"

12:00 p.m.

Tony watched Jefferson walk down the lower path to the Superintendent's from beneath the eave of the dining hall entrance.

"An' just how'm I supposed to know when it's curfew," Tony muttered. "Ain't got no watch that runs."

Even so, his heart was still pounding as the word *prison* resounded in his head. Prison meant no

Ruthie-Marie Beckwith

friends, no job, no girlfriend, no freedom. Bad things happened to people in prison. Mac Jones was to blame for all of this and Dr. Jefferson, too. The thought of losing everything he'd worked for made him feel as dismal as the dreary rain that continued to fall.

He pulled the hood of his poncho back and was reaching for the door handle when he heard his name being called.

"Tah-own-y," called out a falsetto voice. "Ah want to go to the dance with you, Tah-own-y."

Tony turned around and scowled when he saw Charlie leaning up against one of the granite pillars that supported the eave of the entrance.

"Aw, go shave your butt," Tony retorted.

"All you've got to shave is peachy fuzz," Charlie taunted.

Tony clenched his fists and shook the rain off his poncho. He started toward Charlie and then stopped.

"You're not even a man," Tony told him as he pulled his hood back up. "You're just a big fat butt hole. You're so big you don't even fit on the pot." Then, making a face, he marched off into the rain.

He'd gone as far as the west entrance to Building F when he stopped to catch his breath. What he wouldn't give to land just one good punch right in the middle of Charlie's ugly face, he thought. As he turned to head to the dining hall, bright yellow tape that was flapping in the wind off in the distance caught his eye. He shook his head to rid himself of Jefferson's lecture about wandering off and decided to investigate.

Trying to appear casual as he walked toward the yellow ribbon, Tony stopped to look over his

Seven Days at Oak Valley

shoulder four times to make sure no one was observing him. He got as far as the steam plant when he realized that it was the same kind of ribbon that was taped to Dr. Cordell's office door. Here it was anchored to the grate that covered the front window. The other end must've come loose in the wind, he figured.

Tony caught hold of the loose end of the ribbon and stared at the black letters printed on it. "Cah-rime," Tony sounded out, adding, "S'cah-ene". Somethin' about the police, Tony determined. Noting that the padlock was missing from the door, he reached out and jiggled the handle. The door was unlocked. He gave it a nudge, trying to decide whether or not to go in. Might be spooky, he told himself, what with Tinker dyin' in there and all. Then again, he reasoned, maybe the police thought it was a crime s'cah-ene. His curiosity got the best of him and he swung the door open and entered.

The interior of the steam plant was dark, except for places where slivers of light pierced their way through the shuttered and grate-covered windows. Water from his poncho dripped onto the floor. Beneath his feet was a mosaic of black and white ceramic tile similar to the tile in the bathroom back in the dorm. Tinker had always kept it mopped and had fussed at anyone who tromped dirt in from outside. Tony had heard Mac Jones laughing about Tinker's insistence at keeping the floor in a place like a steam plant clean. Tinker had told him that everything that existed was worth being taken care of.

Tony scanned the room and walked over to the main boiler. He looked up at the massive pipes that

Ruthie-Marie Beckwith

were supposed to carry hot steam to all of the buildings at Oak Valley. They were still cold from being inactive all summer. He looked up. There was no sign of any rope hanging from any of the pipes. The police must've taken it.

A second, smaller boiler stood next to it, giving off heat. That boiler was the one that heated all the water at Oak Valley, Tinker had told him when Tony first started hanging around the steam plant.

He was just a kid, back then, but Tony remembered asking Tinker if that boiler was heating hot water, then how come there wasn't any hot water in Building G. Tinker had fussed at him and run him off, but eventually Tony wore him down and was readmitted to Tinker's domain.

He turned back toward the door, studying his muddy footprints as he went. Tinker would have skinned him alive for making a mess of his floor, Tony thought. Then, just before he reached the door, his foot sent the stub of a cigar flying across his path. He reached down and picked it up. It had one of those bright yellow and red bands on it, like the one's he always saw Dr. Jefferson smoking and, maybe once in a while, Mac Jones. Jones probably swiped them when Dr. Jefferson wasn't looking. Still, he wondered how the cigar stub had ended up in the steam room as he slipped it into his pocket next to the cufflink and closed the door behind him.

12:05 p.m.

"I know, Mama," Grace said into the telephone handset cradled between her neck and shoulder. "No, I don't know how long I'd be staying." She rolled her

Seven Days at Oak Valley

eyes in exasperation. "No, Mama. I said that I'd explain everything when I get there. Look, I've got to go. Yes, I'll be careful. Yes, Mama, you and Daddy, too." She hung up and looked up to see Jefferson dripping water on the hallway floor.

"Is lunch ready?" he asked.

"No," Grace responded, "I mean, yes. I mean come here and sit down. I have something I need to tell you."

"Can't it wait until later?" Jefferson asked her. "I'm already running behind and I still need to prepare for my meeting with Russell in the morning."

"Winfred," Grace cut in, "I need to tell you I'm going to Memphis."

"Memphis," Winfred echoed. "This isn't a good time for us to be going on a trip. There's no way I can get away right now to go to Memphis."

"No, Winfred," Grace interrupted. "I said *I* was going to Memphis, not us. I'm going to go stay with Mama and Daddy for a while."

"A while?" Winfred asked, "When do you plan on getting back?"

"I don't know. I need some time to myself to think."

"Mind if I ask about what?" he persisted. "Or do I even need to ask. Thinking about him, I suppose."

"John and I were just good friends," Grace stated evenly. "You're blowing it all out of proportion."

"Cherish our time together," he countered. "Isn't that what you wrote him? That you 'cherished' your time together?"

"You're really reading way too much into that note. Besides, he's dead now, isn't he!" she all but shouted at him.

"Yes, he's dead," Jefferson snarled. "But I'm still here."

"You're just as possessive and jealous as you've always been. Except now you're even jealous of a dead man. I can't take being held captive out here in the middle of nowhere."

"You knew what it would be like when I took this job," Jefferson stated.

"Yes, I knew," Grace said, "but what I didn't know was that you'd have goons like Big Mac Jones reporting on my every move. I can't even run over to Laurelville without it becoming a major incident."

"Come on, Grace," Jefferson said softly. He moved toward her, changing tactics. "I don't mind you going shopping and getting your hair done. I've told you to go. Go have a good time. Just don't be gone so long that I start to worry, that's all."

"Winfred, I am more than capable of taking care of myself," she told him.

Jefferson grabbed her arm and pulled her toward him. "You are, are you?" He gripped her arm tightly while looking down into her face.

She wrenched her arm free, "I'm going to Memphis and that's final. There's nothing here that can keep me from leaving."

Jefferson sat back down. "When are you leaving?"

"First thing in the morning."

Leaning back in the chair as he studied her face, he replied, "Well, then, I guess we still have time for lunch."

Seven Days at Oak Valley

12:30 p.m.

Tony's stomach grumbled and he began to regret his decision to skip lunch. From east to west, gray clouds the color of his poncho filled the sky. "Rain all day for sure", he complained to himself, hoping it would stop before the Relief Ladies arrived. He'd been looking forward to another shot at a moonlit walk with Debbie. Across the open expanse of the Green he spotted Sam walking with one of the nurses and a worker toward the infirmary. The worker looked like he was all but carrying Sam. Tony watched until they made it through the infirmary door, relieved to see that Sam was gonna get checked out by the new doctor.

Arriving at Building F, he climbed the three stairs that ran the full length of the front of the building and swung open the door. In one smooth move, he placed the day's mail for the building in the IN tray, snatched up the outgoing mail, and flipped it into his sack. He paused to gaze down the hall and caught the eye of one lone girl sitting on a bench outside Mrs. Blackstone's, Building F's social worker, office.

Not seeing anyone else around, he decided to get a closer look. He pulled his shoulders back and ran his hand over his head. As he walked towards her, he hitched up his pants and worked on his best Elvis smile. Pausing momentarily at the crack in the office door, he slipped past it and slid onto the bench next to the girl.

"Hello, beautiful," he said in a low voice as he ran his hand over his head. "Where have you been all my life?"

Ruthie-Marie Beckwith

The girl on the bench giggled, blushed and turned her back to him.

Undeterred, Tony continued, "What's your name, gorgeous?"

"Angela Johnson," she replied slowly, emphasizing the consonants. As she turned back toward him, Tony noticed a hearing aid in her right ear.

"My name's Tony," he informed her. "You new here?"

Angela nodded, causing her long blond hair to shimmer across her back. Tony stifled a gasp. He looked down next to the bench where two suitcases sat side by side.

"You comin' in today?"

Angela nodded and her lower lip began to quiver.

He sat quietly to her left and waited as she struggled with trying not to cry. Voices from the office drifted into the hall.

"We wouldn't have had to do things in such a hurry," he heard a man's voice say. "It's just that my wife's doctor told her that with her heart condition she just wasn't up to takin' care of Angela any more."

"That your dad talkin'?" Tony whispered.

Angela whispered, "Yeah. Mama's in there, too."

Tony listened as he heard Mrs. Blackstone tell Angela's parents that there would be no parent visits for six months.

"That can't be true!" Tony heard Angela's mama declare.

"I just don't think that's right!" added her father. "Six months! Why by the time we get to see her again, she'll have forgotten what we look like!"

Seven Days at Oak Valley

Mrs. Blackstone didn't sound moved by their protests. She sounded like she had firm control of the interview when she explained, "I assure you, it's in Angela's best interest. She'll need some time to adjust. We here at Oak Valley need time to complete her assessments and help her begin the process of getting used to not having Mama and Daddy around all the time."

The sound of her mama's weeping carried out into the hall. He stretched out his shirtsleeve and offered it to Angela to use to wipe the tears that had pooled in her light blue eyes. Angela took the cuff of his sleeve swiped it across her face. Tony felt a shiver go up and down his spine.

"Things aren't all that bad, here," Tony told her, casting about for something to distract her from what was happening in Mrs. Blackstone's office. "They do have fun things to do every once in a while."

"Like what?" Angela asked, swallowing the bait.

"Like tonight, for instance," Tony explained. "There's these Relief Ladies that come and sponsor a party every week. They pass out cookies and stuff."

"Does Angela like to sing?" Tony heard Mrs. Blackstone ask.

"She really enjoyed being in our church choir," Angela's mama responded. "She kept up real good, too. Her hearing aid made a world of difference. After she got it, she was hardly ever off key and everyone was extra nice to her, being how she's retarded and all."

Tony winced at the word retarded.

"That's wonderful!" Mrs. Blackstone gushed. "I bet she's a perfect candidate for our girls chorus. They're really good! We have a teacher from over at

Jefferson High that has done wonders with the girls. They even performed for the Governor last year."

Angela giggled as Tony began another distraction—mimicking Mrs. Blackstone. He took advantage of her smile to lean over and ask, "Would you like to meet tonight at the Relief Ladies party?" Adding in his deepest voice, "I'd be honored."

Angela smiled and shook her head in agreement. The sight of her blond hair swaying sent another shiver up his spine.

"I'll meet you there," Tony told her, "but don't tell anyone else about it, O.K.? I really know my way around here and I want to be the one to show you the ropes."

"Okay," Angela agreed, "thank you . . . ah . . ."

"Tony," he reminded her. He stood up. "Well, I need to get back to work." He leaned over and whispered in the ear that didn't have the hearing aid, "See you later, alligator." He slipped past the door and stopped to take one more look at his dream girl. He pinched himself to make sure he wasn't dreaming.

"Is there anything else?" he heard Mr. Johnson ask.

"Well, there is one other small matter," Mrs. Blackstone began, "I need you to sign this consent form to give permission for Angela to have a hysterectomy for hygiene purposes. I assure you it's totally routine and nothing to worry about. She'll be well and back on her feet in no time and things will be so much simpler for her."

Tony heard Angela's mother gasp. "But she's only nineteen! She's always been good at taking care of

Seven Days at Oak Valley

her period," Angela's mother asserted. "You just have to make sure she has the things she needs, is all."

"I'm sure she is," Mrs. Blackstone interjected, "but here at Oak Valley, all the girls have had that problem taken care of. It's in Angela's best interest to not have to deal with it anymore."

Tony heard Angela's father cough. "If Mrs. Blackstone says it's for the best," he started.

"I just hate to think of her having to go through with something like that all by herself," Angela's mother continued.

"I assure you, Angela will be just fine," Mrs. Blackstone said.

The sound of Mrs. Blackstone's voice tapered off as he stopped eavesdropping and tiptoed down the hall, wondering what a "historytomy" was. Tony waved at Angela one more time. He watched her parents emerge from Mrs. Blackstone's office. Her mama hugged her and her dad picked up her suitcases. Mrs. Blackstone gestured for them to follow her. Angela walked slowly, taking one step forward with her left leg and then pulling her right leg up beside it. At the end of the hall they turned left and Angela disappeared from view.

1:00 p.m.

"I want to assure you it is extremely unlikely that any of the residents at Oak Valley are responsible for the recent deaths there, m'am," Thomas told the middle-aged woman. She'd been standing at the front desk when he'd returned from lunch, expressing her fears of being out at night with a murderer running loose to no one in particular. He

Ruthie-Marie Beckwith

glanced around the office and noticed his assistant moving toward the bathroom and Deputy Ward leaning back in his chair, trying not to grin.

The woman drew back at his tone and moved toward the door. "I'm just letting you know how some of us here in the community feel, Sheriff, surely you can appreciate that."

"I'm always thankful for the input of the good citizens of Laurel County," Thomas told her, trying hard not to slip into campaign speak. "It's just, in this case, I feel that there are other explanations for what is happening over there." I just don't know what they are, yet, he thought.

Thomas walked her to the door. When he was sure she was out of earshot he asked Ward, "Did you get her name?" Ward shrugged.

"Didn't you think it was important?" Thomas asked in a tenor approaching the one he had just used with their visitor. Ward shrugged again. Thomas started to let one of his famous lectures come streaming out of his mouth, caught himself, and sighed. Instead, he pulled out a white envelope from his jacket pocket and handed it to Ward.

"See if you find this a bit more important and challenging," he told him. "Miss Williams, the receptionist over at Oak Valley slipped it to me on my way out the door this morning. Appears to be some kind of license tag and a note about missing supplies. Let me know when you have something back." He called out to his assistant, "I'll be over at the County Commission if anyone needs me." He grabbed his hat and walked out the door, leaving Ward standing there, staring at the contents of the envelope.

— 154 —

Seven Days at Oak Valley

1:45 p.m.

The telephone ringing interrupted Jefferson's concentration. After the fourth ring he realized that Fisk wasn't at her desk.

"Oak Valley," he answered.

"Yes. Well, good afternoon, Sheriff Thomas. Or should I say it's been a wet afternoon?"

"Don't I know it," Jefferson replied. "No, we didn't need this rain. What we needed is that construction finished."

"Is that right?" Jefferson continued. "You're sure that letter opener was the murder weapon?"

"Yes, I know," Jefferson answered. "Modern science never makes a mistake. Guess that means Tinker must have been the one to kill Dr. Cordell?"

"No other evidence on the opener? That's a shame." Jefferson replied.

"Yes, I realize everything's still under investigation. I hope you get to the bottom of this soon," Jefferson told him.

"Well does this mean we'll still be having you and your deputies as our guests?" Jefferson asked.

"Sure," Jefferson told Thomas, "I'll pass it on to Mac. I'm sure he'll do what he can to help."

"You have a good rest of the day, Billy," Jefferson concluded. He hung up the telephone but another question occurred to him and he picked the receiver back up to buzz Mrs. Fisk.

Ruthie-Marie Beckwith

"Yes, well, please find Mac Jones for me," Jefferson told her. "I need to catch him up on a few things."

Mac was going to have to put up with the Sheriff a while longer, Jefferson thought to himself. Leaning over his desk, he resumed his examination of the invoices laid out before him. He reached over and opened a manila folder that was labeled "Housekeeping, 1978". Similar files beneath it were labeled "Pharmacy" and "Dietary."

He picked up a yellowed sheet of paper and looked at the figures that summarized the procurement of housekeeping supplies for the month of February of the prior year. Next he pulled out another less yellowed sheet that summarized the procurement of housekeeping supplies for this past February. Laying the two documents side by side, he shook his head. The figures from this year were more than three times higher.

He pushed the intercom again. "While you're trying to track Mac down, see if you can get me Margaret Napier over in housekeeping."

Sitting back in his chair, he rolled his head around his shoulders to ease the tension. He looked out the window into the gloomy afternoon before picking up another invoice. The head of housekeeping had some explaining to do, he thought to himself. And perhaps others on his administrative staff had some explaining to do as well.

2:00 p.m.

The floor was wet from being mopped when Tony arrived back at Building K. He did his best to keep

Seven Days at Oak Valley

from tracking in too much mud on his way back to see Miss Lambuth. He didn't want to do anything to warrant another lecture before he had an answer about going to Tinker's service. Thinking about Tinker brought yet another lump in his throat. It was still hard to believe he was gone. Dead. Gone. He wondered who Dr. Jefferson would get to replace him. He was sure Tinker couldn't be replaced.

Tinker had told him he'd been working at Oak Valley since he was a boy. That was back when the boilers ran on coal instead of a generator like they did now. Tinker said his first job had been shovelin' coal into those boilers, day and night.

Tony reached Miss Lambuth's office and was surprised to see it open. Lambuth gestured for him to enter but he shook his head and pointed to his wet feet.

"Don't want to get your floor all wet," he told her.

:That's very considerate of you, Tony," Lambuth responded, "but I'm afraid I've got bad news. I talked to Tinker's wife and she said the family was having a private viewing and service. Family only, is what she told me."

Tony stood wordlessly, taking in what Lambuth had just told him. Family only, he thought to himself. Tinker was like the only family he'd ever had. Least ways he thought of Tinker as family. He swallowed the lump in his throat and blinked back the tears that were blurring his vision.

"Well, thanks anyways," Tony told her. "Guess I best get back to work. I still have two more buildings to go."

Ruthie-Marie Beckwith

Lambuth stood up and handed Tony a manila envelope. "Would you carry this over to the mailroom for me?" she asked.

Tony nodded, took the envelope from her and tucked it into his mail sack. "Anything else?" he asked.

"No, Tony," she replied. "Not right now."

Tony made his way back out into the rain. He trudged along the Upper Path to Building G where all the little kids lived. Tony had spent fourteen years in Building G and he always saved it for last. He shook himself off and opened the door. Mail in Building G went to the Supervisor's desk. He dropped off a small bundle, retrieved a similar sized bundle and placed it in his sack.

Looking around and seeing no one, he tiptoed down the hall to the day room. Two little boys, about the same age as he had been when he first arrived at Oak Valley, lay on the floor curled in each other's arms, sound asleep. Another little boy sat in front of the room's radiator, which had been encased in a wooden frame. It looked like it was going to be a while before the radiator put out any heat, Tony reflected. Across the room to the left, the top half of another door stood open.

Tony walked over and peered into the day room. Sitting on the floor of the five feet square room was a little girl, maybe around three years old. She was dressed in orange corduroy pants that were wet below her waist and a short sleeve shirt. Her short brown hair was full of knots and stuck up in at least ten different directions. Tony whispered to her, "Hey, Cutie. What you doin' in here?"

Seven Days at Oak Valley

The little girl looked up. Her face was mottled with red spots and what appeared to be leftovers from lunch. She reached her arms up to him. Tony bit his tongue to keep from hollering out when he noticed bite marks and scratches up and down both arms. While several of the bite marks appeared new, two had to be old because they oozed yellow pus. The girl whimpered when Tony didn't offer to pick her up.

A female voice behind him caught him unawares.

"What you doing in here, boy?"

Tony turned to see one of the day workers crossing the room toward him. "I heard someone cryin'," Tony replied.

"You ain't supposed to be in here," the worker told him.

Tony looked at the worker carefully. She was someone new. "I'm Tony," he said. "I deliver the mail."

"Well, there ain't no mail in here," the worker admonished. "And no one cryin' that you need to be bothered about."

Tony ignored the scolding and pointed to the little girl. "She was cryin'."

The worker took a step toward him. "She," the worker said, "is being punished. Like I imagine you will be if you don't get about your business."

Tony backed off and headed toward the door. He stepped over the sleeping boys and winked at another little girl who sat twirling a piece of thread between her fingers. As he reached the front entrance, he reminded himself to mention the little girl behind the half door to Miss Williams. Since she'd been able to get someone to help Sam, maybe

Ruthie-Marie Beckwith

Miss Williams could get someone to come over and check on her, too.

Once outside, Tony made his way down the lower path to the mailroom. He opened the door and greeted the mail clerks.

"Wet day," he told them as he hung his mail sack back on its hook.

"You look like a wet puppy," the mail clerk observed.

One of his favorite Elvis songs zipped through Tony's brain. "Nah, more like a wet hound dog." He shook his poncho, sending droplets of water spraying in all directions, "Anything else for me to do?"

"Not today, Tony," the clerk told him.

"See ya' later, then, alligator," Tony quipped.

"After a while, crocodile," the clerk replied. Tony opened the door and stepped back outside. Now all he had left to do for the day was eat dinner and get ready for the party. He hoped the Relief Ladies weren't going to cancel out because of the weather. His mood lightened as he ran back to Building K to search for Joey.

4:45 p.m.

Joey sat on his bed, trying to get the brown wrapping paper off the box Tony had delivered. His parents always put a lot of tape on the boxes they sent him, he thought to himself. He tugged and lifted the box to grasp one end of the tape in his teeth while he pulled the box with both hands. The tape separated from the box, tearing the paper with it. He pried back the lid and stared at the contents.

"What'd you get?" Tony asked.

Seven Days at Oak Valley

Joey replied, "Un'wear. Un'wear an' 'ocks."

"Geez, Joey," Tony observed, "seems like your folks always go to a whole lot of trouble just to send you underwear and socks every time. Don't you ever ask them for somethin' else?"

Joey shook his head. He pulled out the package of underwear and reached in to get the socks. His folks had told him they were sending new jeans, but the box was empty.

"You could at least ask them for cookies or somethin' good to eat," Tony continued. "You know, like Moon Pies or Little Debbie cakes or somethin' like that."

Joey ignored Tony's chatter. He had been so sure his folks were sending more. Maybe his mama didn't have time to run over to K-mart to get the things he'd asked for during their last visit.

Tony looked up when the box hit the floor at his feet. "Maybe they'll send some good stuff next time," Tony told him.

"'Ext time," Joey echoed. He shoved the socks and underwear under his pillow where he'd keep them until Miss Lambuth counted them and wrote the number down in her book. She'd also write his name on them with a big black magic marker, but they'd be long gone after he wore them the first time. Socks and underwear were always the first things to get lost in the laundry. Even when he had his name on things, they still ended up in the clothes room, and not necessarily the one in Building K.

Joey looked down at Tony's feet. His roommate's pant legs were wet almost up to his knees. "'Et," he observed, pointing to Tony's feet.

Ruthie-Marie Beckwith

"I wear my poncho and I still get wet," Tony agreed. "And, by the way, thanks for the shoes."

"Nuttin'," Joey replied.

"I snuck up to the cemetery today," Tony told him. "There was fifteen graves that looked like they were from this year."

Joey's eyes got big. He tried to whistle in response but it came out more like a wheeze.

"'Ots," he responded.

"Yeah, lots," Tony echoed. "And look at this," Tony continued as he reached into his pocket. "I found one of Dr. Jefferson's cigar butts at the steam plant."

"'Eally?" Joey asked. He held out his hand and Tony placed the cigar butt in his palm. Joey lifted up to his nose. "Eew," he exclaimed.

"Got that right," Tony told him. "I don't see how Dr. Jefferson can smoke those stinky old things."

Joey pinched the cigar butt with his thumb and forefinger. He imitated inhaling on the cigar butt and exhaled directly into Tony's face. "'Ot ya'!" he exclaimed.

Tony jumped back, laughing. "I don't know about you but I need some food. I skipped lunch today."

"'Kay," Joey replied. He stood up and reached over to pull his jacket off a hook on the wall next to his bed. "'Ets go."

"Joey," Tony said gesturing to the cigar butt. Joey turned around and handed it to him. "Don't tell nobody about this."

"'Kay," Joey said.

"I mean it, Joey," Tony told him as he slipped the butt back into his pocket. "Nobody."

Seven Days at Oak Valley

"'Kay," Joey said louder to indicate he got the point.

Tony took the steps down two at a time and waited for Joey at the bottom of the staircase. Joey followed, carefully putting one foot on a step and then bringing his other foot to join it, all the while clinging tightly to the handrail. The stairs continued down another level to the basement, but no one ventured down there where the building's laundry and cleaning supplies were locked up, not even to sneak a smoke. People caught down there were thrown right into the tight room, no questions asked.

Proceeding down the hall, Tony slowed his pace to match Joey's. He slipped his poncho over his head and waited for Joey to pull his jacket hood up. Together they ventured out into the darkening light.

7:00 p.m.

Cordelia cringed as the door swung open and Jones strutted through and up to the counter.

"Working late?" Jones asked her.

"Dr. Ford has given us all last minute assignments to complete before the accreditation team shows up," Cordelia replied.

"Your assignment wouldn't be snooping around looking for missing files, would it?" Jones asked.

"I don't know what you mean, Mr. Jones," she told him. "It feels like everyone from three counties has been here either asking about or looking for those files. I'm sure when they're ready to be found, they'll turn up."

In an effort to dismiss him, Cordelia picked up her pen and began editing the notes she'd begun

Ruthie-Marie Beckwith

transcribing for Dr. Ford that afternoon. Jones remained stationary in front of her desk.

She sighed, "Anything in particular I can help you with, Mr. Jones?"

Jones thrust out his chest and laid his right hand on top of the papers she'd been editing.

"Just be sure you report any major lost and found items, to me," Jones told her. "It'd be a shame if Dr. Jefferson had to replace his receptionist for. . ." he paused and brought his hand up to stroke his chin. "What's that big fancy word in the discharge policy?" He laid both of his hands on the counter and let a lazy smile slide across his features. "Malfeasance, that's it."

Cordelia started as the word "malfeasance" came rolling across Jones' mouth with no apparent difficulty. There was more to him than he let on, she thought to herself. But, there was more to her than she let on as well. She chose a straightforward, direct counter attack.

Using the "teacher is not putting up with any more nonsense" voice she had acquired during student teaching, Cordelia shoved herself forward until her face was less than six inches away from his and let loose. "Now you listen here, Mac Jones, you think you can bully anyone you want to around here but you're not going stand there and bully me. I don't care about your threats and I don't believe you could do anything to jeopardize my job. Besides, I'm three credits short of my degree and pretty soon I'll be able to move out of this backwoods county and over to Knoxville, or maybe even Nashville."

Jones started to interrupt but Cordelia cut him off with a threat of her own. "So leave me alone

Seven Days at Oak Valley

before I ask Dr. Jefferson to provide me with some *real* security." She stepped back, crossed her arms, and glared at him. "I have work to do, Mr. Jones. As I'm sure you do somewhere as well."

Jones raised both hands, palms open in apparent surrender. He backed his way to the door. "No offense, Miss Williams, just wanted to let you know how high the stakes are. . ."

"I'm quite aware of how high the stakes are, Mr. Jones, being as how we've had two murders in as many days. Maybe you should worry about doing something about that and leave me to take care of what needs caring for here."

Even with his capitulation, Cordelia felt a need to put another barrier between her and Jones. She followed the edge of her desk to her chair while keeping an eye on Jones as he stomped out of the door. She placed her hands on the blotter and took one deep breath after another. Her hands were shaking and her heart had to be pounding about one hundred fifty beats per minute, but she hoped she'd made it clear to Jones that just because she was petite and perky didn't mean she was a pushover.

7:30 p.m.

"You goin' to the dance?" Tony whispered to Joey. "The Relief Ladies are sponsoring it."

"'Ot goin'," Joey told him. He pointed to his arm, "'Ots."

"You had more shots today?" Tony asked him.

"Yeah," Joey repeated, "'ots."

"What they give you all those shots for, anyways, Joey," Tony asked.

Joey shrugged, "'Unno. "'Oc 'enerson 'arted it."

"Doc Henderson's dead now. You should ask the new doctor, Joey," Tony admonished.

Joey shrugged his shoulders in response.

Tony studied his roommate's pale face, "Your mama and daddy know about all these shots?"

Joey shrugged his shoulders again. "'Unno."

"Well, you could at least tell them about it," Tony suggested.

Joey slipped off his pants and shirt and placed them neatly on top of his trunk. He pulled back the sheet and slipped into bed.

"Sleepyhead," Tony commented.

"'Eep," Joey replied. "I 'ired."

"Well, I'm not tired," Tony said. "And I gotta' date with an angel."

"Angel?" Joey asked.

"A new girl came in today. Her name's Angela and she's beautiful, Joey," Tony told him. "And I saw her first!"

"'Eep," Joey muttered.

"Aw go ahead and sleep," Tony told him. "I'll tell you all about it later." He flipped the light switch as he walked out the door, plunging the room into darkness. No moon out tonight, he noted as he looked back at Joey one more time.

8:30 p.m.

Mac Jones leaned back in his chair and took a long draw on the cigar he had purloined from Jefferson's humidor during his final security check of the day. The muscle in his right cheek twitched as he let the smoke trickle out of his mouth. He reached for

Seven Days at Oak Valley

the black phone that sat on the corner of his desk. Aside from the phone, the desk held only a tray for incoming mail and an orange ceramic ashtray that one of the residents had given him as a gift three years before.

Jones studied the ash at the tip of the cigar. Jefferson had told him the whiter the ash, the finer the soil that had produced the tobacco. More uppity claptrap, he thought as he flicked it into the ashtray, pushed the button for a direct outside line, and dialed a number from memory. He listened for five rings and was about to hang up when he heard a voice answer.

"Russell?" Jones queried. He chuckled and leaned on one elbow to listen more intently.

"No, just checkin' in, Senator," Jones said.

"I'm doing alright under the circumstances."

"Yeah, we still have Sheriff Thomas sniffin' around about Cordell's murder. When will they be done? I don't have any idea. The lab report said the letter opener could be the murder weapon. It fits the size and shape of the wounds, but there wasn't any blood or fingerprints on it. So I guess they'll still be interviewing folks."

"No, I don't reckon' they've ruled out Tinker," Jones reported as he took another draw on the cigar. The ash fell onto the floor before he could make it to the ashtray as he leaned back in his chair and put his right foot up on the desk.

He took another couple of puffs before cutting in, "Anyways, did the merchandise make it there as planned?"

"I know there wasn't any drugs. How do you suppose I was going to get into the pharmacy with Thomas' deputies all over the infirmary?"

"You still comin' up tomorrow?" he asked.

"Plan on comin' by my office before you head out. We can talk about it then."

"I don't know and I don't care," Jones went on, "Thomas is focused on a murder and suicide. He's got no cause to be botherin' himself with a few missin' supplies."

"You just take care of Jefferson and I'll deal with Thomas."

"That would suit me just fine. Have a safe drive. See you in the morning."

9:30 p.m.

Joey was sound asleep when a hand clamped over his mouth and an arm held him down on the bed. Awake, he began struggling but the arm pushed down harder.

"Quiet!" a voice whispered to him. "Where is it, skinny ass?"

Joey tried to point at the empty box that had been shoved over into the corner. While he was still being held, another silhouette moved toward the box, picked it up, and turned it upside down.

"Empty," another voice grunted.

"I said, where is it!" the first voice whispered and with one arm yanked him out of the bed. Joey tried to shake his head in denial but the hand over his mouth held him tight.

Seven Days at Oak Valley

"I'm gonna move my hand, boy, and if you scream, no one is gonna come runnin'," the first voice told him. "You know that, don't yah?"

Joey nodded as best he could and the hand over his mouth dropped away. The arm holding him clamped down even tighter. He'd have bruises for sure in the morning.

"Now where's the stuff?" the voice said. "I'm not gonna ask you again, boy."

Joey pointed to his pillow and the second silhouette moved across the room and picked it up. The silhouette scooped up the underwear and socks and threw them down on the bed.

"That's it?" the voice whispered.

Struggling to nod, he shivered in the dark. His breath was getting shorter and his feet were getting cold. He thought of a prayer his mama had taught him. "'Ow I 'ay me 'own to 'eep," he began.

"Shut up," the first voice told him.

He stopped praying.

"I told you that I'd be around, didn't I?" the voice said.

Joey nodded.

"An' you still ain't got nothin' for me, do you skinny ass?"

"No," he whispered.

"Well, I'm tired of you holdin' back on me, boy," the voice told him. "I know your rich mama and daddy send you better stuff than that." He yanked Joey by the arm and the other silhouette grabbed his other arm. They lifted him up and dragged him toward the doorway and looked out into the empty hall.

Ruthie-Marie Beckwith

"Everyone must be on their cigarette break," the first voice commented as the two silhouettes pulled Joey out into the light. Joey looked up, recognizing the one of the workers from the dining hall confrontation the day before.

"I'm tired of comin' over here all the time and leavin' empty handed," the other worker told him. "Can't let that stand."

As the two workers dragged him to the stairwell and down the stairs to the first floor, he heard the outside door open at the east entrance of the building. That was the entrance the staff used for their breaks. The workers kept their hold on him and took him down the first flight of stairs leading to the basement.

Joey started praying again, "'Ow I 'ay me 'own to 'eep."

The two workers glared at him as voices and footsteps drifted closer from the other entrance.

"You want sleep? Huh, Joey?" the first worker said. "Well, we'll help you sleep, won't we?" he said to his partner and with that they pitched him down the remaining stairs that led to the basement storage room. His thin body bounced off the fourth step, hit the twelfth step on its side, rolled down the remaining four steps and landed on its back. His right arm, his good arm, was wedged under him.

"Sleep tight," the second worker called down to him as a kind of darkness not unlike sleep claimed him.

Seven Days at Oak Valley

9:45 p.m.

The night had gotten off to a bad start, but thanks to the Relief Ladies, things had improved as time went on. Tony had showed up at Building F to retrieve Angela to find Debbie and Wanda Sue struggling with her in the rain.

"You know they're gonna cut off all that blond hair of yours," he heard Debbie tell Angela as Wanda Sue grabbed a fist full of hair and yanked.

"Cut it out," Tony said, shouting at Debbie. "Cut it out or I'll get the supervisor."

Wanda Sue stopped yanking as Debbie looked over her shoulder at Tony.

"Well, Tony Ervin," Debbie said as she turned around. "You're here right on time to walk me to the party."

"I ain't here to walk you to the party, Debbie," he told her as he leaped up the steps to Angela. "I'm here to take *her* to the party."

"*Her*?" Wanda Sue repeated.

Tony reached around Debbie, grabbed Angela's hand, and helped her down the steps.

"Come on, Angela, let's go," he said.

The rain began to let up as they made their way across the parking lot and down the path to Assembly Hall. Tony scouted out two chairs and they sat down.

"I hope those two weren't bothering you too bad," Tony said.

"No, not, too, bad," Angela replied. "You came just when they started to get mean."

"That's good," Tony said and then added, "You let me know if anyone messes with you again, o.k.?"

Ruthie-Marie Beckwith

As Angela nodded, the P.A. system emitted a loud squeal. One of the Relief Ladies stood in front of a microphone on the stage and began appealing to the group of residents to quiet down.

"Now, boys and girls," the Relief Lady said, "I need your attention."

The roomful of residents ignored her for a few more minutes as people located seats near friends and sat down.

Tony looked up to see Charlie heading his way, carrying a metal folding chair. Charlie unfolded the chair, placed it on the opposite side of Angela and sat down.

"Boys and girls," the Relief Lady admonished. The room became quiet.

Moving his chair even closer to Angela's, Tony whispered severely to Charlie, "Scram, meathead."

Charlie leaned over to Angela and told her in a voice loud enough for Tony to hear, "You don't want to hang out with that loser do you, sweet thing?"

Angela looked back and forth at both men and then reached out and took Tony's hand. Tony grinned and squeezed her hand in return.

"Guess you've got your answer, Charlie Butthole Edmondson," he exclaimed. Charlie got up without comment and looked around the room. He spied Debbie three rows up, made a beeline to sit next to her, and shot Tony a smug look as he put his arm around her.

"Tonight we have a special treat," the Relief Lady announced. "Mr. Barfield has come all the way over from Sevier Landing to lead us all in a nice evening of square dancing."

Seven Days at Oak Valley

"Square dancing," Tony muttered under his breath. "Whatever happened to rock and roll?"

"So we need each of you to pick a partner and move your chairs to the side of the room so we can get started. After the dancing, we'll have refreshments."

Chairs scraped as residents and workers shoved them out of the way. Charlie and Debbie took their place with three other pairs of partners. He led Angela across the room to join Ben, Wanda Sue, and two other pairs. The Relief Lady adjusted the volume on the record player and square dancing music filled the hall. Mr. Barfield stepped up to the microphone and began to call the moves.

Tony liked swinging Angela around best of all. She was light as a feather, and he was happy when she leaned on him for support whenever they circled 'round. By the end of the last song, they were both laughing with the three other pairs in their square.

The music ended and the people in attendance moved to two tables set up with a punch bowl and cookies.

"It's usually Kool-aid and store bought cookies," Tony informed Angela. "But sometimes they have High C. Guess it depends on whatever folks give 'em."

"Kool-aid's ALL RIGHT," Angela replied. "You dance real good."

Tony stood up taller and smiled. "The Relief Ladies been comin' ever since I moved up to Buildin' K.," he said. "That's a lot of square dances."

Another Relief Lady was busily serving punch. Tony handed a cup to Angela and picked up two

Ruthie-Marie Beckwith

cookies off the table along with two napkins. They found two chairs and sat down.

"So how's your first day at Oak Valley been?" he asked.

She stopped smiling and looked like she was going to cry.

I've messed up remindin' her, Tony realized. "I'm sorry, Angela. I didn't mean to make you sad. Come on, smile for me. You look like an angel when you smile."

Angela rewarded him with a small smile.

"You look tired," Tony observed. "Let me walk you home."

"OKAY," Angela replied. Tony took her hand and helped her to her feet. He set their empty cups down on the chair behind him and led her to the door. Outside the rain had stopped and the wind had died down. More leaves had been blown to the ground and the earth was soft and soggy beneath their feet.

As they came into the light outside of Building F, Tony leaned over and tried to plant a kiss on Angela's cheek. She giggled as she dodged his effort. He helped her up the stairs and tried again, this time with success.

"Thanks for comin'," he told her.

Angela flashed him a wide grin. "I had fun."

"Will you go with me next week?" he asked.

"Sure!" Angela replied. "You're nice."

"Well, goodnight, then," he stammered.

"Night," she echoed. She blew him a kiss and then slipped through the door.

Tony all but ran back to Building K. He couldn't wait to tell Joey about his good fortune. He replayed the night over and over in his head. It had been the

Seven Days at Oak Valley

best dance of his life—and it hadn't even cost him any cigarettes. Next week couldn't come soon enough. He raced past the front desk and bounded up the stairs to his room. The light from the hall fell directly on Joey's empty bed.

Tony looked around the empty room. Sam was still at the infirmary and Ben hadn't gotten back from the dance. He walked out and down the hall to the bathroom. He ducked his head in but only saw one of the men from the opposite wing standing in front of the urinal.

Walking the length of the dimly lit hall, he peeked into each room looking for Joey. Meeting with no success on that floor, he went back up the stairs and walked the length of the next floor. He began to worry when he failed to find Joey on the either the second or third floors. Making his way to the first floor, he looked in both of the day rooms and peeked through the glass of the supervisor's office. Joey wasn't anywhere on the first floor. Joey didn't seem to be anywhere in the building.

Retracing his steps to the stairwell, he considered looking down the final flight of stairs. No, he told himself, Joey wouldn't go down there for nothin'. Still, he reasoned, he'd better check, just to be sure. He made his way down the last flight of stairs. As soon as he turned on the landing and looked down, his gaze fell on Joey's lifeless form.

Tony raced down the stairs, screaming, "Joey, Joey! Help someone, help! Joey's fallen down the stairs! He's been hurt real bad!"

He kneeled beside his friend and gently pulled Joey's head into his lap. "Help! Joey, oh man, Joey!" he continued to scream until he felt hands on his

Ruthie-Marie Beckwith

arms lifting him up and he saw Joey being carefully moved onto a stretcher and carried up the stairs.

Seven Days at Oak Valley

Chapter Five

Wednesday, October 3rd, 6:30 a.m.

Grace waited until she heard the water running in the bathroom shower before dragging her luggage from the walk-in closet. Jefferson's clothes for the day were neatly arranged on the wooden valet. He must have set those out himself before going to bed the night before, she reasoned. For the life of her, she had never been able to keep up with his things. He must have sent his best shirt out to be laundered but what in the world had he done with his other pair of loafers? Fortunately, she wasn't going to have to worry about it any longer.

She swung the largest of the floral tapestry suitcases onto the bed, zipped it open, and flipped the lid away from her. She had finished packing three pairs of shoes, her lingerie, blouses and skirts by the time she heard the water stop. Her favorite cashmere sweaters were placed gently on top of the skirts. Pausing when she heard the buzz of Jefferson's electric razor, she began moving the toiletries from the top of the antique oak dresser to the small carry-on bag.

The only jewelry she retrieved from her jewelry box were her pearls, her cameo, and the sapphire

Ruthie-Marie Beckwith

earrings she had inherited from her grandmother; the rest had neither sentimental nor monetary worth. Slipping off her wedding ring, she set it on top of his chest of drawers, next to one of the Tiffany turquoise cufflinks she had gotten him for their second anniversary. Now, for the life of her she couldn't figure out what in the world had happened to the other one. Well, if it mattered to him, he could spend *his* precious time searching for it after she was gone.

The door swung open and Jefferson's frame filled the doorway. He was wrapped in his robe and the razor had left his face chaffed. She watched in silence as he surveyed the room, the luggage on the bed, and the drawers of the dresser left open and nearly empty.

"Going so soon?" he asked.

"It's a long drive," she replied.

"You don't have to do this. If you can wait just a few days, maybe we can slip on over to Gatlinburg and relax. What you need is a nice warm fire over at Blackberry Lodge and a room with one of those hot tubs."

Jefferson moved into the room and reached out his arms to her. "I just need a little time to wrap up a couple of things and then I can make it up to you. I swear."

"I need a little time, too, Winfred," she replied, ignoring his outstretched arms. "I've got some things that I need to sort out on my own. Things a warm fire and a hot tub won't necessarily fix."

He reached up to touch her cheek.

"Don't," she said, "just don't."

Jefferson sighed. "So when will you be back?"

"I'm not sure," she replied as she folded the jewelry she'd selected into her monogrammed handkerchiefs.

"I might be there for a while," she added.

"A while?" he echoed. "How long is a while?"

"Maybe a real long while," she said. "I don't know."

She waved her arm over the bed, taking in the nearly full suitcases. "I didn't want you to think I was slinking off behind your back."

"No," Jefferson observed. "Guess that must have happened before you decided to run home to mama."

Grace flinched, leaned over the suitcases, and began zipping them up. "You wouldn't have any idea of what I was doing or not doing," she retorted. "You're too caught up in your own grand schemes to have any idea of what I might need or want."

She turned her back to him, pulled the largest suitcase off the bed, carried it to the top of the stairs and returned for the second suitcase and her carry-on. Jefferson had begun dressing for the day. As he slipped a white shirt over his still muscular arms and chest, she turned away and made her way to the door. She was retrieving her coat and hat when Jefferson came down the stairs.

He didn't offer to help and she didn't ask as she opened the door to take the largest suitcase out to the car. When she returned, he had his hat and coat on as well.

"There's nothing I can say to stop you?" he asked, following her outside.

"No, Winfred, all we had to say has either been said or it hasn't."

"Call me when you get to Memphis."

Ruthie-Marie Beckwith

Grace nodded. She carried the last two suitcases to the car, laid them in the trunk, and walked to the driver's side. At the instant she inserted her key into the lock, Jefferson laid his hands on her shoulders, spun her around and pulled her toward him. His strong arms crushed her to his chest as his hand snaked around her neck and forced her chin up to his face. He leaned down and kissed her forcefully, thrusting his tongue in between her resisting teeth. She brought her arms up and pushed against his chest.

Forcing her to endure the kiss her for a moment longer, he released her, saying, "Don't forget."

"Forget what?" she asked.

"You gotta' dance with the one who brung ya'," he replied. Turning abruptly, he strode off around the corner of the house in the direction of his office, appearing oblivious to the row of purple mums whose blooms were long past their time.

She got in the car and turned the key in the ignition with shaking hands. Only four hundred fifty miles to Memphis. She hoped that it was far enough.

7:00 a.m.

"I don't have any idea why there's been such an increase," Margaret Napier, Oak Valley's Director of Housekeeping stammered. She stared at the two documents Jefferson had handed her only moments ago as though the ink would leap off the page and splatter across her crisply starched white smock.

"We try to do our best with what's allocated," Napier stated simply. "We've been using the same

Seven Days at Oak Valley

amount for all the buildings. I check it off as it's dispensed each week."

Jefferson brought his fingers together, formed them into a pyramid and then lowered one hand. He considered his line of questioning as he fondled the letter opener laying on the blotter, a twin to the one that was found at the steam plant. Mrs. Napier was known for being extremely excitable and prone to "nervous spells", his predecessor had indicated in her personnel file.

"Surely, there must be some explanation," Jefferson stated with extreme patience. Mrs. Napier continued to stare at him with a blank face.

"What I mean, Mrs. Napier," Jefferson said, elaborating, "is that somewhere between you putting your request in and you checking it off, there seems to be a whole lot unaccounted for."

"Well, there's just no way I could have dispensed that much toilet paper," Napier stated with some finality. "Half the residents here don't even use it and the other half could just as well do without."

Struggling to maintain his composure, he tried again. "Mrs. Napier, you and I have already been down that road. All toilet roll dispensers are to have toilet paper present. That is one of the standards that this facility is required to meet and it is your responsibility to make sure we meet it. And furthermore . . . "

"Well," Mrs. Napier interrupted. "I just finished tellin' you that I dispense the same amount of toilet paper each and every week. It's been the same amount as I've dispensed since the last inspection and the same amount as I've dispensed since the one

Ruthie-Marie Beckwith

before that. And we passed both inspections with flyin' colors. Least ways that's what you told me."

"Yes, Mrs. Napier, that's what I told you," Jefferson replied. "But I didn't ask you here this morning to talk about the inspection. I need to know if you are aware of any reason why Oak Valley's consumption of toilet paper is three times greater than it was two years ago?"

"I already told you," Napier said. "I dispense the same amount each week as I always dispense."

Looking up at the ceiling and then at the fidgeting figure of Margaret Napier before him, he let out a long sigh of exasperation. He silently counted to ten and then picked up two more pieces of paper and handed them across the desk to her. She accepted them and held them up to her face, squinting at the figures.

"Those are the figures the procurement office sent over for bar soap," he explained. He hesitated and against his better judgment, decided to press forward. "Do you have any idea why Oak Valley seems to be going through so much bar soap these days?"

"Probably 'cause it's that cheap yeller soap that they send me," Napier commented. "Spit cleans better, if you ask me," she added. "And it doesn't leave near the mess, besides."

"Mrs. Napier," Jefferson told her, "if you feel a different soap is in order, then why haven't you talked it over with procurement?"

"Procurement just tells me that the darn stuff is part of a state user contract, and we're bound to orderin' it," Napier sniffed. "Whatever the devil a state users contract is."

Seven Days at Oak Valley

"A state use contract is one that is put out statewide for a product that can be bought in bulk for the whole system," Jefferson told her, deliberately pointing out the number of times he had corrected her and explained the concept in the past.

"Well, if all they can come up with is that nasty yeller soap, then maybe they should be shippin' it to some other state," Napier sniffed again.

Upon reflection, Jefferson realized he could have predicted the impasse he was having with the head of housekeeping. Napier was old enough to have been on the housekeeping staff since the first Oak Valley cornerstone was laid in 1937. The facility consistently received compliments from visitors for its cleanliness and absence of malodorous fumes, but his head of housekeeping had yet to master the mysteries of documenting the amount of supplies her department used on a routine basis.

Napier continued to fidget and her expression grew increasingly more panicked. Jefferson tried one more tactic. "Do you have anyone in your department who helps you keep up with your paperwork?" he asked hoping that perhaps an assistant could shed more light on the department's discrepancies.

The head of housekeeping looked affronted. "Why, Dr. Jefferson, the paperwork is my responsibility and mine alone," she answered. "It just wouldn't do for me to shove my work onto the other girls."

Jefferson sighed once again. What Napier probably meant to say but had avoided was that there probably weren't that many girls in the housekeeping department who could read or write.

— 183 —

Ruthie-Marie Beckwith

Patronage and peonage did come with their own unique crosses to bear, he concluded.

Feeling that no amount of questioning was going to solicit the answers he sought, he decided to surrender. "I think that'll be all for now, but please try harder to keep up with what your department uses. We wouldn't want to have to go through a big fuss with the legislature over how many rolls of toilet paper folks in East Tennessee seem to use, now would we?"

"Yes, sir, I mean, no, sir," Napier replied as she leapt to her feet, ready to flee his office at the first sign of a dismissal.

"Let me know if you find anything out of the ordinary in the future," he instructed.

"Yes, sir," she told him. She reached over and ran a fingertip along the edge of his desk, then held it up for examination. "I'll get someone on to this," she clucked.

"Have a good day, Mrs. Napier," Jefferson told her by way of dismissal.

"You, too, sir," Napier replied as she bustled out of the room.

Jefferson waited until he heard the bells jingle before gathering the forms he had shared with Mrs. Napier back into their respective folders. He stood up and watched out the window as Napier took the lower path to the Central Support Services building. Overnight the rain had stopped and the sun appeared to be making an effort at casting aside the gray clouds that still lingered in the morning sky.

As he watched Napier make her way across the grounds, another figure caught his attention out of the corner of his eye. Looking down at his watch, he

Seven Days at Oak Valley

cursed softly. Damn, it was only seven fifteen a.m. and Senator Russell was already on his doorstep; a full forty-five minutes early. The man must have left Nashville at three in the morning to arrive so early! He moved back behind his desk and sat down just as the sleigh bells jingled again.

"Senator Russell," Jefferson called out, "is that you?"

Russell stepped into view. "Good mornin', Dr. Jefferson," Russell replied.

Jefferson stood up and moved the folders on his desk to the side. He reached out, shook Russell's hand, and then motioned for him to take a seat. "Take your pick, Senator. Make yourself comfortable while I see if I can rustle up some coffee. Mrs. Fisk doesn't usually come in until 8:00 a.m. I like to get an early start, most days."

Jefferson picked up the phone and punched in the extension for Dining Hall 2.

"Good morning," Jefferson said into the receiver. "No, nothing's wrong. I was hoping I could trouble you for a pot of coffee and maybe some of those breakfast muffins you all are so famous for."

He came around the front of the desk and took Russell's coat and hat and carried them out to the hall tree in the vestibule.

"So," Jefferson began as he sat back down at his desk, "do you think UT's going to beat Vanderbilt this weekend?"

7:30 a.m.

Tony had been waiting outside the dining hall for fifteen minutes before Angela finally appeared. She

Ruthie-Marie Beckwith

had on a brown turtleneck sweater and a brown and orange flowered skirt that ended just above her knees revealing braces that were firmly in place over matching knee socks. He figured that since things fit so good and looked so nice that she must be wearing her own clothes. In his mind, she looked like an absolute dream.

It wasn't until he saw her face that he became alarmed. Her eyes were rimmed with red and it was clear that she'd been crying.

"What's wrong with my Angel," he asked her in his best Elvis voice.

"I miss my mama and daddy!" Angela cried. "I wanna' go home! I wanna' go home!"

He decided that changing the subject might be the best way to get her to stop crying.

"Look," he said, "I brought you something." Holding out a rose he had picked from Jefferson's garden on his way to the dining hall, he cautioned, "Careful, don't let the thorns get ya."

Angela stopped crying and accepted the rose. She'd seen her older sister get roses from her boyfriends over the years, but had never received one herself. She smiled and rewarded Tony with a hug.

"Thank you, Tony. I never got a flower from anyone before."

"Come on, Angela," he said, "let's go get somethin' to eat." He looked over her shoulder and let his gaze take in the whole of the grounds that was to be seen from Dining Hall 2. "'Sides, I got somethin' important to tell you."

They entered the dining hall together. Tony showed her where to get her silverware and then they went through the serving line. Angela followed,

Seven Days at Oak Valley

carefully carrying the tray full of her breakfast as he led the way across the room to a table where both of them could sit together.

He pointed to a mass of orange and white substance on the tray. "Don't eat that stuff," he advised, "it's nasty."

"OKAY," Angela responded.

They ate in silence. At one point, Angela's arm brushed up against his sending small electric jolts up his arm and down his body to his toes. He blushed and hoped that no one noticed.

Tony finished eating well before Angela. She picked at her food and took the tiniest bites. No wonder she was so skinny, he thought, waiting until she laid down her fork before starting to explain.

"Angela," he began, "you've only been here for one day but you need to know some stuff that's been goin' on."

"OKAY," Angela replied. She turned her head at an angle that was best for her hearing aid to catch what he was saying.

"Bad things are happenin'." He swallowed hard, struggling with what he had to say and how to say it.

"What's wrong?" Angela asked.

Tony fidgeted, hesitating a minute longer. "Joey, one of my roommates, got hurt real bad. He fell down a flight of stairs and they sent him to the hospital."

"Sorry, Tony," Angela replied, offering sympathy.

"And other folks have been hurt bad, too," he went on to say. "Doctor Cordell who runs the infirmary got stabbed. . ."

At the word stabbed, Angela's eyes got real big and she whispered, "Stabbed?"

Ruthie-Marie Beckwith

"Stabbed dead," Tony told her, "and Tinker, my other best friend who worked the steam plant, got hung by the neck. Bad things are goin' on here."

Angela stared at Tony. He looked over his shoulder to see if anyone was paying attention to them, but didn't see Debbie or Wanda Sue anywhere in the hall. He hoped his luck held out this morning and he could avoid them.

"I need you to promise me that if I'm not around, you'll go see Miss Williams over at the Infirmary if anyone gives you any trouble," Tony told her. "I'm not sure what she'd be able to do but she's nice and she seems pretty smart, so maybe she'll figure out a way to help you."

"Infirmary?" Angela asked.

Tony stood and motioned for her to go with him to the window. The view from Dining Hall 2 to the Infirmary was obscured by the Children's Ward so he pointed in the general direction.

"Just follow the path down that hill," he explained. "When you get to the bottom, you'll be right at the front door of the Infirmary. It's got a lot of windows in the front. Not windows like these, though, a big tall kind with a glass door right in the middle of 'em. So do you understand?"

"I think so," Angela responded. "Go see Miss Williams if there's trouble."

"Yes," Tony told her and repeated the instruction one more time for good measure, "Go see Miss Williams at the Infirmary if there's any trouble."

Angela shook her head.

"Look, Angela, I need to get to work. Do you know where they want you to go after breakfast?"

Seven Days at Oak Valley

"Back to the dorm," Angela answered. "Mrs. Blackstone needs to talk to me."

"You know how to get back?" Tony asked not wanting her to get lost her first day at Oak Valley.

"'Course," Angela told him. "It's just next door!"

Tony reached out and squeezed her hand gently. "See ya' later, alligator."

Angela looked puzzled.

Tony let go of her hand and said, "'Bye. I'll come find you at lunch. Be careful."

8:00 a.m.

"Is the coffee okay?" Jefferson inquired. Senator Russell nodded his head and waved Jefferson's offer of another muffin aside.

"Coffee's just fine." He uncrossed his legs and leaned forward in his chair to set his cup on the corner of Jefferson's desk. Dressed as he was in a tailored blue serge suit and a red and blue striped tie, he didn't look like someone who had just finished making a three-hour drive from Nashville.

After fifteen years in the Tennessee State Legislature, Russell's poker face had been honed to where it could have been mounted next to the faces on Mount Rushmore. Jefferson pulled out a folder, then shook his head, and returned it to his desk drawer. He selected another and handed it across the desk. Russell opened it up to take a look.

"Those are the most recent construction figures," Jefferson told him. Russell studied the report as Jefferson began his explanation.

"Two hundred and fifty thousand dollars worth of cost overruns and the project isn't even halfway

Ruthie-Marie Beckwith

finished. The weather has been totally uncooperative. And then there is the problem with the slab needing to be re-poured on the second cottage. It took them two weeks with a backhoe and jackhammers to dig out the one that didn't set right. I sure hope that is the last of those kind of problems."

"Things getting back on track, then?" Russell asked.

"Since it stopped raining last night, I can still hold out hope for a dry spell," Jefferson answered. "They've got some of the cinder block up and the site might be sufficiently dry to get the heavy equipment back in. The foreman was supposed to get back with me this morning."

"Hopefully, that won't be much longer," Russell offered. "Weather report said we've got one of our Tennessee warm spells comin' through in the next few days."

"Good thing," Jefferson observed, "since I've got to track someone down to fire up the boilers before things get really cool."

"It's too bad about your steam plant man," Russell commented. "He must've been here since they opened the doors." He paused and then put in, "So, how's the murder investigation going?"

"Far as I can tell, pretty slow," Jefferson replied. "They found a letter opener up at the steam plant that looks to be the murder weapon. Other than that, all Sheriff Thomas has is two dead bodies."

"No suspects?" Russell asked.

"You know Thomas isn't going to tell us anything. I did put him off of thinking that one of the residents was responsible," Jefferson retorted. "Fortunately,

Seven Days at Oak Valley

they keep the dangerous ones under lock and key over at Central State."

"I don't know why they just didn't turn them over to Corrections," Russell observed.

"You know our people wouldn't survive a day in with the general prison population," Jefferson replied. "It takes all they've got to survive a day when they're incarcerated with each other."

"You professional types can argue about that," Russell responded.

"Either way," Jefferson put in, "spending the rest of their days behind locked doors without any chance of getting out should be punishment enough."

Jefferson returned the construction file to his desk drawer, pulled out another and handed it to Russell. Having decided not to disclose the missing medication problem, he reported, "The last thing I've got going besides construction and a murder investigation is trying to track down a whole lot of missing toilet paper and soap."

"Toilet paper and soap?" Russell asked.

"You should've been here when I talked to the head of housekeeping about it," Jefferson chuckled. "She and my boiler man must've been in the running for the oldest state employee award. It's going to take a little more digging to solve this mystery."

"I'm sure you'll get to the bottom of it," Russell told him. "Speaking of things gone missing, since you brought it up . . ."

Jefferson jumped in, "I know, I know. I've had half the records department and most of the medical staff turning things upside looking for those files. They're simply nowhere to be found."

"You don't suppose one of the residents put them somewhere? Maybe using them for drawing paper?" Russell asked.

"Well, the thought had occurred to me," Jefferson replied. "If they are, I guess I'm hoping someone will take notice and eventually turn them back in. Then again, some of these residents are magicians at making things disappear."

"Like toilet paper and soap?" Russell asked.

"Exactly," Jefferson laughed. "Maybe the missing toilet paper is the cause behind all of the plumbing problems we've had to contend with this year. I tell you maintaining these old buildings takes a mighty big chunk out of my budget. Here's hoping the new ones help take the edge off."

Russell stood, signaling that the meeting was over. "Dr. Ford from Rolling Hills report in today?"

"Yes," Jefferson responded.

"Good. I think I'll take a quick walk over to the Infirmary to give him my regards," Russell said as he pulled on a tan, all weather overcoat.

"Keep me posted, Winfred," he instructed, opening the front door to leave.

"Always," Jefferson told him, "always."

8:30 a.m.

Mrs. Blackstone had accompanied Angela to the workshop and given her a brief tour of the building before depositing her into the custody of Mrs. Dawson. Mrs. Dawson looked over her new charge, commenting on her hearing aid and braces to Mrs. Blackstone.

Seven Days at Oak Valley

Angela stood next to Mrs. Blackstone, placidly waiting while she and Mrs. Dawson decided her fate for the day.

"So, how high functioning is she?" Dawson asked Blackstone.

"Her parents said she got a certificate of attendance from a self-contained educable class," Blackstone answered.

"Can she talk?" Dawson persisted.

"Quite normally, even with the hearing aid," Blackstone responded.

"Well, then," Dawson said hurriedly, "tell her to sit over at the table with Debbie Allison and her bunch."

Angela took a seat at the long oak table. She spent the next 30 minutes staring at the scratches in the wood and listening to Debbie and Wanda Sue and six other girls whisper about the dance and Tony finding Joey at the bottom of the stairs. She wondered if there was any particular thing she should be doing while she was sitting at the table as she caught pieces of their conversation—her hearing aid wasn't all that good at picking up low voices.

"I bet you Tony pushed him," Wanda Sue exclaimed.

"Naw, he probably just fell," said another girl.

"So what was he doin' wanderin' around in his underwear?" Debbie asked no one in particular.

"He probably beat up Sam, too," Wanda Sue said.

Not hearing half of what was being said and not knowing who Sam was, she tuned out the conversation and looked around the room. Dawson stood at the head of the table closest to the window, passing out huge gray plastic buckets of different colored wire. She then demonstrated how to remove the colored plastic coating from the wire. Each boy at the table started imitating her, some better than others, but by that time Dawson had moved to the head of the table where Angela sat.

Dawson looked at Angela, again taking note of her hearing aid. She began giving instructions in a loud voice.

"Now, girls," Dawson began. "What I need you to do is to take these wire strippers," she held up one pair of wire strippers for the girls to see, "and then put the wire in the middle like you would if these were a pair of scissors. Then you squeeze the wire cutters closed and pull." Dawson deftly pulled away a strip of black plastic.

"Any questions?" Dawson asked as she gave each girl a bucket.

Angela spoke up, "Why?"

"What, dear?" Dawson asked in a syrupy voice but her expression looked anything but sweet to Angela.

"Why are we doing this?" Angela asked.

"To earn tokens, of course!" Dawson replied. She began issuing further instructions, "One other thing, girls, you'll each have to share a pair of wire strippers. There's not enough to go around." Dawson then moved to another table and began repeating the instructions for the third time.

"Tokens?" Angela interrupted. "What are those?"

Debbie rolled her eyes while Wanda Sue took charge of the table by picking up all of the wire strippers and deciding who would get to use them first.

Seven Days at Oak Valley

"We get tokens for working," the girl sitting next to Angela explained. Wanda Sue looked at Angela's neighbor and shot her a stern look for speaking out of turn. She deliberately passed over giving Angela and her neighbor first dibs at the wire cutters. Angela's neighbor appeared unfazed.

"Then we use the tokens for things at the Canteen," her neighbor finished.

"Canteen?" Angela asked.

"You really are a baby, aren't you An-ge-la," Wanda Sue exclaimed, emphasizing each syllable in Angela's name.

"The Canteen's like a store," another girl at the table told her. "It's where we get to buy things like cold drinks and candy."

"Oh," Angela said, still unclear as to what tokens were and why they just didn't use money to buy things here like she did back home.

"Enough chatter," Dawson pronounced from across the room.

Everyone stopped talking and four of them began working on the wire. The two remaining girls put their heads down and promptly fell asleep. Angela sat with her hands in her lap as she watched Wanda Sue and Debbie strip the wire and the other girls sleep. Her first day at Oak Valley was going to be a really long one, she concluded as she waited for a turn with the wire strippers.

9:00 a.m.

Cordelia finished transcribing Dr. Ford's notes from the previous day and placed them in the IN box for his signature. She remembered how patient Dr.

Ruthie-Marie Beckwith

Cordell had been with her while she'd mastered the Dictaphone, a skill she hoped she would never have to use again once she finished her degree. She was also happy that she didn't have class that night, it being church night and all.

The door swung open and Tony made his way to her desk. She examined his face as he came nearer and decided that he looked like he had the world on his shoulders.

"Mornin' Miss Williams," Tony told her as he forced a smile. He picked up the outgoing mail and set the incoming mail in its place.

"Good morning, Tony," Cordelia told him once he had things situated in his mail sack. She held up her hand before he could reply. "I know what you're going to ask," she continued. "You want to talk to Dr. Ford about your roommates, don't you?" she asked.

"Well," Tony hesitated, reluctant to cross paths with Dr. Ford. "I was kinda hopin' that you could talk to him for me. Then you could tell me what he said."

"Sure, I can do that for you," she answered. "Just wait here for a few minutes and I'll see if he's free."

Cordelia came out from behind the desk and walked down the hall to Ford's office. Her long rust colored skirt swirled around her ankles. Clutching the ends of a shawl that was wrapped around her slender shoulders with one hand, she knocked on the door with the other. She heard a muffled "Come in", so she turned the knob, stepped inside, and closed the door behind her. She paused when she saw that he had a visitor.

"I'm sorry to interrupt, Dr. Ford," she told him. "I didn't know you were with someone."

Seven Days at Oak Valley

"No problem. Miss Williams, let me introduce you. This is Senator Russell." Ford turned to Russell, "Senator, Cordelia Williams. So, Miss Williams, what can I do for you?"

"Tony Ervin is here wanting to know how his roommates are doing, Dr. Ford."

"Tony Ervin?" Ford asked as he raised his right eyebrow.

"He's the mail boy," Cordelia explained. "Joseph Marcum and Samuel Jackson are his roommates over in Building K."

"I see," Ford responded. He picked up a paperclip and began bending it into a line as he gave her the details about Tony's roommates. "You can tell him Joseph is coming back from Knoxville Memorial sometime this afternoon. He's got a mild concussion and a broken leg, but other than that, he'll be fine. He's one lucky boy."

"And Samuel?" Cordelia persisted.

Ford cleared his throat again and told her, "Since you seem to know him, it might be best if you told him. Or if you know someone else who'd be better, you might want to ask them to break it to him."

Cordelia was confused and her expression must have made it evident.

"Samuel Jackson is in intensive care at Knoxville Memorial," Ford explained further. "I'm not sure he's going to pull through."

She gasped. "Not pull through? I thought he was only complaining about a stomach ache yesterday."

"Well, his stomach ache turned out to be something more serious. The gastroenterologist called me and said it appears as though he's got

Ruthie-Marie Beckwith

massive internal bleeding. It may be only a matter of time."

Placing her hand on her heart, she wondered aloud, "What am I going to tell Tony?"

"Do him a favor," Ford told her, "and just tell him about Joseph. We don't have to tell him about Samuel until we know something for certain.

Cordelia returned to her desk. She forced herself to smile as she shared Dr. Ford's news with Tony. "Joseph will be back this afternoon. He's got a broken leg and he'll have a bad headache for a while, but he's going to be just fine."

Tony exhaled a deep sigh of relief. "What about Sam?"

She hoped her face didn't give away any more than she intended, "Dr. Ford said that he sent Sam over to Knoxville Memorial to be checked on by another doctor there. He's still waiting to hear back." It wasn't exactly a lie, she reasoned, but it wasn't the truth either.

"Oh, all right," Tony said, appearing to be satisfied with her explanation. He looked up and down the hall and seeing no one, he continued. "I've got one more question for you. What's rad-i-a-ton?"

Cordelia repeated rad-i-a-ton after him, a puzzled look on her face.

"Here, let me show you," Tony told her.

He reached into his right front pocket and dug out a small piece of paper. He shoved it across the desk and Cordelia picked it up. The word 'radiation' was neatly printed in capital letters.

"Oh," Cordelia exclaimed. "Radiation! It's what they use to make x-rays of people's bones."

"Does it hurt?" Tony asked her.

Seven Days at Oak Valley

"No, not at all," she told him reassuringly. "Not unless someone gets too much by accident. Then it can make the person really sick."

"Sick enough to die?" he asked.

"Yes, but x-ray technicians know how to keep that from happening."

"Thanks," Tony mumbled. "I don't feel so good, either," he told her.

"What's wrong?" Cordelia asked him.

"My stomach really hurts," he said as he grimaced and clutched his abdomen.

"Do you want to see Dr. Ford?"

Tony shook his head. "No, I just wanna' go back to my building and lay down."

He must still be upset about his roommates, she reasoned. "Would you like me to write you a note to give to the building supervisor?"

"Yeah," Tony said in a voice that came out more as a groan. "Then I can show it to the clerks over at the mail room, too."

"Sure," Cordelia said sympathetically. She pulled out an Infirmary visit form and filled out the time and day and wrote "stomach ache" on the line for illness. She reached into her top right hand drawer to retrieve her stamp and inkpad. She stamped the form and caught her breath as she checked it.

"It has Dr. Cordell's name on it," she said handing it across the counter. "But it's still okay."

Tony thanked her and put the paper in his pocket. She watched him drag himself out the door. Through the glass she could see him turn in the direction of the Central Services Building. His shoulders drooped as he moved out of view.

Ruthie-Marie Beckwith

Cordelia picked up the rubber stamp and put it back in her drawer. So much going on, she reflected. More than anybody could possibly keep up with and the day had only just begun.

10:30 a.m.

Jones had spent the last thirty minutes pacing when Russell appeared at the door of his office. He grabbed his coat and hat and stepped outside to meet him.
"Let's go for a ride," Russell said.
"My car or yours?" he asked.
"Let's take mine," Russell replied. The two men walked up to the main parking lot and climbed into the dark blue Oldsmobile sedan that had "State Legislature" stamped on the license plate.
Russell pulled out a cigarette pack from his shirt pocket, "Smoke?"
"Don't mind if I do," Jones replied as he reached for the pack. Fishing in his shirt pocket, he retrieved a Zippo lighter that was engraved with "Oak Valley Training School" on one side and "10 years of dedicated service" on the other. The sedan filled with smoke as Russell turned the vehicle onto Highway 11E in the direction of Laurelville. Jones cracked open his window and flicked his ashes out.
"So, what's on your mind, Senator?" he began.
"Same thing that's on your mind, I hope," Russell retorted, "business."
"Business is bust until Thomas finishes nosing around the grounds at all hours of the day and night," Jones observed.

Seven Days at Oak Valley

"You sure have quite a number of dead bodies piling up over here," Russell noted. He glanced at Jones who calmly took another draw on his cigarette.

"Ain't any of my doin', ain't any of my business," Jones replied.

"Well, you might want to make it your business," Russell told him. "The sooner Thomas nails someone for Cordell's murder, the sooner we can get back to business. And, by the way," he added, "lay off the housekeeping supplies. Jefferson told me about interviewing the Director of Housekeeping this morning about missing toilet paper and soap."

Jones shrugged, "Margaret Napier? She couldn't have given him much insight about that. She barely knows where her office is and she's worked here since time began."

"I don't care what Mrs. Napier can or can't do," Russell told him in a curt voice, "It's Jefferson who's asking the questions, not her."

"All right, all right," Jones responded. "We'll lay off the toilet paper and soap. Besides, there are bigger ticket items than those anyways."

"It probably was a good thing that Dr. Cordell met with such tragedy," Russell observed. "He never was much of a team player."

Jones took a long side-glance at Russell before flicking his cigarette butt out the window. Russell stubbed his out in the ashtray.

"So, that all you got on your mind?" Jones asked.

"I just want you to keep your nose to the ground," Russell warned. "It took too long to build things up over here to have it come to a screeching halt. Give Jefferson a couple of folks to hang out to dry so he'll back off, too, while you're at it."

Ruthie-Marie Beckwith

"Sure," Jones told him as they turned back into the gate and drove past the Oak Valley State Training School and Hospital sign. He added, "I just happen to have a couple of people in mind."

Russell's car hit a speed bump and he muttered a curse. "Damn things should never have been invented!" he exclaimed as he pulled into a parking spot.

Jones opened the door and slid out of the car. He ducked his face back into the vehicle long enough to share one last thought with Russell. "They're just there to keep folks from going too fast, Senator," he said. "You might want to give that some consideration." Having delivered that rejoinder, he closed the car door and walked back to his office, softly whistling in the mid-morning sun.

11:15 a.m.

At precisely eleven fifteen, Jefferson heard the sleigh bells jingle. Fisk called out a greeting loud enough for him to hear in the next building. Jefferson remained at his desk, eavesdropping on the conversation.

"Good mornin', Tony," she exclaimed.

"Mornin', Mrs. Fisk," Tony replied in a monotone voice.

"What's wrong, Tony?" Mrs. Fisk asked.

Tony moaned and replied, "I don't feel so good. Here's your mail."

Jefferson heard Mrs. Fisk make a clucking noise like a mother hen and respond, "There's probably something goin' around. Have you been to the Infirmary?"

Seven Days at Oak Valley

"Yes, m'am. I got me a pass to go back to the building and lay down but my boss down at the mail room, he wanted me to make sure that Dr. Jefferson got his mail before I quit workin'."

Jefferson pushed the intercom on the telephone and Fisk picked up. "Is that Tony?" he asked her.

"Yes, sir," Mrs. Fisk replied into the handset.

"Would you send him in, please? I have something I need to talk to him about."

"Certainly, but I tell you, he doesn't look so good. I hope he doesn't get sick all over the carpet in your office."

"Just send him in, Mrs. Fisk," Jefferson said. "I'll worry about the carpet."

Ms. Fisk gazed at Tony who by now was clutching his stomach and moaning even louder. She pointed toward Jefferson's office. "Dr. Jefferson wants to talk to you for a minute, Tony. I hope you're feeling better."

"Thank you, m'am," Tony responded. He let the mail sack fall to the floor and dragged it behind him into Jefferson's office.

"This won't take but a minute, Tony. You do look kind of peaked," he said.

"Yes, sir," Tony responded, returning both hands to rest on his abdomen. "I don't feel so good."

"I'm not going down to the house for lunch today, so I guess it's a good thing you'll be heading back to your building. I just needed to know if you might have come across any brown folders full of papers as you've been going around picking up the mail."

Tony let out a moan and brought his hand up to his mouth. Jefferson scooted back, beginning to take Mrs. Fisk's counsel to heart.

"No, sir," Tony finally replied, keeping his hand over his mouth and his eyes on the carpet. "I ain't seen no folders no where. Just mail and them big brown envelopes with the strings on them. That's all."

The telephone rang. Jefferson ignored it. After the second ring, he heard Mrs. Fisk say, "Superintendent's Office." He turned his attention back to Tony.

"Well, then," Jefferson said, "I guess that's all for right now. You best get on back to your building. I hope you're feeling better shortly."

Continuing to hold his stomach as he slowly pulled his mail sack onto his back, Tony replied, "I just gotta' turn in my bag, and then I'll go on back."

"I'm sure you'll feel better by morning, Tony," Jefferson told him. "It's probably just some kind of bug that's going around."

"That's what Mrs. Fisk told me," Tony responded in a low voice. He paused at the doorway to say good-by to Mrs. Fisk and left the building.

The intercom on Jefferson's desk buzzed and he reached for the phone. "Yes?"

"While you were talking to Tony, Joseph Marcum's mama called. She and Mr. Marcum want to meet with you this afternoon about Joseph's accident."

"What accident?" Jefferson bellowed into the phone. "Why wasn't I informed?"

"I left the incident report on your desk, this morning, Dr. Jefferson. It must have gotten mixed up in your papers. Would you like me to help you look for it?"

Seven Days at Oak Valley

"No," Jefferson told her. "I'm sure I can put my hands on it now that I know I need to look for it. What time did they say they were coming by?"

"Three o'clock, or thereabouts, Mrs. Marcum said. They're going to follow the ambulance back to Oak Valley from Knoxville Memorial."

"Ambulance! What ambulance?"

"Joey Marcum was treated over at. . ." Mrs. Fisk began.

Jefferson exploded. "Is everyone at this place conspiring to keep me in the dark? I have told and told the medical staff I am to be informed of admission to the infirmary."

"Your memorandum didn't specifically say to a hospital. . ."Mrs. Fisk trailed off.

Jefferson covered the mouthpiece with his hand and counted to five. When he felt calm enough to continue, he lifted it up and told her, "I thought that since they all have college degrees over there that informing me of any admissions to the Infirmary and a hospital would go without saying."

"Yes, sir." Mrs. Fisk agreed. "That should be the case."

"Very well," Jefferson went on. "See if you can get our new physician on the phone. I'll need an update from him before the Marcums arrive. Then, see that I'm not disturbed for the next hour or so, I'm going to work through lunch and see if I can get caught up on this pile of paperwork you left for me."

11:30 a.m.

Thomas pulled his patrol car over by the side of the road and reached for the greasy brown paper sack

Ruthie-Marie Beckwith

that held one of his wife's famous pimento cheese sandwiches, an apple, and a Little Debbie Cake he'd added on his way into work. What his wife didn't know wouldn't hurt her. He locked the car and climbed down the bank of the Lower Pigeon River, right where the Senator Roy Russell, Sr. Bridge spanned its widest breadth. Below the bridge, it meandered through bottomland before it cut a direct path to Oak Valley where it ran rapidly enough to support the mountain trout that served as the basis for the annual fishing rodeo.

He sat in a patch of shade under the bridge and looked up at its thirty-two year old girders. Before the bridge was in place, anyone wanting to get over to Laurelville took the ferry. State Senator Roy Russell Sr. had done a lot for this county. Too bad his son had turned out to be more of a politician than a public servant. Russell Jr. seemed to spend more than his fair share of time over at Oak Valley, too. His comings and goings had tweaked Thomas' curiosity for at least the better part of the past two years. Nothing seemed all that right over there anymore.

Thomas ate his sandwich in three bites, contemplating the lack of progress on this case. His deputies had turned up next to no evidence. Other than the letter opener fitting the wounds, the yellow rope, the pills, and a solid distrust of Jones, he had nothing concrete to move forward on. He had that plate number traced and was waiting to hear back from the TBI who had been more than delighted to hear from him. He wasn't sure what to make of the missing supplies and he was still waiting for the results of the background check he'd run on Jefferson.

Besides Jones and Jefferson, he couldn't think of any other suspects who warranted further examination at this point. Hell, as of yet, he hadn't even uncovered any possible motives, motive in his opinion usually being the strongest indicator of who was responsible for wrongdoing. Well, he did have that last box of paperwork that Deputy Ward had fished out of Cordell's office to go through. As much as he hated paperwork, he hoped Cordell's bore greater fruit than what the Sheriff's department afforded.

He stood, tore the wrapper off the Little Debbie Cake and took a bite, savoring the chocolate and sating his craving for sugar. He tossed the apple into the river and watched as it bobbed up and down, the current taking it downstream and out of sight.

12:15 a.m.

After Tony turned in his mail sack, he wasn't sure what to do while he waited for Joey to get back from the hospital. He was still worried about Sam, too. At the rate his roommates were getting hurt, he probably ought to be worryin' about Ben as well. But Ben usually made out okay. He was the kind of person who stayed pretty much invisible, doing what he was supposed to do and never calling attention to himself. If Ben was missin', nobody except him would probably notice for weeks.

Tony sat on a bench outside the Central Support Services building. The sun had come out and the sidewalk and grass were drying up pretty good. He

Ruthie-Marie Beckwith

weighed his options, continuing to hold his stomach in case someone asked him what he was doing. He knew he couldn't wander around too much, or someone was bound to send him back to Building K or worse. On the other hand, he wanted to be outside when Joey came back, just to ease his mind. He made a decision, stood, and headed out.

The leaves crunched beneath Tony's bare feet. He'd left his shoes back in the locker, hoping they'd dry out some now that it'd stopped raining. He continued downhill and across the field where Special Olympics was played every year. He'd stopped bein' in Special Olympics when he got the mail boy job. His favorite event had been the softball throw; after that he liked the hundred-yard dash, even if Charlie Edmondson did come in first every year.

Beyond the athletic fields, Tony followed the path that ran along the river. It was overgrown with some kind of bush that had prickly branches. One branch swung in the wrong direction and scraped up his left forearm, drawing a thin line of blood. He raised his arm to his mouth and sucked on the scratch to make the bleeding stop.

As he had hoped, the boat dock at the end of the path was deserted. The two rowboats that were used in the annual fishing rodeo were beached on the brown pebbly gravel that lined the shore. When he was back in the little kid's building, he and his buddies like to dig in the pebbles for Indian money. He carried Indian money around in his pockets for days until some turned up in the laundry by mistake and he'd gotten a reprimand.

Seven Days at Oak Valley

The river was up because of the rain and Tony smelled the musky earth mixed with fresh water. The current seemed pretty fast. Tony pitched a stick out into the center of the river and watched as the river caught it and took it downstream. He sat on the bank, stretched his legs, and looked up at the sun. He probably had a couple of hours to kill before Joey got back.

The sun peaked earlier this time of year and fell faster to the horizon. The rain had ended during the night and a warmer breeze was coming in from the west. Events of the past four days raced through his mind. He tried to piece together what he had heard and found. Missing files. The cufflink with the blue stone. The trucks in the night.

Questions rose up like the monsters in the stories the workers told the little kids to scare them on Halloween. Tony felt like he'd spent his whole life trying to fight off the questions that he always occurred to him but didn't seem to occur to anyone else. Tinker had always warned him that curiosity killed the cat. Now here he was again thinking of questions he had no business trying to get answered.

Had Jones been the one to kill Tinker and Dr. Cordell? Did Tinker and Dr. Cordell see something they shouldn't have? Come to think of it, had he had seen something he shouldn't have? Was he going to be next? Maybe the ones that had hurt Joey had really been after him!

Guilt flooded his mind. He didn't want to be responsible for what'd happened to Joey anymore than he wanted to be responsible for what had happened to Tinker. Curious cat or not, somehow he'd have to find out who was hurting people.

Ruthie-Marie Beckwith

Pulling the things he'd found out of his pocket, Tony focused his thoughts on each item. The cufflink was fancy, too fancy for Jones. He'd never seen Dr. Cordell wearing a shirt that needed cufflinks, either. The cigar butt was sure to be Dr. Jefferson's but then, like he'd thought before, Jones could have stolen it, too. After focusing as much as he possibly could, he was left believing the murderer was either Jones or Dr. Jefferson, and neither one of them would be happy if they found out he was nosing around.

Tony wished he had someone to talk this over with, but Tinker was gone and so was Joey. He'd just have to wait until Joey got back, that's what, and this was the best possible place to wait in Oak Valley. He had it all to himself. He stretched out on his side and as the water tumbled by, he wondered where it ended up after its long journey through the mountains.

1:45 p.m.

Sheriff Thomas was back at this desk for all of five minutes after yet another unproductive trip to Oak Valley with Deputy Ward when Julie came trotting in with a stack of paperwork. He moaned outwardly and wondered why her position was named "administrative assistant" when she neither administered nor assisted. The county commission must have had another management consultant come in, even though Laurel County had only five commissioners and a total of fifteen people on the payroll. He counted his blessings that he was an elected official and didn't have to subject himself to the whims and wishes of the Commission.

Seven Days at Oak Valley

"Here it is," Julie reported. "All present and accounted for."

"Any phone messages?" he asked.

"In the stack", she replied as she walked out the door and headed down the hall to the ladies room.

Julie spent more time in the ladies room than she did at her desk, he reflected. The only time he could recall his wife spending that much time in the ladies room was when she had been in the family way with their firstborn child. The thought of Julie being in the family way elicited another groan. She'd never get any work done, if that was the case.

Thomas had held the office of Sheriff for twenty-two years. He'd gone through eleven elections, four of which were uncontested and two of which had opposition backed openly by the County Commission. But he tried to be fair and he stayed over-involved in civic events; flipping pancakes for the Lions, getting dunked by the Rotaries, and catching fish for Oak Valley. The good citizens recognized his contributions, on and off duty, so he had been fortunate enough to be re-elected time and time again.

In the two decades he had held the illustrious Office of County Sheriff there had been only four murders. One had been a wife who had caught her husband slipping out behind her back and fired a shotgun at him; killed him dead even though she only meant to take out a kneecap. Another had been a double homicide up at the Interstate exit, the perpetrators had gotten as far as New Mexico before they were caught and brought back to Laurel County to stand trial. And the fourth, Dr. John T. Cordell, was what was disturbing his peace of mind and

Ruthie-Marie Beckwith

taking time away from his fishing. There might be a fifth if Tinker's hanging was in fact murder like the coroner had speculated.

Thomas looked up at the three big mouth bass mounted on the wall next to his prize buck. Wouldn't be any fishing to be had until he'd caught whoever had thrust that letter opener into Cordell's heart. He put his hand on his thigh to stop his leg from jiggling like it did every time he was frustrated and he was particularly frustrated by this case.

Thomas picked up the WHILE YOU WERE OUT pink slip of paper and looked at the phone message, a request from the high school principal for an extra patrol car at the football game on Friday night. Laurel County High was playing their biggest rival, Washington County, and the principal wanted to deter any problems. People in Laurel County took their ball pretty seriously.

Shoving the rest of the pink slips aside, he shuffled the documents until half-way through the pile he found the partial results of the background check from the State of Oklahoma, Department of Public Welfare, Division of Mental Retardation. At the bottom, the word "confidential" was printed in capital letters. He skimmed the first two pages; standard copies of credentials and licenses.

Julie had actually done a good job talking the Oklahoma people out of those. The last page was a portion of a personnel evaluation that was partially blacked out except for the name and date. Attached was a note Julie had written and initialed, "PSM". Thomas looked at the initials and shook his head. It must take too much energy for her to write out "please see me".

Seven Days at Oak Valley

Reaching over the stack of papers, he pushed the intercom and waited. Moments later, Julie appeared at his door.

"You don't have to come when I buzz," he said. "You just need to pick up the telephone." She nodded blandly, continuing to chew gum as he motioned her in and held up the page with her note.

"Please see you?" Thomas asked.

Julie nodded and swallowed her gum. "See, after I got the first couple pages, I called them up and got the guy in personnel to find out when you'd get the rest. He was a total wreck. He'd just found out that the Alabama concert sold out before he could get tickets. I couldn't believe it! I told him that I was never goin' to see a live concert livin' out here in the sticks like I do, and besides, what I get paid wouldn't even buy a half a ticket, let alone a whole ticket, let alone tickets, as in more than one."

When she paused to take a breath, Thomas took advantage of the moment to interject, "The note if you please."

Rolling her eyes, Julie said, "I was getting to that. So anyways, because we were so simpatico on the phone, the guy tells me that your guy, that is the guy you wanted me to check up on, the Dr. Jefferson guy, was really bad news. He was so bad news that the Commissioner asked for his resignation and basically made it where he couldn't have gotten a job anywhere else in Oklahoma and maybe even Arkansas. So I guess that's how he ended up here, huh?"

Thomas ignored her question to ask one of his own. "So, did he say anything about why Dr. Jefferson was asked to resign?"

Ruthie-Marie Beckwith

"Well, that was on the form, you know, the one that's all blacked out because of some agreement or something. But my guy tells me over the phone that it was something to do with his wife, a dead baby, and acting crazy..."

"Dead baby?" Thomas blinked, not sure he had heard correctly. In the two years he'd been around them, Jefferson nor his wife had ever let on like they'd had a child.

"Yeah," Julie continued. She gave him an irritated look at his interruption and shook her head from side to side. "That was the really sad part. A baby boy. Only two months old. Anyways, my guy says the baby died on the way to the hospital. Something about meningitis and the doctor out there at the 'facility', that's what he called the place, being too drunk to recognize it until it was too late."

"And the crazy part?" Thomas prompted.

"Oh, yeah. Apparently after the funeral, your Dr. Jefferson guy went back to the facility and beat the livin' daylights out of that doctor. My guy said it took three workers to pull him off 'em."

"Anything else?"

"No, that was it."

Pleased for a change with the information she'd gathered, Thomas told her begrudgingly, "Thank you. You did a good job." Then he waved her off and sat back in his chair, mulling over her report.

The information Julie had unearthed gave him the additional rush of adrenalin he'd needed to finish digging through the stack of paperwork on his desk. The second from the last piece of paper was the DMV run-down on the license plate number that skittish Miss Williams had given him the day before.

Seven Days at Oak Valley

"Well," he said out loud, "this is mighty interesting." It appeared that the license plate went with a pickup truck that belonged to one Senator Roy Russell. So what did a pickup truck owned by a Senator have to do with his investigation? He grabbed the keys to his patrol car and headed out the door. No time like the present to find out.

3:00 p.m.

The ambulance that ferried Joey back to Oak Valley turned into the entrance and made its way down the drive toward the Infirmary. Tony saw it and Joey's parents' car pass by from his perch on top of the water tower. He shimmied down the ladder and set off across the grounds to greet his fallen roommate. The workers had just loaded Joey into a wheelchair and were in the process of wheeling him into the Infirmary when he caught up with the entourage.

"Joey," he called out. "Wait! Hold up!"

The workers paused but Mr. And Mrs. Marcum waved them forward. Tony broke into a trot and caught them just before they passed through the open door. Joey's right leg was in a cast up to his thigh and propped up on the leg of the wheelchair. His head was still bandaged and a bruise the size of an orange marked his cheek.

"Hey, Joey," Tony said and reached out his hand.

"'Ey, 'Ony," Joey replied. He weakly lifted his arm but before he could connect with Tony's, his father stepped between them.

"You've done enough damage already," Mr. Marcum lashed out in a tone laced with loathing.

Stung, Tony stepped back, his face a cloud of confusion.

"Damage?" Tony questioned.

Marcum took Tony's question as an opening to launch into a diatribe about his son's relationship with Tony.

"I knew you were trouble the minute I laid eyes on you."

Mrs. Marcum tugged on his sleeve but he brushed her aside.

"I wished I'd done something about it then, but Joey seemed happy and that's always been enough for me," Marcum continued. "But rest assured, I'm going to do something about it now. For someone to push a crippled boy down the stairs just for fun is criminal and I aim to see that you end up somewhere where you can't hurt my son again."

"Joey," Tony started after taking in all Marcum had to say. "Tell your dad it wasn't me who pushed you down the stairs—it was me who found you! Tell him," Tony pleaded.

Joey looked up at his mom who was continuing to urge the workers to take him into the building.

"He's already said what happened," Marcum stated. "The whole time he was in the emergency room, all he did was say your name over and over again. That's good enough for me and I'm sure it will be good enough for Dr. Jefferson." Marcum looked at his wife and waved her and the workers onward.

"Stay away from my boy," Marcum said ominously and with that Joey was wheeled away without a word passing between them.

Tony stood on the sidewalk and watched them disappear into the Infirmary. He couldn't believe that

Seven Days at Oak Valley

Joey's parents thought he had pushed Joey down the stairs. He couldn't believe that Joey had told his parents that it was him. But he did believe there was going to be even more trouble and this time his best friend wouldn't even be there to help out.

The workers came out of the building and walked briskly to the ambulance. Tony saw them shake their heads as they passed him by. After what Mr. Marcum had said, Tony thought, everyone at Oak Valley was goin' to believe that he had done something horrible to the best friend he ever had. He only hoped that wasn't what Joey believed and that somehow he could help Joey convince Dr. Jefferson that it had been somebody else who had left him broken at the bottom of the stairs.

3:45 p.m.

Jefferson had asked Miss Williams to call his office when Joseph Marcum returned from the hospital in Knoxville. She'd followed through and now he was sitting in the small conference room in the Infirmary basement, listening to Mr. Marcum say as many disparaging things about Tony as he possibly could. He'd been listening for fifteen minutes, trying to find a way into what had become a one sided conversation.

"Mr. Marcum," Jefferson tried to interject, "I know you're upset..."

"Darn right, I'm upset," Marcum retorted, taking control of the conversation once again. "My wife and I get a call in the middle of the night from someone I've never heard of sayin' my boy was found layin' in a pool of blood at the bottom of the stairs and he's

Ruthie-Marie Beckwith

the only one that can tell me how it happened? What kind of operation are you runnin' here, Dr. Jefferson?"

"I assure you," Jefferson responded, "there will be a full investigation into this accident. . ."

"Accident!" Marcum roared. "Haven't you been listenin' to a word I've said? I'm tellin' you that Joey was pushed down those stairs. Pushed intentionally by another boy who's done nothing but torment him since the day they were put together!"

Mrs. Marcum spoke up, her voice softer than her husbands. "I wouldn't necessarily say torment, Will. I think it was more like teasin'."

"Martha," Marcum retorted, "teasin' is nothin' but torment to a boy like Joey." Marcum turned back to Jefferson. "And that's why Joey's mama and I put him here in the first place! To get him away from the tormentors of the world."

Jefferson took a deep breath and then calmly repeated himself. "Mr. Marcum, I assure you that there will be a full investigation of this, err. . ., incident. I promise that I will interview Tony Ervin and if I feel as though he had any involvement whatsoever in causing Joey's injuries, he will be dealt with in an appropriate manner. In the meantime, I'll see that he doesn't have the opportunity to come anywhere near your son. Please accept my assurance of that."

Mrs. Marcum looked her husband, her desire for the conversation to come to an end written all over her face.

Marcum responded begrudgingly, "Well, I guess that'll have to do. But I want your word."

Seven Days at Oak Valley

Jefferson stood and extended his hand across the table, "You have my word on it."

Marcum shook his hand and looked at his wife. "Well, Martha, we have a long drive back."

"But, I want to check in on Joey just one more time before we leave," Mrs. Marcum countered.

"Okay," Marcum replied. He glanced at his watch as Jefferson led them back into the hallway. They waited in silence for the elevator to accompany them back to the main floor. The elevator doors opened and they stepped in.

"Then let's get visitin', Martha," Marcum's authoritarian exclamation shattered the momentary peace. He moved to his wife's side and took her hand in his. Tenderly he added, "I want to make sure he's settled in, too, you know."

Mrs. Marcum smiled at him, "Yes, dear, I know that, too."

Jefferson found himself envying the pleased expression Mrs. Marcum gave her husband in return.

4:00 p.m.

Jones was at home grabbing a sandwich when his beeper went off. His trailer occupied a five acre wooded lot at the end of a dirt road. He'd hand-cleared half of the lot before his wife had deserted him and after that he lost interest in making any additional home improvements.

He reached into the refrigerator for a Coke, bypassing the Budweiser because he drew the line at drinking on the job. Jones sat down in the threadbare La-zy-boy recliner and pulled the telephone into his lap. He dialed the telephone

Ruthie-Marie Beckwith

number on the beeper and counted four rings before a male voice answered on the other end.

"Jones, here," he said.

"No, I'm back at my place, came home to grab a bite to eat."

Jones stood up and dragged the telephone across the small living room and into the kitchen. He wedged the handset between his neck and shoulder and reached up for the bread that was perched on top of the microwave. The microwave had been a present to himself about the same time an eighteen-wheeler had lost its load on I-40 one rainy night early that spring.

He took a swig of Coke and opened the refrigerator.

"Well, how in the world could he have gotten that tag number?" Jones asked.

"You told them what?" Jones shouted into the phone. "You can't report a truck as stolen when I've got someone up here still drivin' it around. Why in the world did you claim it was stolen?"

"You should've put him off," Jones yelled. "Then I would've been able to help you cover for yourself. Now I gotta' go find Carl, who's drivin' that truck who knows where, and get him to park it somewhere out in the middle of nowhere so someone else can find it or steal it, just to cover your backside."

Not seeing anything that could go into the microwave, he grabbed the Hellman's and package of bologna, and kicked the refrigerator door closed. Based on what he was hearing, Jones thought Russell deserved a swift kick, too.

"Well, it's more than just a little inconvenience, if you want to know," Jones told him. "Just because

Seven Days at Oak Valley

you pushed the panic button when you got a call from Motor Vehicles because some county sheriff just happened to inquire about a truck that just happened to belong to a state senator."

"Sure, sure," Jones continued as he spread Hellman's across a slab of bologna. "Well, it looks like this whole operation is takin' a dive and I'm not about to take a dive with it. You need to line me up another job somewhere. Maybe at one of those fancy new prisons you guys have built all over the place. Hell," Jones added, "even the Turney Center would do at this point."

"No," he said with his teeth clenched as he hunted around for the pickle jar. "That's not how it's gonna be. You owe me and I do plan on collecting. Call me when you got somethin' else lined up and not before."

Jones slammed the phone down and pulled up a chair at the small metal table. He devoured his sandwich and a dill pickle in four bites and stood to put his plate in the sink. Better go track down Carl before he gets picked up for grand theft auto, he thought. He should have known Russell would bail at the slightest whiff of trouble. Then again, he considered, the opportunities might turn out to be even better wherever he ended up next.

5:45 p.m.

"Heard you beat up your roommate and pushed him down a flight of stairs," Wanda Sue jeered at Tony on his way through the serving line.

Ruthie-Marie Beckwith

Tony ignored her, picked up his tray and carried it to the table where Angela sat. She looked up at him but didn't speak.

"Hey, beautiful," Tony greeted her, "how was your day?"

"You gonna beat her up, too?" Charlie yelled across the room at him.

"Ignore them," Tony said to Angela. "They don't know what they're talkin' about. So what've you been doing today?"

"I stripped wire," she told Tony.

"They strippin' wire again?" Tony asked.

"For tokens," Angela replied.

"Tokens are for babies," Tony replied.

"You have a job," Angela stated almost as a question.

"Yeah," Tony told her. "I'm the one that makes sure the mail goes through, least ways here at Oak Valley."

"Do you get tokens?" Angela asked innocently.

"Naw," Tony told her. "I just get outta' the workshop, is all. But that's a whole lot better than sittin' there all day with retards like Charlie."

Angela toyed with the food, twirling her fork in the compartment closest to her.

"Not very hungry, huh?" Tony asked.

"No," she replied in a small voice.

Tony reached out and grabbed the orange off her tray. "Mind if I take this?" he asked.

"No, it's okay" Angela responded.

"I usually get a bunch of oranges when they have 'em," Tony informed her. "Not everyone can peel 'em, you see, so I get 'em and put 'em in my locker. Did you get a locker, yet?"

Seven Days at Oak Valley

Angela nodded and Tony winced as feedback from her hearing aid pierced the air. He pointed and she reached up, fiddled with something, and the sound stopped.

"I keep all my 'portant stuff in my locker," he continued. "Only Joey knows where I keep the key."

Mentioning Joey reminded him of the fact that two of his three roommates were laid up. He searched the hall with his eyes and saw Ben sitting in the far corner all by himself.

"Hey, Angela, let's move and go sit by my Ben," he said, adding, "Ben's my other roommate. You might've seen him at the dance. My roommate Joey is the one who fell down the stairs and broke his leg."

Angela stood and reached for her tray.

"I'll carry it for you," Tony said, picking up both trays. They walked across the hall, ignoring the comments from Wanda Sue's crowd, and slid onto the bench next to Ben.

Ben looked up and went back to eating.

"Ben, this is Angela," Tony said. Ben looked up once more while his spoon scraped up a portion of watery applesauce.

"Angela, this is Ben." He explained, "Ben don't say much."

"You have two roommates?" Angela asked. "I got three. One of 'em is Wanda Sue."

Tony rolled his eyes at Wanda Sue's name. "No, I got three just like you. My other roommate, Sam, he's in the hospital." Tony decided he didn't want to scare her on her first day, so he told her, "He's got somethin' wrong with his stomach."

"Oh," Angela said.

Ruthie-Marie Beckwith

Ben held his orange up as Tony finished eating. Tony took it and started to squeeze it into his pant's pocket, but Ben grunted at him and pointed at the peels on Tony's tray. He pulled the orange back out, peeled it, and handed it to Ben.

Picking up their trays, he walked slowly with Angela as she made her way laboriously through the maze of people, tables, chairs and wheelchairs. As they reached the line to deposit their trays, Charlie breezed by, brushing up against Angela, almost causing her to topple over. Tony hollered, "Watch where you're going! Moron."

"Least I'm not a murderer!" Charlie responded. "Or a 'tempted murderer."

Tony clenched and unclenched his fists as they walked outside. He took one last look over his shoulder in Charlie's direction and turned to face her. "I never murdered nobody," he grumbled, "but I know someone who needs murderin'."

Angela started down the lower path in the direction of Building F and he called out, "Be careful! See ya' later, alligator!" He heard her laughter ringing in his ears all the way across the Green as he headed back to Building K.

8:30 p.m.

Joey lay in the hospital bed in the Infirmary watching the one other patient breathe through a mask that was fastened to his face. Under the covers he had on a hospital gown and nothing else. He'd already been subjected to the indignity of using a bedpan because the only nurse on duty in the building hadn't wanted to help him go to the

Seven Days at Oak Valley

bathroom. The four other nurses who worked second shift were out in the buildings, giving people their nighttime medicine.

The first thing Joey had said after they had undressed him and transferred him into the bed was, "'Ots," but no one had understood his question about the shots.

The nurse had simply said, "Don't worry, dear, we'll make sure you stay warm enough. We've got lots of nice soft blankets here." Then she rushed off. The person in the bed next to him was already using the only blanket Joey could see.

The first thing that Joey had said after his parents had left was, "'Ony." No one had understood that either. His head hurt and he really wanted someone to come and explain what was wrong to the nurse. She was new and the chances of her understanding anything he had to say were slim. He decided to give her one more chance.

Joey hollered out, "'Urts, 'urts, 'urts." He kept yelling until the nurse appeared in the doorway. "'Urts," he said more softly because the yelling had made his head hurt even more. He pointed to his head, "'Urts." She had a puzzled look and then comprehension slowly spread across her face.

"Your head hurts?" she asked.

"'Aya," Joey said as he nodded his head in affirmation. "'Urts."

"Let me see if Dr. Ford ordered anything for you to take for headache," she told him then bustled from the room. She took what seemed to Joey to be forever to come back and hand him two white pills and a glass of water.

Ruthie-Marie Beckwith

"Here, you go," she said. "Now take them like a good boy."

Joey put the tablets in his mouth and swallowed. He took a sip of the water and set it on the table next to the bed. "'Anks," he told her as he closed his eyes and laid his head back on his pillow. He kept his eyes closed and tried to think happy thoughts so he could go to sleep.

He was at the point of dozing off when he heard footsteps entering the room. He opened his eyes to a slit so he would still look asleep to anyone who might be wanting to poke him or take his temperature or something. Through the slits he caught sight of the person's stomach and he opened his eyes a tad bit wider to catch the person's face.

"'Ony!" Joey exclaimed.

"Shhh!" Tony whispered. "You'll get me thrown out of here!"

Joey repeated Tony's name three more times before Tony stepped closer to the bed and threatened to put his hand over his mouth.

"You okay?" Tony asked, taking in the bandage still around Joey's head and the tip of his cast peeking out from beneath the sheet.

"Yeah," Joey whispered.

"Good, I missed you."

"Me, 'oo."

"Everyone's sayin' I pushed you Joey, but I swear I didn't, I swear."

"I know."

"If you know, why didn't you tell your mom and dad it wasn't me?" Tony demanded.

Joey rolled his eyes at the mention of his parents. "'Umb," he explained.

Seven Days at Oak Valley

"Your parents are dumb?" Tony asked and Joey nodded his head. "Will you at least tell me how you ended up at the bottom of those stairs? I swear, when I saw you layin' there, I thought you were a goner."

Joey frowned. His head hurt and it was hard to move, but he didn't think he was a goner. He was plain lucky, that's what he was.

"I 'e o.k.," Joey whispered, trying to reassure his friend.

"How did you end up down those stairs, Joey?" Tony persisted.

"'On't 'emember," Joey lied. He didn't want Tony getting mixed up with those workers. If they had done this because all he had to offer up was some underwear and socks, no tellin' what they would do if they ended up on report because of him.

"Are your folks comin' back tomorrow?" Tony asked.

"'Eah," Joey answered, nodding his head. He winced. Nodding his head still hurt, even with the pills. "I 'ired."

Tony's eyes widened with concern. "You get some rest, then. I need to go. Need anything? I can sneak back tomorrow."

Closing his eyes, Joey whispered, "No."

"Later, then," Tony told him as he slipped quietly out of the room.

Ruthie-Marie Beckwith

Chapter Six

Thursday, October 4th, 6:30 a.m.

The harsh rhythm of a jackhammer sounded like an overgrown woodpecker as it shattered the morning calm. Tony was making his way from Building K to the Dining Hall deep in thought when the noise attracted his attention and he veered off in the direction of the construction zone. Construction trucks lined the makeshift drive that had been created as an alternative route for the delivery of materials and heavy equipment to the site. He stopped at the fence and watched as a forklift moved a pallet of cinderblocks to where one of the buildings was going up.

His stomach growled, reminding him of his original intent. He dragged himself back in the direction of the dining hall. He could have stood at the fence all day, fascinated with the process of building something but he had his own work to do. The morning sun was low in the sky and was just beginning to peek above the hills. He had barely enough time to grab somethin' to eat and get to the mailroom.

He walked faster than normal across the grounds and strutted into the dining hall. A quick look around

Seven Days at Oak Valley

located Angela sitting with her roommates and Ben sitting by himself, as usual. He grabbed his tray, decided to leave Ben alone and walked over to Angela's table.

"Here comes the murderer," Wanda Sue said aloud for no one in particular to hear.

"Put a lid on it, Wanda Sue," Tony growled.

"Who you gonna kill next?" Wanda Sue retorted.

"I don't know," Tony told her, "maybe someone who looks like you!"

He shifted his attention from Wanda Sue and onto Angela then asked, "Sleep good?"

"Sort of," Angela replied, eyeing Wanda Sue nervously.

"Don't worry about her," Tony said firmly. "She just has a big mouth."

"OKAY," Angela replied.

Tony started shoveling scrambled eggs that had a greenish tinge to them into his mouth. When he was finished, he picked up his milk carton, put it to his lips and drained the contents in three huge gulps. He grabbed his tray and Angela's as well and deposited them on the conveyor belt that ran into the dish room.

"Come on," Tony told her when he returned to the table. "I got something important to tell you that I don't want Miss Blabbermouth to hear," Tony added, saying "blabbermouth" loud enough for everyone at the table to hear.

"Ta-hon-y and Angela, sittin' in a tree," Wanda Sue began chanting. "K-I-S-S-I-N-G."

Angela blushed. Tony drew her away from the table and towards the door. Once outside, he slowed his pace so Angela could keep up. They walked down

Ruthie-Marie Beckwith

the upper path toward the workshop and mailroom. He reached out and took Angela's hand, but she drew it away.

"What's wrong?" he asked.

"Nuthin'," Angela replied warily.

"You worried about Wanda Sue and that bunch?" he asked. "She doesn't know what she's talkin' about." He stopped walking and looked Angela in the eyes. "I do want you to be my girlfriend, though."

Angela blushed again.

"You're cute when you get all red like that," he said. "And you've got the prettiest smile." He reached out, took her hand again and asked in his best Elvis voice, "Please be my girlfriend."

"OKAY," Angela said tentatively. "I've never had a boyfriend before."

As his heart pounded, he squeezed her hand and said, "Then I'll be your first one!" They resumed walking. "My roommate Joey's gonna be o.k.," he shared. "Sam's still in the hospital."

"Oh," Angela responded.

Midway down the upper path, Tony stopped to look up at the Superintendent's office and then resumed walking.

"Dr. Cordell, our doctor got murdered," Tony told her.

"I know," Angela replied. "I know. Debbie told me. She said somebody named Tinker got hanged, too."

Tony's face clouded over. "No way Tinker murdered himself," he replied.

Angela shuddered and he drew her toward him. "Don't be scared, Angel," he told her. "I'm lookin' out for you. I won't let nobody murder you. But," he

Seven Days at Oak Valley

added, "I am gonna find out who it was that murdered Tinker. I may even find out who murdered Dr. Cordell, too."

The expression on Angela's face turned into concern. "You could get in trouble," she said.

"I'm not worried about that," he told her with more bravado than he truly felt at the moment. "Tinker was my buddy and I don't like it that folks are sayin' he murdered himself."

"Mama and Daddy will be real mad if I get in trouble," Angela said in a worried tone. She drew back and let go of his hand.

"You won't get in trouble," he said as they approached the workshop. "Don't worry, sweetheart. I'll keep you out of it."

"OKAY," she said tentatively.

"You better get goin'. Mrs. Dawson won't be very happy if you're late," Tony told her, pointing to the entrance. "See ya' later alligator."

Angela giggled and Tony felt his heart expand. Tony waited until she was inside to wave at her through the plate glass door. When she waved back he smiled a big smile that lasted all the way to the mailroom.

8:30 a.m.

Jones pulled up in his security car outside the mailroom of Central Services. Scooting up from the seat, he dug in his pocket and retrieved his lighter. In lieu of lighting up, he flipped the lid of the lighter open and shut, taking pleasure in the clicking sound it made. He was going to take even greater pleasure in seeing one of Jefferson's pets get the comeuppance

Ruthie-Marie Beckwith

that was, in his opinion, long overdue. He got out of the car when Tony emerged from the mailroom with his mail sack slung over his shoulder and across his chest.

Jones called and motioned for him to approach. "Ervin, over here!"

Tony gave him a puzzled expression and dragged his feet in the direction of the vehicle.

That boy is slower than molasses, Jones thought as he waved his hand, motioning for Tony to hurry up.

"Come on," Jones urged. "Dr. Jefferson wants to see you. Sent me to fetch ya'. Good thing you're where he said you'd be. Get in."

Tony slung the mailbag off of his shoulder, held it up and asked, "What about my mail sack?"

Jones glanced at the sack. It was too large to fit in the front seat with the boy. He pulled out his keys and walked around the car to open the trunk. Tony walked to the back of the car and watched as Jones rearranged things to make room for the sack.

"Never gonna let Jefferson borrow this car again," he muttered as he moved aside two fishing poles, a minnow bucket, net, a set of golf clubs, and a tangled mass of yellow nylon rope. "This is a security car, not a recreation vehicle," he exclaimed. He finished shifting the contents around.

"Set it in there," he ordered, "and be careful you don't get it hung on one of those lures."

Tony set the mail sack in the trunk next to the yellow rope and Jones closed the lid. Jones slid into the driver's seat and motioned for Tony to get in.

"Come on," he said, "I ain't got all day."

Seven Days at Oak Valley

Jones took a moment to look over at Tony's appearance. The boy looked like a ragbag but at least he smelled okay. Some of the residents stank so bad he didn't think they ever took a bath, particularly the ones in Building B. He turned the car around on Dogwood Loop and reached over to the ashtray. Jones picked up the end of the cigar he'd been workin' on since the night before. After the first bitter taste of being relit, they didn't taste too bad. He watched the boy's eyes get real big as he pulled out his Zippo lighter, flipped the lid, held it to the tip, and took a long draw on the cigar.

"What's the matter?" he asked. "Never smoke a cigar before?"

Tony shook his head.

"Well, don't start," Jones advised.

Jones grunted at the sight of the first shift workers making their way across the campus from the upper parking lot. Most of them he wouldn't give two cents for and wouldn't trust as far as he could throw 'em. But, it wasn't his job to do the hiring; he only participated in the firings, which were far too rare in his estimation.

"Come on," he said as he opened the car door after parking in the lot behind the superintendent's office, "it's goose cookin' time."

Tony got out of the car and followed Jones around to the front door. The sleigh bells jingled as they entered the vestibule.

"Mornin', Miss Fisk," Jones said as he pointed to Tony. "Tell Dr. Jefferson that his package has been delivered."

"Just have a seat, boy," he said, pointing to the chair closest to Fisk's desk.

Ruthie-Marie Beckwith

Touching his cap, he made a quick nod in Fisk's direction and told her politely, "Have a good day, ma'am." He stepped outside, anxious to get back to office to check on the status of the esteemed state senator Roy Russell's truck. "What an idiot," he grumbled out loud. "If all those senators are as dim-witted as Russell, it's no wonder Tennessee's in the shape it's in."

8:45 a.m.

Tony rubbed his head and his chin as he sat for what seemed like hours in the chair across from Jefferson. The electric razor he got to use once a week had gotten most of his stubble. He stole a glance at Jefferson and observed that Jefferson didn't look as though he'd taken time to shave that morning.

Jefferson placed the papers he'd been reading into a small pile and looked up. Tony worried a small crack in the Naugahyde on the left arm of the chair.

"Tony," Jefferson began.

Tony waited.

"I need to talk to you about some rumors that are going around about you. Mr. Jones tells me that it might be possible that you were responsible for pushing your roommate Joey down those stairs the other night."

Tony shook his head and inwardly cursed both Wanda Sue and Big Mac Jones.

"Now, I met with Joey's parents yesterday and told them I'd get to the bottom of this unfortunate incident. So, I need you to tell me everything you know about Joey's accident."

"Joey's my friend," he responded. "I'd never push him down a bunch of stairs."

"People do get angry with their friends," Jefferson countered. He leaned back in his chair and pulled out a cigar from the humidor. "People even do things that hurt their friends. Particularly when they're angry."

"I wasn't mad at Joey," Tony told him. He watched Jefferson pull out a black square with a hole in it use it to cut the tip of the cigar. The yellow and red band disappeared from view as Jefferson put his forefinger and thumb around it. Chills zipped like lightening up and down Tony's spine when saw the cigar band was a perfect match to the one he had found. Jefferson sat back and lit the cigar. Tony tried not to screw up his face at the smell.

"So you weren't angry with Joey," Jefferson continued, "Maybe you were just a little impatient with him for going so slow down the stairs and gave him a shove to hurry up?"

Tony decided to remain silent.

"You're going to have to tell me eventually, Tony. Let's just get it all out now," Jefferson told him in the sweet, syrupy kind of voice that all the workers at Oak Valley used when they were trying to fake being nice.

The buzzer went off on the telephone at that same moment Tony's wounded pride won out over silence. "I swear I didn't do it!" he blurted out as Jefferson picked up the receiver.

"Yes," Jefferson said into the phone. "Did you tell them I was in a meeting?" Jefferson asked. He listened for a moment and then said, "Very well, tell them I'll be right out."

Jefferson hung up the telephone and set his cigar down in the ashtray.

"You stay put," he instructed as he got up and walked to the door. "This will only take a minute."

The door closed behind Jefferson and Tony let himself breathe again. Through the door he could hear voices arguing. He reached over, lifted the lid of the humidor, and picked out a cigar with the matching band.

Watching the door the whole while, Tony took only a minute before deciding what he would do. Trying to be extra careful as he slid the cigar into his pocket, he wondered what he'd do if Miss Williams wasn't at work today. She'd know what to do, once he explained why he'd taken it from Jefferson's office.

The door swung open and he jumped. He felt the cigar pressing against his skin and forced himself to relax. Jefferson emerged from the vestibule.

"So, where were we?" Jefferson asked as he sat back down. "You say you didn't have anything to do with Joey's fall."

"Yes, sir, I mean, no, sir," Tony answered.

"Which is it?" Jefferson asked, somewhat distractedly.

"I didn't have nothin' to do with it," Tony told him. "I just found him, that's all. He wasn't in bed after I got back from the dance so I went lookin' for him and I just found him layin' there."

Jefferson looked skeptically at Tony, reached for the cigar, took a draw of it, and sat back in his chair. "I know you've been at the bottom of mischief here from time to time," he told him, "but up until now, you've never actually hurt anybody."

Seven Days at Oak Valley

Jefferson stopped there. To Tony, he looked like he was considering something horrible, like the prison he'd told him about the day he'd lectured him about curfew.

"You get back about your business," Jefferson concluded. "And, I don't want to hear anything more about you from anyone, you understand?"

"Yes, sir," Tony said as he stood up. "I'm just gonna finish with the mail."

"Well, finish your rounds and come back here when you're done," Jefferson told him. "I don't want to have to send anyone to fetch you, understand?"

"Yes, sir," Tony told him as he shuffled out the door and pulled it behind him. But first, he told himself, he needed to do something about the cigar that was poking through his pocket.

9:15 a.m.

Cordelia was surprised to see Tony standing at the counter as she made her way back from Dr. Ford's office. "Tony," she exclaimed, "it's too early to be visiting your roommate. You'll have to come back later."

"I'm not here to see Joey," Tony responded, "at least not right now. I'm here to see you."

The last sentence sounded a little like an Elvis impersonation, she thought. She stifled a grin by yawning and quickly apologized. "Excuse me! Dr. Ford has been keeping us here all hours of the day and night. I sure will be glad when this inspection is over."

Tony shifted his weight from one foot to another. She waited for him to explain what he wanted, watching as his eyes darted up and down the hall and then back to her desk.

"I need your help," he said finally, his voice shaking. "Used to be Tinker I could talk to but he's gone. Joey's hurt. Sam, too. Ain't nobody else."

Cordelia came out from behind the counter and stood next to him, careful to keep her voice down.

"Joey's gonna be okay," she said, trying her best to reassure him. "He's got a broken leg, but it'll heal in time."

"Ain't about that. . ." Tony told her clearly struggling with whether or not to trust her.

He had trusted her once, Cordelia reasoned, that day he gave her that tag number. If she was patient enough, he might open up again. She waited by his side. She took long slow audible breaths, and it appeared to have a calming effect on him. He began to relax in front of her.

"So what's this about?" she asked as he shuffled his feet once more.

"The murders," he stated.

Not expecting that reply, she stiffened and looked nervously up and down the hall. He caught her eye and she put her finger to her lips. "Tell you what," she told him. "Why don't we go down to the conference room where you can tell me more about this in private?"

Cordelia motioned to Tony to follow her. They waited without speaking for the elevator doors to open and stepped inside. Cordelia pressed the call button and together they descended into the basement, back to where it all began.

Seven Days at Oak Valley

9:30 a.m.

Sheriff Thomas studied the young man sitting at the table before him. His hair was shaved off and his face bore a patch or two of stubble that he must have missed during his morning shave. The red and blue plaid shirt he wore was three sizes too big and the corduroy blue pants he had on were at least one size too small. In short, Thomas thought, he looked like very much like the typical Oak Valley resident. Except this one had come to him as he'd pulled into the drive next to the Infirmary and had handed him a Partagas cigar.

Thomas looked around the small conference room. Nothing had changed since his first meeting in this room earlier in the week, he thought. He had a dead body, two dead bodies if he counted the steam plant worker, and that was all. Thinking to revisit one or two of the employees who his deputies had interviewed, he'd come back today to see if they could shed some light on who might have wanted Cordell dead. Instead, he sat in this drab conference room with an unsmoked, Partagas cigar laid out on the table, waiting for what was sure to be a wild story from what seemed to be a very nervous young man.

Miss Williams, the receptionist, who'd handed him the lucky license plate number, had volunteered to sit in on the interview. He'd agreed, since she seemed to know the boy and might have better luck getting his story out of him, given that she worked at Oak Valley and all. Clues in this case seemed to be coming from the unlikeliest people and places.

Ruthie-Marie Beckwith

"So, Tony," Cordelia began, "Sheriff Thomas wants to know where you got the cigar."

Tony sat deathly still at the table. Thomas decided that a bribe might be in order. "Look, son, just tell me where you got this cigar and why you think it's so important and then you and me can take a short ride for some ice cream, okay?"

The bribe of ice cream didn't have the desired effect. Tony still sat mute before him.

"Does this have anything to do with Joey?" Cordelia ventured.

"Who's Joey?" Thomas inquired.

"His roommate," Cordelia explained. "He was hurt real bad two nights ago. Rumor is Tony had something to do with it."

"I didn't do anything to Joey," Tony protested, his indignation taking precedence over his fear.

"If you said you didn't do it, let's just say I believe you," Thomas replied. "Let's just talk about the cigar for now."

"Dr. Jefferson smokes these cigars, that's all," Tony confessed.

"So why'd you bring it to me?" he asked.

"Tinker was hung," Tony said simply.

Thomas sat back in his chair, considering whether to tell Tony that Tinker was dead before he was hung, and decided against it. Instead, he inquired, "So do you have anything else you want to give to me?"

Tony looked at Cordelia who nodded. He dug in his shirt pocket, pulled out a cigar stub and laid it on the table.

"A cigar butt," Thomas raised his eyebrows. "Why are you carryin' around a cigar butt?"

— 240 —

Seven Days at Oak Valley

Tony hesitated. Miss Williams waited. "It was at the steam plant," he answered.

"What were you doin' up at the steam plant?"

"Just lookin'," Tony replied.

"Just lookin'," Thomas repeated as he slid his chair back and leaned against the wall. "Anything else?"

Tony remained still another minute. Thomas watched as Tony dug deep in his pant's pocket, pulled out his fist, opened his hand, and laid a cufflink with an inlaid turquoise stone on the table. He raised his right eyebrow. Now, this was getting more interesting.

"Where'd you find this?" Thomas asked. Tony looked to Miss Williams for reassurance.

She nodded as Tony responded, "It was under the bookcase."

"Bookcase?" Thomas asked. This interview was going to take forever if he had to pry loose the facts one tooth at a time.

Miss Williams inserted herself. "Tony, try to tell Sheriff Thomas the whole story."

Tony sighed. He kept still for a few more minutes, then squared his shoulders and sat upright in his chair.

"The bookcase in Dr. Cordell's office," he began. "It was under the bookcase. That's where I found it. I was looking for money."

"Whose cufflink do you suppose it to be?" Thomas asked.

"It's got blood on it," Tony replied, pointing to the cufflink. Thomas picked up the cufflink with his handkerchief and examined it more closely. He cursed his deputies' oversight and set it back on the table.

"Whose cufflink do you suppose it to be?" Thomas repeated, beginning to take far more seriously what this young man might have to say.

"It's too fancy to be Mac Jones'," Tony answered. "Dr. Cordell didn't have shirts like that," he added pointing at the frayed cuff of Thomas' own ill-fitting attire.

Tony appeared reluctant to name who he really felt the cufflink belonged to. Miss Williams, though, realized his intent and burst in, "You don't think that it belongs to Dr. Jefferson, do you?"

Thomas watched Tony shrink further into himself and lowered his gaze to the items on the table.

"So what do you want me to do with this cigar, cigar butt, and cufflink?" Thomas asked.

"Arrest him," Tony stated flatly.

Cordelia started to respond but Thomas raised his hand to halt her. He leaned over the table and stared into Tony's eyes. "So you want me to arrest Dr. Jefferson, the superintendent of Oak Valley State Training School and Hospital, for smoking cigars?"

Unable to contain herself Cordelia inserted, "Tony, you know Sheriff Thomas isn't going to arrest Dr. Jefferson. He doesn't have any cause to do that, do you Sheriff?"

"No, Miss Williams, I do not," Thomas told her, adding, "but I do have work to do." He turned to face Tony. "Son, it takes a whole lot more evidence than this to arrest someone. I need things like a weapon, fingerprints, bloody clothes. . ."

"Bloody clothes?" Tony echoed. His expression brightened.

Thomas nodded, "Bloody clothes. Things like that is what's required for me to get a warrant from a Judge. I need a warrant before I can go out arresting anyone."

"I know where there's a bloody shirt. It was with these shoes," Tony reported as he bent over and pointed to the muddy loafers he wore on his feet.

Thomas stared at Tony as this last fact clicked into place. "Where did you get those shoes, son?"

"They aren't the ones the Relief ladies gave me..." Tony started.

Thomas, sensing another tangent, interrupted him, "Where did you get those?"

"They was in a black sack at the 'struction zone. With the shirt," Tony explained. "Me and Joey found 'em. On Visitor's Day."

"Visitor's Day?" Thomas asked.

"Sunday is the official day of the week that family members encouraged to visit," Miss Williams explained.

"Me and Joey was exploring," Tony went on. "We found these shoes but the shirt had holes in it and was all stained. Well, it could've been blood..."

Thomas hesitated, wondering if he was setting foot on the path of a wild goose chase. "Where's the shirt now? Can you take me to it?"

"We stuffed it back in the sack and put it in the hole of one of those blocks," Tony replied.

Thomas sat back and contemplated his options. He stood up and motioned for Tony to follow. "Why don't you show me where it is, son, and then you can get back to work." He followed Tony's glance to the

Ruthie-Marie Beckwith

items on the table. "Don't worry," Thomas told him, taking out his handkerchief along with a small plastic baggie, "These'll be safe with me."

Thomas then pulled out an ink pen and wrote on the baggie, "Cordell, Thursday, October 4th, 1978." He looked at his watch and then wrote, 10:05 a.m. on the small label attached to it. He'd hoped that the employees might have some additional insight to offer, but first, he decided, he might go on a small fishing expedition.

10:30 a.m.

Tony let a moan of disbelief escape his mouth as he stood at the entrance to the construction zone. Two concrete trucks were lined up on at the gate, waiting their turn to enter and dump their loads. Men wearing yellow hats were running around shouting at each other while trying to dodge the few remaining puddles. The fresh scent of cut lumber teased his nostrils and a round of hammering made it hard to hear what the sheriff was trying to say.

"It was right over here," Tony shouted above the noise. He pointed to the building where the foundation was being poured. "First it was there," he told Thomas, "and then we moved it over there," he added, pointing at the building where a cement block wall was rising swiftly in the morning sun.

Tony waited while Thomas stared at the wet concrete layered between each block. It was starting to set. The workers must be very anxious to get back on track, he thought. Thomas looked up to where he had pointed at the cement blocks. Tony led him through the site and into the corner of the building.

Seven Days at Oak Valley

The crevice that had been there on Sunday had been mortared over. Worse still, it was four feet lower than how high the wall currently stood.

"It was there," Tony repeated. Thomas stared at the blocks, squared and trimmed, then turned and began walking across the site to where a man with yellow hard hat and several helpers stood looking at a big sheet of paper with blue lines on it. Tony followed, but hung back when Thomas interrupted them.

"Did any of your men find a black sack with a stained shirt it in over near that wall?" Tony heard Thomas ask the man with the paper. The man shook his head and looked back at his paper, but Thomas wasn't going away.

Tony watched as Thomas tapped the man on the shoulder and told him, "This is a police investigation." The man looked up. Thomas repeated himself. This time, the man carefully folded the paper and handed it to one of his helpers. Thomas turned and started back to the block wall, gesturing for the man to follow him.

"Like I said, Sheriff," the man told Thomas, "nobody turned in anything like that." Thomas looked over at Tony.

Tony drew himself up to his whole six feet, "That's where we left it, I swear."

Tony watched the sheriff look up at the sky as if he was praying, then back down at his feet.

"Looks like I might have to have you stop for the day," the sheriff told the man. "At least until I can get a court order for you all to tear out that corner, and a warrant to search the premises." Then he added, "I

— 245 —

Ruthie-Marie Beckwith

sure do hope you all won't have to tear up that new foundation as well."

Tony crept back as the man began to curse. The sheriff let the man go on a few minutes. Tony took advantage of his inattention to slip further and further away from the two men. As he crossed through the open gate, he could still hear them arguing. He looked over his shoulder one more time and saw more and more of the workers lay down their tools and move into a circle around Thomas and the man. At that point, he took off running north of the site in the direction of the cemetery. He didn't stop until he got to marker number 8627.

11:15 a.m.

Thomas paced the hall outside the chambers of his honor Judge Robinson. He knew that what he was going to ask was going to sound like one of the most harebrained requests the Judge had been asked to entertain in recent memory. Well, maybe not the most harebrained, there was that time Robinson had been asked to settle a dispute over the septic field lines the tractor of one of the local farmers had busted up.

Thomas was on his tenth pace across the lobby when the door opened and the Judge's secretary ushered him in. "Mornin', your honor," he greeted Robinson as he took off his hat.

"Sheriff," Robinson responded, gesturing to one of the brown leather chairs positioned in front of his antique mahogany desk.

"I'll get right to the point, Judge," Thomas explained as he sat on the edge of the chair farthest

Seven Days at Oak Valley

from Robinson's presence. "I need an order to stop work over at Oak Valley and a warrant to search the new construction zone."

Robinson smiled. Thomas took that as a positive sign and laid out the story of Tony and his clues. Robinson stopped smiling. Thomas stopped talking.

"You want me to issue an order and a warrant based on the word of a retarded man?" Robinson asked incredulously.

"I know it sounds crazy, Judge," Thomas began, hoping to soft peddle the "retarded" part.

Robinson interrupted, "Got any motive?"

Thomas hedged, "Not one specifically, though me and my men are still interviewing folks. I did get a background check back from Oklahoma that intimated Jefferson was having problems with the Missus."

"Hell," Robinson exploded, "half the men in this county are having problems with their wives and the other half aren't smart enough to know it."

Thomas decided to take the high road and remained silent. Robinson stopped himself and looked down at his hands, clasped together almost as in a state of prayer.

"Come back when you have a solid motive," he instructed Thomas. Thomas nodded and stood, anxious to extract himself from the Judge's querulous glare.

"Yes, sir," Thomas replied. "I'll just let myself out," he told him.

He burst out of the courthouse and was down the steps and into his car faster than he'd moved since the 100-yard dash at church camp forty years ago. The engine turned over with a purr, the new Chevy

Ruthie-Marie Beckwith

Impala police model being one of the more dependable vehicles the County Commission had supplied him with in recent memory.

It was a harebrained idea, Thomas admitted. Yet, something in his gut told him that Tony had been on to something; the same something that he'd been leaning towards himself. He sat there with the engine still running and replayed the interview with Tony in his mind. He focused to the moment when Tony had disclosed that he and his buddy had found a bloody shirt. What was it that he had done? He'd pointed to his feet, yes, that was it. Tony had pointed to the shoes he was wearing!

Thomas gave himself a severe mental kick and turned the car in the direction of his office. He should have gotten the shoes, he told himself. If they were with the shirt, they would be evidence as well. But, now, given the way the Judge had reacted, he was definitely going to need something more than just the shoes to convince him. Motive, he thought. With over one thousand folks living over at Oak Valley and who knew how many employees, there could be that many motives and then some.

What he needed, Thomas thought, was a chance to clear his mind. Maybe he'd just go back over to the office while he did some of that mind numbing paperwork that had built up over the week. Surely Tony and the shoes wouldn't going anywhere before he got some time to run back over there and retrieve them. With that settled in his mind, he considered another course of action. Before he picked up the shoes, maybe he'd go and see what would crawl out from under Jefferson's rock if he gave it a nudge.

Seven Days at Oak Valley

Thomas smiled. Yes, he thought, time to see what Winfred had to add to the equation.

12:00 p.m.

Jefferson looked down at what was had become a cold cup of coffee. He'd been taking a break at the Canteen to catch up on the paper when the next thing he knew, Thomas was sitting across the table from him.

"I know this is going to sound rather preposterous, Winfred," Thomas began. "But, I just got finished talkin' with one of your residents who had a very interesting story to tell."

Jefferson raised an eyebrow, already suspecting which of the residents had told Thomas the "very interesting story". Even so, he decided to play along. Intent on finding out what Thomas really had in mind, he asked, "Which resident?"

"That's not important," Thomas countered. "But what he had to say was rather interesting. Seems he found one of your cigars and cufflinks and wanted me to arrest you for murder," Thomas said with a smile.

Jefferson mustered a small laugh. "Arrest me for murder?"

"I knew you'd find it amusing," Thomas told him. "That's why I rushed on over here to share it with you."

"Where did he say he found the cigar?" Jefferson asked.

"He wouldn't say," Thomas answered. "But he thought he had you dead on for murdering Dr. Cordell and maybe even Tinker."

Ruthie-Marie Beckwith

Laughing again, Jefferson grimaced inwardly as he felt Thomas' scrutiny on his every move. "I don't suppose I need to offer you up an alibi to go along with this fairy tale, do I Sheriff?" he countered.

"Only if you want to make it a good yarn to share during the Fishing Rodeo next spring," Thomas suggested.

"Just so you'll have some peace of mind, Billy," he told him, "I was at home with my dear wife at the time you said Dr. Cordell was stabbed."

"Well, of course you were," Thomas observed. "I'm sure Mrs. Jefferson would be happy to confirm that."

"I'm sure she will," Jefferson said without missing a beat, "just as soon as she gets back from visiting her mama and daddy over in Memphis."

"I'm sure it can wait," Thomas, said still smiling. He stood. "Don't go too hard on the boy," Thomas advised as he turned to leave, "I'm sure he was just lettin' his imagination run wild."

Jefferson watched Thomas out of the window at the Canteen until he reached his vehicle and was leaving the grounds. He stared at the battered white Formica tabletop where his cold cup of coffee sat and considered Thomas' most recent revelation. Despite his admonishment to go easy on his informant, Thomas hadn't quite gotten around to telling him the name of the resident he'd talked to. Nonetheless, he had a good idea of who it was. Pulling on his coat and hat, he strode across the Green that lay between the Canteen and his office, feeling like the eyes of the entire universe were staring down at him.

Seven Days at Oak Valley

12:30 a.m.

Angela made her way to the workshop by herself. Over lunch Tony had told her about meeting with the sheriff about a cigar butt, a cufflink, and his shoes. She couldn't follow everything he'd told her, somethin' about the steam plant, whatever that was, and a friend of his named Tinker. Tony had too many dead people in his life, she concluded. Was the dead man from the steam plant the same one that Wanda Sue was talkin' about? She wasn't sure she wanted to know; it was all so confusing.

After lunch, she'd promised him she'd be careful. By the time he'd headed back to work most of the other folks from the workshop had already passed her by as she made her way down the upper path. She'd been here two whole days, she realized. All she could think of was goin' home. Tony was real nice, but she didn't want to get in any trouble. He seemed to attract trouble like a bear to a honey pot.

That morning at work she'd watched as Mrs. Dawson had lectured Tony on somethin' about his shoes and the Relief Ladies. She looked down at her shoes. They were custom made to fit into her braces. She wished they came in more colors than just plain old ordinary brown.

Angela wasn't looking forward to sitting at a table all afternoon. Today they were bagging nuts and bolts that were part of a picture frame. She wondered how many tokens she'd get at the end of the week and what kind of things the Canteen sold. She'd ask Wanda Sue when she got back.

As she passed by the Infirmary, an ambulance pulled up to the front. She stopped to watch the

Ruthie-Marie Beckwith

workers open up the back of the vehicle and unload a black boy on a cart.

Dr. Ford came out and began arguing with the ambulance workers.

"There must be some mistake!" Dr. Ford shouted at them. "There's no way this boy is ready to be sent back! His condition could hardly have been stabilized!"

That must be Tony's other roommate, she thought to herself. Tony would be relieved when she told him he'd come back. Maybe he'd find a reason to come by the workshop again and she could tell him.

"Angela," Mrs. Dawson called out to her as she entered the workshop and walked slowly toward her table.

"Yes, ma'am," she answered.

"You're late again," Dawson said in a stern tone. "I didn't say anything yesterday because you're new, but I don't want it to happen again. That'll cost you two tokens today and two tokens for being late from now on. Understand?"

Angela nodded. She sat down and scooped a cup full of nuts and bolts out of another plastic bucket. She wondered if she'd have any tokens left after a week of being late. Maybe, she thought, she'd be better off skipping lunch altogether.

1:00 p.m.

Jefferson buzzed the intercom and Fisk picked up.

"See if you can get me that new superintendent over at the secure facility," he said.

"The one at Central State?" Mrs. Fisk asked.

Seven Days at Oak Valley

"Yes," Jefferson affirmed as he hung up. Ten minutes later, the intercom buzzed and he answered.

"Howard?" he asked.

Jefferson ran through the obligatory small talk before getting around to the purpose of his call. Aware that he'd have to lay some foundation for his request, he gave Howard a chance to lob a few questions his way.

"Yes, it's true," Jefferson told him when Howard asked about the murders. He let Howard squeeze in one final query and cut off the line of inquiry, certain that everything he was revealing would make its way from one end of the state to the other before the sun went down.

Doing his best to maintain some semblance of collegiality, Jefferson told his counterpart, "No, no, nothing yet, the county sheriff's been all over the place. I'll be glad when he gets this thing wrapped up."

"Ford's over here from Rolling Hills providing coverage, but thanks for offering." He leaned back in his chair, drumming his fingers on the desk. He'd forgotten how talkative Howard could be.

"Yes, I agree. It's a hell of a thing to have happened right before inspection. But, I imagine we'll come through it okay."

"Look, Howard," Jefferson continued, now clear on how to frame his request. "I've got a resident over here that's been causing us a pack of trouble."

"No, I don't think he's right for the dual diagnosis center. Besides, that's not supposed to open until sometime next year. I know you take mostly those

Ruthie-Marie Beckwith

sent over from the court. . ." Jefferson said and listened to Howard's arguments.

"Well, mainly because I think he's a real danger to others," Jefferson explained further. "He's already put two other residents in the hospital."

"Yes, I know you run a pretty tight ship over there," Jefferson agreed. He looked at his watch. "Well, it does sound as though you've got one who's ready to come back."

"No, no, I think I can make room for him. Just send his paperwork on over with him. Now what's his name again?" he asked as he cradled the receiver on his shoulder and reached for a piece of paper.

"Well, I can have my guy over there sometime after dinner," Jefferson stated. "He doesn't have any family so we don't have to deal with that roadblock."

"I definitely owe you one, Howard. I appreciate it, partner."

"Oh, one more thing. His name is Anthony Bedford Ervin. Yeah, that's Ervin, E-R-V-I-N."

"Sure," he said, wrapping up the conversation. "Well, keep in touch, and thanks."

Jefferson hung up the telephone and stared out the window. A story that the former assistant commissioner had shared when he'd first been appointed superintendent crept back into his mind.

"Winfred," the assistant commissioner had told him. "On the first day on the job as a new superintendent, my boss gave me three envelopes. He said to open an envelope whenever I hit a major crisis that I didn't think I could solve. So, a few months went by, and sure enough, along came my first crisis. Remembering my boss's words, I reached

Seven Days at Oak Valley

into my desk and opened my first envelope. Inside it said, 'Blame the prior administration.' And so I did.

A couple of years went by and along came my next crisis. I didn't know what I was going to do but then I remembered the two envelopes still in my top desk drawer. I reached in and tore open the second envelope. 'Say you will study the problem,' the message inside the envelope said. And so I did and things went along smoothly for quite a while after that.

Finally, as things will happen, another crisis came along. I had studied the problem as long as anyone would tolerate. I went to my office and pulled open my desk drawer. I reached in and pulled out the final envelope. I ran my letter opener across the fine engraved paper and pulled out the letter that held the final advice my boss had to share. Prepare three envelopes, the paper had read."

He and the assistant commissioner had had a good chuckle over that little story, Jefferson recalled. Things didn't seem so funny at the present moment, however. Hopefully, it wasn't time for him to prepare three envelopes he thought to himself. He looked out the window and watched Miss Williams make her way across the Green in the direction of the Canteen.

3:00 p.m.

Cordelia sat by the window inside the Canteen so she could look out at the fall afternoon. On clear days, the grounds of Oak Valley resembled one of those Ivy League colleges like they had up north. Waiting for her hot chocolate to cool, she observed Tony, Mac Jones, and Miss Lambuth walking down

Ruthie-Marie Beckwith

the sidewalk from Building K. As they turned up the sidewalk toward the Infirmary, Cordelia pulled her shawl around her shoulders and abandoned her hot chocolate.

Miss Lambuth was standing by her desk when she arrived out of breath from the Canteen.

"I'm sorry," Cordelia said. "How can I help you?"

"I need to get Anthony Ervin's medical records and a prescription for any medicine he might be taking," Lambuth said.

"Can I tell Dr. Ford something specific?" she ventured.

"Tell Dr. Ford he's being transferred, that's all. He'll understand," Lambuth explained.

Transferred, Cordelia thought. Transferred where?

She walked down the hall toward Dr. Ford's office, passing by Tony and Jones as they emerged from the men's room. Tony looked dazed and confused. Jones nodded at her and she stopped to greet him.

"Afternoon, Mr. Jones," she said in her sweetest voice, hoping he wouldn't recall their argument.

"Afternoon, Miss Williams," he replied and smiled.

"Miss Lambuth said that y'all are taking Tony somewhere..." Cordelia started.

Jones cut her off. "Yes, we are and it's about time if you ask me."

Cordelia looked at Tony who stood staring at his shoes. "Is he going on an outing?" she asked, keeping her expression neutral.

Tony looked up at her and she could see him trying hard to blink back tears.

Seven Days at Oak Valley

"Nope," Jones stated with an air of authority. "This boy's landed himself a spot at the secure facility."

"The secure facility?" Cordelia gasped.

"Yes, ma'am, that new prison they carved out of Central State for ones like this'n," Jones told her, "and we'd be getting along a whole lot faster if you'd get on with taking care of whatever it is Miss Lambuth needs."

"Sorry," Cordelia said, not knowing anything else to say. Jones didn't appear to have forgotten their argument after all. She scurried down the hall and knocked on Dr. Ford's door.

Cordelia was fuming by the time she'd gotten Dr. Ford's signature on all of the right forms. As she made the required copies, she noted where Dr. Jefferson had accused Tony of harming his roommates. Cordelia knew that couldn't possibly be true. Those boys thought the world of each other. She returned to her desk with the requested paperwork and handed it to Miss Lambuth as Tony was being loaded into the back of Jones' security car. This wasn't right, Cordelia thought as she watched the car turn the corner.

"It just isn't fair," she said out loud. Tony didn't belong at a place with hardened criminals.

"It just isn't fair," Cordelia exclaimed again as she went to her desk to pull out the notes she'd taken at her last class. There it was, the name of that advocacy organization, *The Association for Retarded Children,* along with a Nashville phone number. The paper rattled in her hand as she debated dialing. There probably was a good chance she'd get fired if anyone found out she'd called an outside agency for

Ruthie-Marie Beckwith

help for Tony. Then again, maybe they'd keep her name out of it. Besides, she was only three credits away from her new life.

Tony didn't deserve to be shipped off like a sack of flour, regardless of what he'd done, she thought as she dialed the number. At twenty years old, Tony wasn't exactly a child but maybe they'd be able to help anyways. If not, then she'd just have to keep calling until she found someone who could.

4:10 a.m.

Thomas sat at his desk and looked at the one box of Cordell's paperwork he hadn't gotten to. The second day of the investigation his deputies had hauled it over, along with three others, and stacked them in the corner of the office. Too bad they'd missed that cufflink. They'd all be getting reprimands for that oversight.

His own mistake of the day lay heavily on his mind. By the time he'd gotten done interviewing folks and making his rounds at Oak Valley in hopes that someone could shed some light on a motive, he'd missed the opportunity to retrieve the shoes. Miss Williams had told him tearfully that Tony, with the shoes still on his feet, was on his way over to Nashville to some kind of prison that was just for the mentally retarded.

After that he'd called Judge Robinson to complain that a potential witness had been shipped off across state, but when he'd told the judge it was Tony, Robinson had slammed the phone down in his ear. "Robinson needs to remember that election time was just around the corner," he muttered as he

Seven Days at Oak Valley

turned his attention to the box sitting on top of his desk.

Thomas generally did paperwork as a way to let his mind settle. Yesterday he'd tackled the first two boxes, but then he'd been sidetracked by a call about some boys shootin' target practice at an old barn that wasn't even in use anymore. He'd no sooner got back when one of the County Commissioners called all in a dither. So now, here it was at the end of the day, he thought, and he was just getting to the thing he'd wanted to do most.

He moved the box to the floor and piece-by-piece began studying the last of Cordell's paperwork. Most of it was routine notes and memos about this committee or that resident. Stopping to put his glasses on, he studied one paper that had risen to the top. As he read about missing medical supplies and medicine, particularly Valium and other controlled substances, parts of one puzzle seemed to click into place. He set the memo aside and continued hunting through the box.

A piece of flowered stationary lay on top of the final paperwork at the very bottom. Flowered stationary wasn't the official letterhead for Oak Valley. Pushing his glasses further up on the bridge of his nose, he scanned the feminine handwriting. "I'm afraid for both of us, now," he read out loud. "You've no idea how jealous he can be, even over the simplest things. If he were to find out," the note continued, "there's no telling what he might do. Please, don't call me again. My heart can't bear it. Yours, Grace."

Thomas held the letter up to the light. The date was neatly written in the upper right hand corner,

Ruthie-Marie Beckwith

September 27th, 1978. Three days before Cordell's body was found dead in the Infirmary. He wondered what Jefferson might have to say about this piece of paper.

Taking one last look in the box, Thomas fished another document out, a letter addressed to the U. S. Department of Health, Education, and Welfare. Edits Cordell must have been in the process of making stood out in the margins along both sides of the paper. The words "radiation experimentation" and "human subjects" caught his eye as he scrutinized the document. Standing up so abruptly that his chair almost tipped over, Thomas called out, "Ward?"

Ward appeared in his office doorway. "I'm going over to Judge Robinson's chambers again. Hopefully he's still in." Ward stepped aside as Thomas exited his office. "Meet me there," Thomas instructed, "so you can ride out to Oak Valley with me. I think the superintendent might have some explaining to do."

5:15 p.m.

Jefferson was sorting through the stack of mail Mrs. Fisk had left in the center of his desk when Thomas showed up unannounced with his deputy in tow. Four inches deep and bound together with two huge rubber bands, he'd whittled the pile of paper down to two when he was interrupted by the sound of those damn sleigh bells.

"I need a moment or two of your time," Thomas had called out to him.

"I'm up to my elbows in a bureaucratic backlog, Billy," Jefferson called back. "But come on in and make yourself comfortable."

Seven Days at Oak Valley

"Do I need to get an attorney, Billy?" Jefferson joked when Thomas removed his hat and left Ward standing right outside the door. He gestured for Thomas to make comfortable in one of the desk chairs and the interview had gone downhill faster than a timber hauling truck losing its brakes on Monterey Mountain.

"So what's on your mind?" Jefferson asked while making a half-hearted attempt to keep going through the mail.

"Seeing as how you're busy, I'll get straight to the point, Winfred," Thomas replied. "I was going through the last batch of the three boxes of paperwork my deputies hauled out of Dr. Cordell's office..."

"Only three?" Jefferson smiled and waved his hands over the piles he'd created on his desk.

Thomas nodded. "It was more than enough, given what I was able to unearth. I'd about given up, but in the bottom of that third box I came across a couple of letters that I think warrant further investigation."

Jefferson raised an eyebrow, "Letters?"

"I'm afraid so. One was a letter that Cordell addressed to the United States Department of Health, Education, and Welfare," Thomas explained.

"HEW," Jefferson put in. "The other?"

"The other was a note penned to Cordell by Mrs. Jefferson."

Jefferson groaned inwardly. He'd never thought to ask if she and Cordell had an on-going pen pal relationship on what all else he suspected. He took a minute to compose himself by leaning over and tossing the extraneous junk mail that Mrs. Fisk had failed to screen out into the wastebasket.

"The letter to 'H-E-W' as you put it, Winfred, may or may not be relevant to this investigation. However, when I read about how Cordell alleged that some of the residents here have been unwitting guinea pigs in a series of radiation experiments, I thought you might be able to shed some light on it."

Jefferson forced his expression into one of utter disappointment. Under the circumstances he'd thought that with Cordell dead, the best course of action was to paint Cordell himself as the responsible party. In fact, he'd been mentally preparing himself for exactly these types of questions should the occasion arise.

"Quite frankly, Billy, I have no idea what you are talking about. Granted, Cordell was only Medical Director here for a short period of time, but within that time I never heard anything from him about something as absurd as using our residents here as human subjects," Jefferson told him. "Of course, that doesn't mean that I was fully aware of everything Infirmary did while he was alive," Jefferson told Thomas smoothly. "It's always an on-going battle to get medical professionals to share what is happening to their patients, even in a state facility such as this."

Thomas sat back in his chair and looked to be deep in thought. Jefferson took advantage of the lull in the sheriff's questioning to begin stacking the correspondence that he needed to address with Mrs. Fisk the next day into a tidier pile. He gathered up the letters along with his notes and pulled out a desk drawer to retrieve a paperclip. Across from him,

Seven Days at Oak Valley

Thomas reached into a pocket and pulled out handkerchief and a small plastic bag.

"You don't happen to know who might be the owner of this fine example of men's jewelry. . ." Thomas had started to ask him. Then, Thomas had jumped up and leaned across his desk.

"I need you to put your hands on the desk, Winfred."

Jefferson complied with Thomas' request. Astonished by the sight of the cufflink Thomas had stored in a plastic bag, Jefferson looked from it to Thomas' face. He reared back in his seat and asked, "Now wherever did you happen to find. . ." Jefferson's effort at trying to retake the higher ground dissipated when he witnessed Thomas nudge aside the pile of meaningless memos from central office to reveal his letter opener.

Thomas picked it up with the handkerchief, and held it closer to his face. He squinted and read the inscription aloud, "*NAMD Fellow, nineteen seventy-seven*. Interesting. I believe that Dr. Cordell was also a National Association of Mental Deficiency fellow," Thomas observed. "You don't happen to know what year it was that he was conferred as NAMD fellow, do you Winfred?

"I have no idea, sheriff," Jefferson growled.

"Well I am a little puzzled by this," Thomas told him. "It seems that the date on this letter opener doesn't match the date on your certificate up there on the wall, Winfred. With so many unanswered questions floating around, I'm afraid that we're going to have to continue this conversation down at the office."

At that point, Thomas had reached into his inside pocket and produced a warrant. "I guess it's a good thing I thought to drop by and get the Judge to sign one of these. What else do you think we might find, Winfred, after a thorough search of the building?"

Thomas had given him time to get a glimpse of it and he realized then that he was going to need someone good to get him out of it. All that was left to be said had been his second request for a lawyer.

"Don't look so disappointed," he'd told Thomas. "I'm sure you'll have a chance to ask me whatever you want after I get to make my phone call."

Jefferson listened without comment as Sheriff Thomas read him his rights, silently cursing Grace for setting him up like this. Just when it looked as though things were going to work out. At that point, that deputy of his had come in with his handcuffs. Then together they had taken him outside and in clear sight of the entire grounds, loaded him into Thomas' patrol car.

"Now, don't you think this is a bit overdoing it?" Jefferson yelled as Thomas loaded him into the back seat. After that, Thomas hadn't had much to say, which was good for a change.

Jefferson was already rolling around options in his mind. He'd need to resign, of course, he thought to himself. Just to be able to leave in good standing. Once this rough spot was smoothed over, he'd head to Memphis to deal with Grace. There was no telling what he'd have to promise her this time. Of course, she'd come back to him, he reasoned. She always did. Things always had a way of working out before.

He ran down the list of lawyers he knew. Most of them had small practices that dealt with bankruptcies and divorces and such. But surely one of them could point him in the direction of a good lawyer who would be able to pick this case apart in a heartbeat.

Jefferson ran down the evidence Thomas had against him. A letter that was just a misunderstanding, a letter opener that who knew how many people had handled, a cigar butt, a bloody shirt that may or may not be found, a cufflink he could have lost in Cordell's office anytime over the two past years, and a mentally defective delinquent as a witness. Who was going to believe that? No one, he thought. He began to relax and felt his confidence return. No one at all.

6:45 p.m.

Thomas slathered a piece of the yeast roll with real butter and popped it in his mouth. He took a swallow of the sweet tea Lyla Jean had promptly delivered to his table and sank deeper into the red naugahyde covered booth seat. He'd come to the café tonight instead of having dinner with Mrs. Thomas for two primary reasons; Lyla Jean's fried chicken was better than his wife's, although he'd never be the one to tell her that, and, it being fried chicken night, he could pretty much count on Andy Knowles showing up after he'd put tomorrow's edition of the Laurelville Daily Register to bed.

There not being a great deal of news in Laurelville to report more often than not, Andy was able to get done in time to hustle himself over to Lyla Jean's. In fact, Lyla Jean had a place setting ready and waiting for Knowles right next to the community

Ruthie-Marie Beckwith

table where he could eavesdrop to his heart's content. It being fried chicken night pretty much guaranteed that most of the county's single men and the married ones with a good enough excuse to dine out could be found at the café. Knowles typically overheard enough gossip to fill up the Saturday edition and part of Sunday's as well. After tonight, Thomas was pretty sure he'd be handing over at least a month's worth of press and possibly one of those newspaper awards Knowles had always coveted.

Moments after Lyla Jean put Thomas' plate on the table, Knowles walked through the door. All the heads at the community table swiveled in his direction. Knowles nodded cordially and swept his gaze around the café. Thomas raised his hand and beckoned for Knowles to join him in the booth instead of his usual table, all the while doing his best to appear resigned at having to face the scrutiny of the fourth estate.

Lyla Jean appeared, pitcher of sweet tea in one hand and a glass of ice in the other, ready to make the switch irrevocable. The volume of conversation at the community table returned to normal when its occupants realized Knowles wouldn't be taking notes on the local gossip of the day. Thomas relaxed as well and took a bite of a drumstick, happy for Knowles to take the lead.

"I tried calling your office several times today, sheriff," Knowles proclaimed. "Each time I was put off by that assistant of yours. Doesn't she know anything about the First Amendment and the freedom of the press?"

Thomas chuckled at the thought of Knowles trying to get anything useful out of Julie. He made a

Seven Days at Oak Valley

mental note to give her another compliment. One more and he might have to consider keeping her on.

"The demands of the citizenry keep me pretty well occupied," Thomas replied, his standard response whenever he was questioned about his time or whereabouts.

"Would those happen to include the arrest of a double murderer over at Oak Valley?" Knowles asked, never one to beat around the bush. Thomas attributed Knowles directness to Knowles' mother having been a Yankee and a New York Yankee, at that.

"Now, Andy," Thomas admonished. "You know I can't comment on an on-goin' investigation."

Lyla Jean reappeared with Knowles' plate and Thomas took advantage of the interruption by buttering another piece of yeast roll and popping it in his mouth. Knowles settled his napkin in his lap and took inventory of his vegetables. Lyla Jean preempted his complaint by telling him that she'd be right back with his fried okra and then headed back to the kitchen. Thomas took another bite of the drumstick and waited for Knowles' next volley.

"Is there anything you can share about the murders, sheriff?" Knowles inquired. "You know the voters like it when they read about public officials doing the job they were elected to do."

Thomas wasn't about to be swayed by Knowles' commentary on public service. He was, however, interested in divulging one particular bit of information to Knowles. He just had to get Knowles to ask the right questions.

"I imagine the Governor will be issuing some kind of statement in the morning," Thomas replied.

Knowles waved the yeast roll he was buttering in Thomas' face. "I've already spoken with the Governor's press secretary. There are holes in that statement big enough to drive a Sherman tank through. I was hoping Laurel County's own arresting officer would be willing to fill in a few of those gaps."

"Not about *this* case," Thomas interjected, and added, "I mean, not at this time, Andy."

"Not about this case," Knowles echoed. He took a forkful of mashed potatoes and appeared to be mulling over Thomas' apparent slip. "What other case is there, if you're not talking about the murders?"

"It's not actually a case, per se," Thomas temporized now that Knowles had appeared to take the bait.

"Well, what's it about then, if it's not actually a case?

Thomas held back. He forced his most solemn expression onto his face. This disclosure had to be handled with more finesse than his previous, more mundane leaks to the press. He'd long ago recognized the usefulness of good public relations and had courted Knowles accordingly. Now, he was more interested in distancing himself from what was bound to be a major political headache if not a full-blown migraine. In his experience, it sometimes worked better to have a trial begin in the court of public opinion rather than the local courthouse across the street.

"It's just a simple thing, really, Andy," Thomas began. "It all started with a license plate number that one of the residents over at Oak Valley gave to a receptionist..."

Seven Days at Oak Valley

Knowles' ears perked up at the mention of Oak Valley but he remained silent as a priest waiting to hear a dying man's final confession. Thomas waited while Knowles reached into his shirt pocket and pulled out the worn leather covered notepad that he carried with him wherever he went.

Knowles thumbed through the pad to an empty page and then asked, "A license plate number?"

Thomas lowered his voice. "Well, being as how this is off the record," he related, pausing long enough for Knowles' nod of his head as affirmation of such before continuing. "You know by now how much I dislike having the TBI sniffing around and meddling in my jurisdiction."

"TBI?" Knowles echoed, his pencil switching into full gear as he began taking notes.

"Those very same," Thomas reiterated. "It was bad enough that the little gal who gave me the number thought that the vehicle in question was being used in some kind of theft ring..."

Thomas paused to give Knowles' pencil time to catch up. He picked up the thread of his account when he heard Knowles repeat, "Theft ring."

"It seems that the truck with the license plate in question is registered to the highly regarded state senator Roy Russell, Jr. And, according to my witnesses," he embellished, "it has been used on numerous occasions to transport misappropriated supplies off the grounds of Oak Valley."

Knowles finished writing his last statement while Thomas polished off the last yeast roll. He watched as Knowles returned the notepad to his pocket and took a stab at his now cold fried okra with his fork.

Ruthie-Marie Beckwith

Lyla Jean appeared with blueberry cobbler and removed the remains of their dinner.

Thomas pushed his serving of cobbler aside. He watched Knowles attack the dessert with great fervor, his appetite having been more than stimulated. Then, to be sure that the hook had been adequately set, he offered, "I'm sure you can see how my colleagues at the TBI would react to any investigation I might launch around these allegations."

"Without a doubt, without a doubt," Knowles answered. Thomas picked up the check before Knowles could reach it and walked with him to the cash register. The community table had cleared out and Lyla Jean was busy filling up all the salt and pepper shakers for tomorrow morning's influx of customers.

"I think I"ll head back over to the office for a bit," Thomas told Knowles as he paid the bill. "There's always loose ends to wrap up in these kinds of cases."

"Say hello to the missus," Knowles replied. "I think I'll head back over to the paper for a minute or two myself."

Thomas stepped outside and leaned against one of the four parking meters the Laurelville City Council had installed to raise additional revenue. He breathed a cautious sigh of relief, hopeful that he had dodged what promised to be a political nightmare. Things never turned out well when one elected official began questioning the activities of another. As it stood now, Knowles had stepped his foot firmly on a trail that Thomas' gut told him would lead to more than the pilfering of a few supplies by a Tennessee state senator and his crew of thugs.

Seven Days at Oak Valley

Chapter Seven

Friday, October 5th: 9:00 a.m.

Tony sat behind a small table in a room the size of the tight room back at Oak Valley. He was still wearing the clothes he'd had on when Jones had loaded him up into the back of his security car and told him he was taking him on a drive to Nashville. Across the table a man dressed in a shirt and tie with no jacket was getting something out of his briefcase. The man reached across the table and handed him a small white card. Tony picked up the card and studied it.

"Anthony," the man began, "my name is Bruce Demonbreun. I'm an attorney here in Nashville. I work for the Association for Retarded Children." He looked to see if Tony understood what he was saying.

"A friend of yours called and told us that you were in trouble and might need some help."

As Tony wondered who the friend might be, he lost track of what the man was saying.

"Do you have any idea why you are here?" Demonbreun asked.

Tony looked at the card and sounded out the man's name, "De-mun-bree-un."

"That's right," Demonbreun nodded and smiled. "Demonbreun. And like I said, I'm an attorney. I'm here to help you, that is, if you want help. Do you know why you were sent here?"

Tony shook his head. The last thing he remembered before he was loaded into the security car was showing up at the workshop to walk Angela back to her building. Then Jones had appeared and there'd been a long ride to Nashville.

Once they'd gotten to Nashville, they'd driven up to a place that looked a lot like Oak Valley, except it had a huge fence around it with barbed wire at the top and you had to go through a locked door to get in. Even Jones' had had to turn over his keys and stuff at the front desk. While Jones was busy signing a bunch of forms, a couple of workers had searched him; like he had anything on him worth taking.

Demonbreun cleared his throat. The sound jolted Tony back to the present and the little room.

"I don't know," Tony mumbled. He felt dizzy and his mouth tasted like fuzz. Must be the shot they had given before they put him back in the tight room.

"Are you sure you weren't told why you were sent here?" Demonbreun persisted.

"Well," Tony began hesitantly, "Tinker got dead and the Doctor too and Joey fell down the stairs and Sam's in the hospital and Angela was waitin' on me and then Big Mac put me in a car and here I am."

"That's quite a story," Demonbreun told him. "Maybe you can tell it to me a little bit at a time. Don't worry," he added, "I've got all the time in the world. Why don't we start at the beginning?"

Demonbreun reached down and retrieved a yellow pad from his briefcase. "I'm going to make a few notes while you talk, so later I can remember what you said." He waited while Tony tried to pick a good place to start.

"Well," Tony began, "I had these cigarettes that I traded Joey, he's my roommate, for a pair of shoes. That was last Saturday. I was hoping to get to see Debbie Allison but I got there late 'cause Dr. Jefferson was outside in his garden . . ."

9:45 a.m.

Grace answered the phone on the third ring. "I've got it, mother," she called out. She tucked a stray hair behind her left ear and held the handset up to her right. Then, out of the habit of a lifetime, she pulled the receiver around the banister and held it in her lap as she lowered herself onto the fourth step of the stairway. Settled in, she told the caller, "This is Grace Jefferson."

"Sheriff Thomas?" she repeated, confused by an unexpected intrusion of Laurelville into her Memphis respite.

"Who is it?" her mother called out to her from the sunroom that overlooked the garden. Her mother had been savoring her morning cup of coffee while Grace had been doing her best to evade her mother's questions about her failing marriage to Winfred.

Grace covered the mouthpiece with her hand and answered, "It's Sheriff Thomas, Mama." She heard her mother's footsteps coming toward her from the back of the house and resumed speaking when her mother appeared in the archway of the parlor. "Of course I remember you, Sheriff Thomas," she replied.

Ruthie-Marie Beckwith

"Arrested?" Grace stammered and then asked, "Winfred?"

"No, I hadn't heard," she replied. "Last night?" Covering the handset again, she whispered to her mother, "Winfred's been arrested!" Her mother moved toward her and Grace shifted position to make room for her mother to join her.

"Are you certain? Winfred a murderer?" Grace asked. "I just don't know what to think. A murderer?" she repeated. Her mother put her arm around her and gave her a gentle squeeze. The passage of time slowed. Each word Thomas spoke began to sound as if it was coming from the end of one of those wind tunnels they had over at the Piney Bluff research facility.

"No, I'd planned to be in Memphis for only a week or so. I've family here and wanted to spend some time with them. We didn't see much of each other when we were in Oklahoma, you see. . ." her voice trailed off and her mother gently took the receiver from her hand.

"Sheriff?" her mother spoke into the telephone. "This is Elizabeth Nash, Grace's mother. I believe Grace will need to call you back. Your news has given her a bit of a shock, you see?" Grace's mother reached over and squeezed her hand. "Yes, I'm sure knows she how to reach you," she told the sheriff as Grace nodded in numb agreement.

The conversation lingered on while Grace felt herself drifting further and further from her parent's familiar shore. Then she felt her mother's body stiffen slightly beside her and, cordial to a fault, she heard her mother end the call by assuring Thomas that Grace would return his call, ". . . after she's had some time to recover."

Her mother returned the handset to its cradle and pulled Grace into her arms. "If I'd only known the trials that man would put you through," her mother began.

"Mama, don't start," Grace pleaded. "Just don't start."

"I get the feeling that you haven't told me the half of what you've had to endure. . ." her mother persisted.

Grace untangled herself from her mother's arms as she felt an crushing wave of incredulousness sweep across her soul. The life she'd left behind had followed her home. Even now it threatened to overturn the small raft of hope she had sought to reclaim as she had gotten closer and closer to the Shelby County line.

Grace stayed seated on the stair next to the phone while her mother moved into the parlor and stood by the bay window that faced the street. Her mother was watching for her father to get back from the errand she'd sent him on while she'd tried to pry out Grace's problems out of her, Grace concluded. Daddy never was one to get information first hand.

She shivered and hugged herself, wondering why Sheriff Thomas had decided Winfred had done all of those terrible things. There must have been some sort of evidence, she realized and wondered what the evidence could be. Would she have to testify? There was a great deal she hadn't told her parents and she wasn't anxious for the whole ugly story to come out. How disappointed they would be, even over something as simple as a single kiss. No one was ever going to believe it was nothing more than that.

The honking of a horn made Grace look up and from the stair she caught a glimpse of her father's blue Buick as it turned into the drive. Her mother continued to stare out of the window, a much older replica of herself, frozen by the revelations she knew were to come. Grace ran her hand across the worn carpet tread as she waited for her father to emerge through the door. She'd had so many conversations on this particular stair step over the course of her life, but this was sure to be the longest one of all.

10:30 a.m.

In the absence of any authority, Cordelia had taken ownership of Tony's trunk. She'd convinced two of the workers in Building K to haul it over to the parking lot and secured it in her hatchback. After that, she'd walked over to the office and finished out the day. She'd called the Arc's office and left a message with the secretary that the trunk was now in her possession. Afterward, she'd wrestled it out of the back of her car and into her living room. She'd studied the lock briefly and decided, absent the key, it would have to be pried open.

When her alarm had gone off that morning, she shut it off with a swat and went back to sleep. Now she sat outside on the patio of her small apartment waiting for that lawyer to get back with her. He was supposed to have met with Tony by now, but then she remembered it was only 9:30 in Nashville, it being on Central time.

Seven Days at Oak Valley

What had she gotten herself into, she wondered. Everything over at work was in an uproar and when Dr. Ford had insisted she come into work on her only day off in two weeks she had told him in no uncertain terms that he'd have to find someone else to man the switchboard.

Cordelia wondered what the lawyer would be able to do for Tony. She wasn't sure that coming back to Oak Valley was in his best interest. Not with how he was mixed up in the murders and most likely had gotten in Sheriff Thomas' way. He didn't seem too happy when he'd come back and found Tony missing, however. He'd launched himself out of the Infirmary and nearly backed into one of the wheelchair vans on his way out of the parking lot.

Cordelia forced herself to stop fretting about work and stood up. She had laundry and housework and a long list of things to do before she headed over to Roane State. Surely she would have heard something by the time she got back from class, she thought as she slid the plate glass door aside to go back inside. Her reflection snagged her attention and she stepped back to study the woman standing before her. Her hair still looked like a red curly bird's nest but overall she appeared to be made, in some intangible way, more alive. The woman in the glass stood taller and her expression was full of determination.

Cordelia pushed the screen aside and secured it and the glass door behind her. She crossed the kitchen with a slight spring in her step, hoping that the pantry might offer up a cake mix or some other confection she could whip up before she left for class.

Ruthie-Marie Beckwith

That lawyer might appreciate a little extra hospitality when he came to fetch Tony's trunk.

1:00 p.m.

The door to the little room opened and Mr. Demonbreun entered. "Did you have any lunch?"

Tony shook his head, "Not hungry."

Tony felt the attorney's eyes examining him from top to bottom. Tony wanted to tell him he was okay, but he was too depressed to say even that. Demonbreun cleared his throat and took out his yellow pad.

"Maybe this will cheer you up," he announced as he flipped through what seemed to be twenty more pages of writing.

Tony raised his head and studied Demonbreun's face. He didn't understand what his attorney could be so happy about. All of Tony's worst fears had come true. Just because he'd believed that Tinker hadn't suicided himself. He knew he was right about that, but curiosity had killed the cat. That was what Tinker had always told him. And she'd been right all along.

Demonbreun cleared his throat again. Tony gave him his full attention; maybe he had a bad cold or something.

"I spoke with the assistant commissioner after we talked, Tony," Demonbreun announced. "That's the boss of all the superintendents," he explained further. Tony sat up straighter. For some reason it hadn't occurred to him that the superintendents had a boss.

"When I told him your story, and given as how Dr. Jefferson has been arrested," Demonbreun

Seven Days at Oak Valley

continued, "he was quick to agree that your being sent here was a grave mistake."

Tony couldn't believe his ears, "Dr. Jefferson's been arrested?"

Demonbreun placed his pad on the table. "Yes, Sheriff Thomas arrested him late yesterday afternoon," he explained. "The sheriff is also keen on having you back in his jurisdiction. That is, back at Oak Valley. For some reason, he considers you a potential witness."

It was hard to take it all in. Dr. Jefferson arrested! The sheriff wanted him back. "So do I get to get out of here?" Tony asked after thinking it all through.

"Well, this is where I need you to make a decision, Tony," Demonbreun stated. He leaned across the table. "When I talked to the assistant commissioner, he said that he'd be happy for you to go back to Oak Valley. However, given as how poorly you've been treated, I asked him if the Department couldn't find room for you in one of the new group homes that they're opening up here in Nashville. He checked with one of his staff and told me that there is one opening up in about six months."

"Group home?" Tony asked, not understanding what Demonbreun was trying to say.

"It's a new way of helping people like you," Demonbreun answered. "Eight or so residents like you get to live in a house and be part of the community. A regular house and they're also working on helping folks get jobs, too."

"A regular house?" Tony echoed. "I wouldn't have to live at Oak Valley any more?"

Ruthie-Marie Beckwith

"A regular house, probably one with four or five bedrooms and house parents to stay with you. The hitch is you have to stay here until the house is ready to open. They won't transfer you back between state regions again."

Tony tried hard to take it all in. His brain felt like a ricochet rabbit was bounding around inside it. A regular house. Staying in prison for six months. A regular house. Staying in prison for six months. A refrigerator. A real bedroom. His own closet, maybe even his own clothes. His trunk. His trunk...

"What about my trunk?" Tony asked.

"Don't worry, I asked Miss Williams to look after it for you. I'm sure she's taking good care of it."

Tony thought about the records laying in the bottom, under all of his other treasures. "There is something in my trunk I think you should have," he began. "You see, there are these files that have these triangles on them and one of them has Joey's name on them and the other ones are for dead people."

As the words, dead people, came out of Tony's mouth, Demonbreun interrupted. "I think I've heard enough stories about dead people for the moment, Tony. There'll be plenty of opportunities for you to tell your story after you get out of here."

Tony stopped talking.

"What I need to know right now, is whether or not you want to go back to Oak Valley or stay here and wait for that group home to open," he explained. "The assistant commissioner is anxious for this to be settled and for you to be situated." He paused, as if to make sure he had Tony's full attention before continuing, "Frankly, Tony, they made a big mistake when they transferred you here and they know it.

They know that I could make a really big stink about how they treated you. So, they came up with this deal to try to make us go away."

Tony thought about the deal. His attorney hadn't told him what to do. He was actually treating him like a real man. A real man who could live in a real home, even if it meant leaving his friends behind. "Can I say good-by to Joey and Angela?" he asked.

"I might be able to arrange a phone call for you," Demonbreun ventured.

"I wouldn't want to call them from in here," Tony told him. "I don't want them to know I'm in prison."

Demonbreun gave him a sad looking smile. "Yes, this is pretty much a prison, Tony. Perhaps after you get out, then. You'll keep my card?"

"Sure," Tony answered. He stood, reached out and offered his hand to Demonbreun. Demonbreun shook it as Tony told him, "Tell that assistant that I'll take the deal."

Demonbreun shook his hand harder and patted him on the back. "I don't think you'll regret it, Tony. I'll be in touch." He banged on the door and the guard let him out. Tony pulled his chair back out to wait for the guard to return for him.

2:00 p.m.

Cordelia set her coffee cup on the kitchen counter and looked at her watch. Her first full day off in a week and here she was sitting and back to moping. She was sure she'd done the right thing calling the Arc for Tony. She still hadn't heard back from that lawyer. Patience is a virtue, she reminded herself.

Ruthie-Marie Beckwith

Looking at her watch again, she calculated how much time she had remaining to study for her Friday night class. She still found it hard to believe she'd signed up for a class that met on a Friday night, particularly on her only day off. But it was the last class she needed in order to graduate. The teaching program at Roane State was a good one and she hoped having a job at Oak Valley would look good on her resume when she finally got her certificate. Now that the special education law had gone into effect, school systems across the state were desperate for teachers of the retarded.

Cordelia sat down at her small kitchen table and pulled out her *Alternative Textbook in Special Education*, by Burton Blatt, a professor at Syracuse University. He was world famous, but the book seemed a little radical to her. Nonetheless, it was her last seminar and she was learning a lot. Soon she'd have her diploma and be sending out her resume. Until then, she'd just have to settle for being a receptionist at Oak Valley's Infirmary.

4:00 p.m.

Joey watched with increasing curiosity as a woman with long blond hair slowly made her way toward the bed where he'd lain for the past two days. She smiled when she reached his side.

"Are you Joey?" she whispered.

"'Es," Joey responded.

"My name's Angela," she explained as she pushed a lock of hair back over her shoulder and leaned against the bedrail. "Tony's gone," she stated simply.

"I know," Joey replied. "Miz 'Illiams 'old me."

Seven Days at Oak Valley

"They took him away in a police car," Angela told him. "He must be in a lot of trouble."

"'E 'ouble 'fore." He smiled. "'E 'ways 'ouble. 'Ut 'e 'ets it 'ixed."

"Oh," Angela said. "Are you sure he'll get this fixed, too?"

"'Es," Joey responded and laughed. "'E 'ways 'ets it 'ixed."

Angela laughed with him until she saw a wave of sadness pass over his face like a dark window shade.

"'Am's 'ead," he related.

Angela's brow furrowed as she deciphered what Joey had said. "Sam's dead?" she repeated.

"Yes," Joey said as he laid his head back down on the pillow. Tears started running down his cheeks.

Angela reached out and took his hand. She stood there holding it until the nurse told her it was time to head to the dining hall for dinner.

"Bye 'Gela," he told her as she turned to go.

"I'll be back," Angela told him. "And so will Tony. Don't worry, Joey. See ya' later, alligator."

Joey flashed her one last smile for his benefit and closed his eyes as she disappeared through the doorway.

Ruthie-Marie Beckwith

Epilogue

Monday, October 15th: 9:30 a.m.

Cordelia looked at two documents lying on the desk before her. One was a copy of Dr. Jefferson's resignation sent out by the assistant commissioner along with a letter announcing the appointment of Dr. Ford as superintendent of Oak Valley. She wasn't surprised by that after he'd pulled everyone together right before the accreditation team showed up and given them a pep talk worthy of Tom Landry. Following that, everyone had pitched in with a passion. They'd come through it o.k., not with flying colors, but better than to be expected given everything that had transpired the week before.

Dr. Jefferson's letter cited personal problems and expressed regret at having to step down as superintendent so quickly. Personal problems, indeed, Cordelia fumed. After a great deal of fuss and bother, Sheriff Thomas had been successful in getting an order to dig up what looked to be half of the new construction zone and sure enough, right where Tony had said it would be, was the black garbage bag. Inside, just like Tony had said, was a white shirt covered with blood.

Seven Days at Oak Valley

It hadn't taken much after that to get a search warrant for the superintendent's house and the rest of Oak Valley itself. All of this had been happening with the accreditation team looking on the entire time. Dr. Ford had pulled off a small miracle as far as she was concerned.

The Sheriff acted like he'd found even more evidence, but Cordelia was sure what mattered most was the evidence that Tony had uncovered. More importantly, she hoped Thomas came up with enough evidence to link Dr. Jefferson to the murder of Tony's friend, Tinker.

Thinking of Tony turned her attention to the second document Dr. Ford had given her to put in Tony's file. It was a commitment order to that place in Nashville where Tony had been sent. Drafted by Dr. Jefferson, it hadn't been signed. Mr. Demonbreun had put a stop to it before it ever ended up in the hands of a judge.

Cordelia glanced around her desk to see if anyone was watching and tore the paper into tiny pieces, watching as each one fluttered like confetti into her wastebasket. Confetti. Wasn't much cause for celebration around here after the accreditation team left, except maybe Mac Jones turning in his notice two days after Dr. Jefferson was arrested.

As it looked now, Tony was going to end up in some group home in Nashville. Mr. Demonbreun had made the long trip to Laurelville to fetch Tony's trunk. He seemed like a very compassionate man. He'd met her at her house to take possession of Tony's trunk and after he removed the lock, she was amazed to see what it had contained; the partial contents of a carton of cigarettes, a pack of matches,

Ruthie-Marie Beckwith

a broken Timex watch, an assortment of Special Olympic medals, a torn plastic poncho, and the missing medical records.

 Cordelia didn't want to know how or why Tony had gotten his hands on those, particularly after Mr. Demonbreun had flipped through them and gotten her to swear that she'd never laid eyes on them. He'd said he didn't want to get her mixed up in the tremendously complicated problem that what was in those files was sure to create. She might have to testify about them someday, but for now, he didn't want her to say a word about them to anyone.

 After he'd eaten a slice of her best double chocolate cake with chocolate icing, Mr. Demonbreun returned the records to the trunk, relocked it, and loaded it into his car to haul back to Nashville. He'd reassured her that Tony was going to be all right and that things were working out for him. He passed on Tony's best wishes to give to his roommates.

 One other piece of good news had crossed her desk following the departure of the accreditation team. She hoped that Joey's parents would be satisfied with their son's promised transfer to the newly opened Hope Mountain Group Home in Kingsport once he had recovered from his injuries. The group home was, after all, one of the first ones in the state and it was closer to their home in Bristol.

 The intercom buzzed and Cordelia withdrew from her contemplation of past events. She pushed the button and heard Dr. Ford's voice boom through the speaker, even though she could hear it just fine through the door. She'd tried to explain to Dr. Ford that her career objective was not being a superintendent's secretary but he'd pretty much ignored her, telling her that she was the only one who could competently use the Dictaphone and was therefore indispensable. She'd have to help him find a replacement before she graduated in December.

"Yes, Dr. Ford," she answered into the handset. She despised talking over the intercom. "Yes, sir. I'll let you know as soon as Angela gets here with the mail. Yes, sir, I know she's slow, but she can read and seemed to be bored out of her mind when I went over to the workshop looking for Tony's replacement."

She waited as Dr. Ford issued several other directives and turned when she heard the sleigh bells ring. "The mail's here," she reported and hung up. Angela gave her the brightest smile Cordelia had seen on her face so far. Cordelia had had a knock down drag out fight over them wanting to cut her hair. Ridiculous, she thought to herself. There were far better ways to deal with lice.

Angela carefully placed the incoming mail in the proper tray and just as carefully placed the outgoing mail in her sack. "You're in a hurry, today," Cordelia remarked, examining Angela to confirm that she was wearing her hearing aid.

"Dance tonight," Angela answered as she opened the door and turned back to wave. "See you later, 'GATOR," she called out as the door closed behind her.

"After a while, crocodile," Cordelia called in return. She turned back to gather up the stack of messages that Dr. Ford would need to return before he left for the day.

Discussion Questions

1. How has the author used the confines of a week, seven days, to build suspense? In what ways does this illustrate both the inertia of bureaucracy as well as the on-going turmoil that lurks beneath the surface of the institution?
2. Tony, the protagonist, has an intellectual disability. How is the author's portrayal of him as someone with an intellectual disability similar to or different from other literary figures such as Forrest Gump or the character Tom in Jack London's story, "Told in the Drooling Ward"?
3. In what ways does the bucolic appearance of Oak Valley belie its darker nature? How does it contribute to visitor's ability to ignore or deny the negative impact of the setting on the residents who live there?
4. Joey, whose speech is difficult to understand, represents the unrelenting vulnerability of the residents to injury and harm. How does the author use his victimization as a means to demonstrate the resiliency of the residents?
5. Different characters in the book are placed in juxtaposition to one another. For example, at the beginning Cordelia and Grace are both subservient to the powerful males that surround them. What other characters are placed in juxtapositions? How do the unfolding events of the murder investigation impact the evolution of their characters?
6. Tony and Sheriff Thomas each carry out an investigation of the murders and other suspicious events that are happening at Oak Valley. How do their different approaches serve to eventually expose the real culprits? When Tony presents his evidence to Sheriff Thomas, why does his demeanor change from self-confidence to self-consciousness?
7. What primary theme did the author emphasize throughout the novel?

8. Did certain parts of the book make you uncomfortable? What do you think the author was trying to get across to the reader by including them?

9. In what ways do you feel Tony and Grace each project a sense being out of place at Oak Valley? How do their efforts to find love and friendship impact the other characters?

10. Set in 1978, the emergence of community services and supports for individuals with intellectual disabilities had yet to occur in most parts of the United States. Since then, how has the presence of such individuals impacted society's understanding and acceptance of them?

Notes

Ruthie-Marie Beckwith, Ph.D. has labored for the past twenty years seeking to liberate individuals with disabilities from oppressive and death-making institutions. Following graduation from the prestigious George Peabody College of Vanderbilt University, she has worked as a disability rights activist throughout the country, promoting the dignity and worth of all people, regardless of their disability. Over 1,000 people in Tennessee and elsewhere owe new lives in community settings due to the efforts of those she has organized and supported. She resides in Murfreesboro, TN.

Seven Days at Oak Valley, although fiction, is based on the experiences of the institution survivors she encountered as a nationally recognized expert in the field of disability rights. At their peak, over 180,000 people lived in state run institutions across the United States. These residents, invisible to those outside the institution walls and often forgotten by their families, demonstrated incredible resiliency and courage on a daily basis.

Fraught with abuse, neglect, and professional exploitation, residents of the nation's institutions learned to mask their ingenuity and resourcefulness. Later, when returned to their home communities, their stories served to expose their true understanding of the conditions they endured. Murder is one of the conditions that was more common than is known and often fiction is no stranger than the truth. And the truth, perhaps this time, will set one of the residents of Oak Valley State Hospital and Training School free.